Highly Flawed Individual

T.C. Roberts

Contents

For my Parents,

who've always supported my (at times questionable) choices throughout life.

Free Book!

Nothing Changes You Like That First Trip Abroad

Not only will you get a glimpse at a younger Archie Flynn but you can join my quarterly newsletter to stay in the loop about future book release dates, as well as discounts and promos.

https://books.timroberts.au/prequel

Chapter 1

This Too Shall Pass

Fuck me, what a time it's been.

If I told you all that had gone down lately (which I promise I will), you'd think I was so full of shit that even flies would drop dead on contact with me. But truth is stranger than fiction, as they say, so I need you to bear with me.

Most people report that when they turn thirty, nothing much changes. But for me, the shit certainly hit the fan, and then some. And it's all culminated in me being where I am now – Sydney Kingsford Smith Airport, International Terminal, Gate 52, about to skip bail and flee my beloved homeland for a life of... who-knows-what. Think I'm gonna become one of those so-called digital nomads because, well, what other choice do I have?

I keep repeating, "This too shall pass" inside my ever-restless head.

I remember the day I learned about mortality. That one day, I too would die. I was about six, and Gramps had just passed. I asked Mum if she would die too one day.

"Yes," she replied, "but not for a long time."

After this deeply disturbing news sunk in and meddled with my still-developing emotions, I asked the inevitable.

"Does that mean I will die one day too?"

"Yes," Mum replied, "we all do. But it's nothing to be afraid of."

Nothing to be afraid of!? I remember thinking. "What happens after?"

"You go to heaven."

Without getting all spiritual, let's just say I didn't buy what Mum was selling. As a result, the great unknown caused me to fall into a deep sorrow for the rest of the day, a part of which I think still remains deep within my subconscious. I struggled to sleep that night. The next day, Dad sensed I was sad and asked why. I told him that I didn't wanna die.

All he said in response was, "Never mind, son, *this too shall pass.*"

I didn't ask him what he meant. Did he mean that how I was feeling would pass? Or did he mean us, our life, would one day cease to exist? Both were true, but the latter thought stuck with me to this day. Yet strangely, as I stare at my Boeing 747 getting ready to board outside the window, the idea still comforts me.

You see, I'm at a crossroads – a real sliding doors moment. Can you relate? If so, you will know that it sucks balls. It's anxiety-inducing. Another cliché that keeps popping into my head is "a change is as good as a holiday". Yeah, except if that change is a one-way ticket to the other side of the world – no accommodation booked, no itinerary, no fucking idea. And everything you own, which isn't much because you had to sell most of your prized possessions at the last minute on Facebook Marketplace at such a discount that makes your eyes water, is coming with you. The great unknown awaits. But it's all good because *this too shall pass.*

Let's just get the basics out of the way, so we can get to the juicy stuff. The name's Archie. I turned thirty a few months ago. That's all you need to know about my background, for now.

I've done my research on this modern-day nomad life. Here's the bag-packing essentials checklist from one of the many blogs I read in the past few days on the subject:

Laptop – ✓
Power bank – ✓
Power converter – ✓
Mobile phone – ✓
Backup charger for phone – ✓
Backup charger for laptop – ✓
Dual SIM card phone – ✓
Local SIM card – X

And that's it. Apparently, that's all you need to live the life of a twenty-first-century digital vagabond. However, that list assumes you already have some online work to sustain you. Which I don't. But I'm working on it. More on that later. I got other shit to worry about first.

Yeah, okay, about that. Enough holding out on you.

You're gonna judge me. Yeah, you are. As I mentioned, I am about to skip bail. But I'm no criminal by any means. Christ, I'd never been arrested until this year. But I've been thrown in the lock-up twice since. I know what you're thinking – how does someone who has never been in trouble with the law all of a sudden score a trifecta with the cops?

Well, here's the first shit-sandwich – it all started with an STD.

For those fortunate enough not to know what this acronym is, STD stands for Sexually Transmitted Disease. Or, Sexually Transmitted Infection – STI. Both terms basically mean the same thing – you caught some nasty shit through sexual activity. See, I knew you were gonna judge me. But here's the thing – it turned out to be not much at all. It's totally gone now. But that didn't stop it from royally fucking up my life.

So, how did an STD cause me to break a good behaviour bond and land me a day in court with a high probability of jail time? Luckily, I could afford a good solicitor and was granted bail. Not so lucky for the justice department, as they didn't confiscate my passport because of my clean record and all. So yeah, I abused that privilege, but before you judge me again, I didn't really have a choice. Firstly, if this went to court and I was convicted, the story would have leaked to the press, and I would have been painted as this church fetish pervert (more on that later). My life and career would be over. This is a big city but a small town. I grew up here, people know me. I'd be finished, as the priest would say – excommunicated. You'll meet Father Bob later.

Secondly, I'm not built for jail. Really, I'm not. I'm a lover, not a fighter. Fair dinkum, I'm such a lover boy that I like to love multiple women at the same time. But I'm not an arsehole. Well, at least I don't think I am. I'm open and honest about it with all my girlfriends. But there's a fair chance I have some serious love and sex addiction issues. I even went to a Sex and Love Addicts Anonymous meeting once. Yep, it exists. But I stopped attending because while I could identify with other sex and love addicts in the group, this only made me build a rapport with the gay dudes. There's plenty of flamers in SLAA...

Now, where was I? I tend to go off on tangents, so bear with me. Oh yeah, I'm not cut out for jail. I'm somewhat handsome, if I do say so myself. Not in the classical sense, but more in an unusual, can't-quite-pin-it-down way, if that makes any sense. Could be my strong chin, or perhaps my dimples when I smile. Whatever it is, chicks seem to dig me.

I just can't hold onto them. The point is – I go to jail, I become somebody's bitch. And there's no way I'm getting bummed. Especially for something that wasn't my fault.

So, now I have a one-way ticket to Colombia, of all places! Why the fuck did I choose Colombia? Because Colombia has no extradition treaty with the Australian Government. They also have this thing called a Digital Nomad Visa which I can apply for, and then stay in the country long-term. The cost of living is low compared to Australia so I can survive a while until I sort my remote income. Then I can begin my new life as a travelling fugitive cyber-gypsy. That's the plan, anyway.

Hang on, there's an announcement over the loudspeaker.

"Flight 374 to Santiago is now boarding. Group D, seated rows 18 to 34, please proceed to the gate."

That's me. Santiago, Chile stopover en route to Colombia. Am I really doing this?

My body seems to think so as I reach for my carry-on, stand up and join the queue to board Flight 374 to a country most famous for its cocaine. Soon I will be past the boarding gate and onto the plane. Once the plane takes off, I'm past the point of no return; officially a fugitive. Faaarrrrkk. My mind has been doing head-miles again over the past few months. I fail to hear the female flight attendant calling me forward when I reach the front of the queue.

"Sir! Your passport and boarding pass, please?" she says, her chestnut-brown eyes glinting and hair tied back in a tight ponytail.

I snap out of it, and hand over my passport and boarding pass. Only now I notice how attractive she is. Young, brunette, wearing the striking red Virgin uniform that always seems to raise a flight attendant's sex appeal a few notches.

"Thank you, Mr. Flynn," she says flirtatiously, providing me a micro-dose for my insatiable appetite for self-validation.

I simply nod and make my way down the boarding tunnel, an umbilical cord leading me into a new world. Once the cord is cut, that's it, there's no turning back. It feels both exhilarating and terrifying at the same time. A deep sense of guilt mixed with anxiety riddles me, engulfs my whole body, up the spine and swirls around my frontal cortex. Suffocating me. I feel dizzy as I imagine the police holding up the flight and pulling me off the plane, embarrassing me in front of all the passengers. Someone filming the drama with their phone, perhaps posting it online.

Look, they caught the church fetish pervert trying to flee!

I settle into my business-class seat and reflect on the past week. The shit really hit the fan after I woke from fainting inside Father Bob's confession booth in St. Patrick's Church. Slightly disorientated, the first thing I noticed was my arm entangled in the mesh separating the confessional booth from the priest, having seemingly punched through it with my fist. Thankfully, Father Bob was not on the other side. The second thing I noticed was my jeans and designer underwear pulled halfway down my thighs beneath a torn, open cassock! My dick was out, still semi-hard and drenched in bodily fluids. The third, and worst, thing I realised was that Father Bob was standing outside the confession booth door. His expression read somewhere between shock, confusion and utter revulsion.

Now, before you get all judgy again, it's not what you think. Everything happened fast from this point on. Instead of pulling my pants up, my first instinct was to ask Father Bob, "Where's Jezebel?" Yeah, I wasn't thinking straight, okay. Of course, Father Bob didn't answer, only turned away and disappeared. I knew what he was about to do. The same thing Father Bob did the last time I got my willy out in the confession booth.

I totally understand how this sounds. But this is not a story about a pervert. I won't lie – I am a highly flawed individual, but a church pervert I am not. Besides, why would I wanna tell *that* story? Just bear with me.

You see, Father Bob was gonna call the police. And rightfully so. I would do the same if I were in his position. However, that didn't stop me from trying to persuade him otherwise. Only, I could barely move. I was still light-headed. It was like a long-dormant volcano had finally erupted in my groin. I was spent, and my legs felt like jelly. When I attempted to stand up, I got dizzy. So, Father Bob had to call the police. He'd had enough of my behaviour. And fair enough, I don't blame him.

But I don't blame myself, either. This one's on Jezebel.

Jezebel Ekas, a devout church-going Catholic and a professional fighter. I know, talk about an oxymoron, right? St. Patrick's is her church, a historic cathedral in The Rocks. And *she* seduced *me* inside the confession booth. It was so mind-blowingly orgasmic that I passed out. And instead of helping me, Jezebel did a fuck-and-run, leaving me at the scene of the crime!

She could not face up to the shame, should word get out about what had taken place on that fateful day. But mostly, it concerned her burgeoning career which was increasingly attracting media attention. Just as I would've begged Father Bob not to call the cops, Jezebel begged me not to tell them the full story. So me, being a fool in love for the first time in my loveless life, took one for the team. The old cliché about "the things you do for love" rings true. Because now, I look like some kind of cassock-wearing pervert. All because Jezebel wanted to protect her precious reputation and career, which involves her beating the shit outta other women. She chose her work over me. Over true love. So, excuse me for sounding bitter but, yeah, that one hurt.

Obviously, I was arrested, and because I was already on a good behaviour bond for a series of other misdemeanours (which we will get to later), I was thrown in the lock-up.

I hired a lawyer, Frank Murphy, who I was fairly certain was on the gear and appeared to be in a mid-life crisis of his own. Frank advised I could be looking at five years unless I could prove I'm not a pervert.

The things you do for love.

Frank did, however, secure me a $32,000 bail, which I paid in cash. Thanks Jezebel! My court date was set for two months down the track. But I had nightmares about going to jail. As I said, I ain't cut out for it. I know that as soon as some big muscly bear eyes me up and down, takes in my semi-athletic 5'11 dadbod, and then stares into my hazel-green bedroom eyes, I'll be his bitch in less than a week.

Fuck that.

Of course, Jezebel was forever grateful, and tried to contact me to express her appreciation. Or, perhaps, to check that I was still sticking to my story of blacking out and not remembering what had happened. Not remembering that I made sweet love with Jezebel. Not telling the truth that, after Jezebel heard Father Bob enter the church, she tried to move me but couldn't so she fled – leaving me to literally clean up the mess!

No, I instead tell them that I cannot remember any of that, leaving them, and the judge, to assume that I was masturbating on my own inside Father Bob's confession booth, and then falling asleep with my dick still out.

Surely you can see why I resent Jezebel after all this. I told her it's best we don't speak until this all blows over.

So, here I am on hot summer's evening, the Australian fortress borders having just reopened in February 2022, and I'm about to skip the so-called lucky fucking country. So much has happened – lockdowns, the loneliness, an "STD", Jezebel, my father, my mother, me quitting my job. It's all pretty overwhelming, to say the least. Never had I ever felt the need to fly the coop before. I know it's wrong. I know I *should* face the law, even if I am innocent.

I'm in my window seat now, in the emergency exit row. I consider getting up and running off the plane, but I've been too lost in my thoughts to realise the plane is moving down the tarmac. Before I knew it, the plane was tearing down the runway, and in seconds we are airborne. Oh, well, I guess that's it then – no turning back now. I'm officially a fugitive.

How the fuck did it come to this? It didn't begin in the confession booth. No, the shit hit the fan way before then.

Chapter 2

Goodbye Stranger

Six months earlier – Sydney, 2021

I was focusing hard on remembering my date's name. We met on one of those crappy dating apps. You know, the beauty-contest type. I've got nothing. I'm waiting for an opportune moment to whip out my phone, open the app and find her name. I can't right now because we're dancing. What I can tell you is she has wavy blonde hair and I'm twirling her around her living room, dancing to Supertramp's "Goodbye Stranger" which is appropriate because the song is about one-night stands, or ONS in modern-day dating app vernacular. But I don't think my nameless date realises this. I listen to the lyrics and cannot help feeling like it's the perfect soundtrack for this date night. All my date nights, to be fair.

Here's the thing – the one-night stand can be a beautiful thing. Yes, there can be shame and regret that goes along with it. But, conversely, a one-night stand can also benefit both parties equally. And I'm all for equality. A mutual, fleeting moment of pleasure. Alcohol generally plays an important role, but not so much that you don't remember anything – that would defeat the purpose. The memories are the best part. They are my reassurance. My validation that I am worthy.

You should know that I've recently emerged from a dry patch. Not because I lost my mojo or anything – that's never happened. But because of the spicy flu that recently swept the globe. But we're not gonna talk about that. No one wants to talk about that depressing shit since we've all lived through it.

What you need to know is that sex is like a drug to me, and I've been denied my meds. So, now, I'm making up for lost time. Nameless and I met at a swanky bar in the city where the suits hang. We then migrated to a small, hole-in-the-wall whiskey bar in one of those narrow back-alleys. After a few stiff ones, she suggested we continue the party back at her apartment. Naturally, I concurred. I needed my fix. And I found the smell of her Victoria's Secret perfume – a heady bouquet of clementine, blackberry and cappuccino charged by her own natural pheromones – seriously arousing. Yes, I have an uncanny ability to identify the aromas of a woman's perfume, much like a sommelier sniffing a glass of fine wine. She was drawing me in, and my loins were firing on all cylinders. Admittedly, we were more than a little tipsy by this point. I realise this as Goldilocks stares drunkenly into my eyes.

"What did you do to me, Archie Flynn?" she asks.

Christ, not only has she remembered my name, but my whole name. Hang on, I don't recall ever telling her my last name. "You been stalking me online?" I ask.

"Ha, of course. Doesn't everybody? Didn't you stalk me?" she responds as she slaps my bum, leaving her hand on my right buttock and squeezing it hard, before twirling away and seductively dancing for me. Her eyes and mouth turn slightly aggressive. But I'm not perturbed. Instead, I see a name-fishing opportunity present itself.

"I did. But I couldn't find you. Do you use a different name online, by any chance? Like a nom de plume?" Jeez, I'm clever.

"Nope. Use my real name, dummy. You didn't look hard enough," she says as she takes my hand, leading me towards the hallway.

Inside the bedroom, we collapse onto the bed in a fit of passion. Clothes quickly come off. "Oh, Archie," Goldilocks says as we kiss and fondle until we're completely naked. She's on top of me, grinding up against my crotch. Just then, my phone rings. I roll her over and grab it from my jeans pocket discarded on the end of the bed, but she aggressively pulls me back.

"Don't you fucking dare," she warns.

"I'm switching it off," I say defensively, genuinely concerned for my safety. I pretend to turn my phone off, but put it on silent instead, while checking to see who called. Sheree. Shit. Were we meant to meet up tonight? I'd totally forgotten.

My date was now resting on her elbows, staring with a mix of lust and scepticism. I placate her by sliding my hands up her thighs before going down on her. The bottle of Veuve Clicquot we just finished was still catching up with me, entering my bloodstream as I take her in my mouth. For some reason, and despite my drunkenness, in the midst of going down on her, I remember her name. I'm so elated that my wet, shiny head pops up and I shout, "Sally!"

But she stops moaning, raises her own head and looks at me like I'm crazy.

"Who the *fuck* is Sally!?"

I leave her apartment building at 12:36 a.m. wearing only my suit pants and unbuttoned white business shirt. She lost her shit and didn't give me time to get dressed, so I'm out here like a schmuck holding my shoes, socks and jacket. And my iPhone keeps ringing! It's Sheree, of course. I struggle to juggle all my possessions while answering the call.

"I'm sorry, I'm on my way right now, five minutes max," I tell her while multitasking as I finish getting dressed.

"Jeez Louise!" is all she gets out before I hang up on her.

To add to the shit-show, it's raining. It hasn't stopped raining. They call it La Nino or El Lina or some shit. It's relentless. My phone almost drowns as I book an Uber. Five-minute wait. Five minutes too long. "Grant me patience, Lord, but hurry," I say to myself as I find shelter from the rain underneath an oak tree.

It seems to take an eternity for the cab to arrive, but I make it to Sheree's apartment building across the harbour in Cremorne Point, on the city's leafier north shore, at roughly one a.m. Drenched from the rain, I press the buzzer embedded into the sandstone entrance to The Ritz, an ostentatious building that screams new money.

A slightly slurred, husky female voice comes over the intercom. She's been drinking.

"You're late."

"I got held up at the office," I lie. "You gonna let me in? I'm drenched."

The door clicks and I enter, dripping water on the sandstone tiles. Up on level eight, a middle-aged lady opens the door. She wears a nightgown and holds a glass of white wine. This is Sheree Hutchinson – single mum, lonely, horny. Much like half of Sydney right now. I met her through her husband, of all people. Relax, she's separated, but not divorced. I'm not a home-wrecker. Her husband, Charles Hutchinson, a crooked banker who basically rips people off for a living, moved out, leaving Sheree to reside in their four-bedroom penthouse with her nine-year-old daughter, Belinda.

"You're so late, I got drunk," she declares unnecessarily. She swings open the door, gesturing me inside with her arm stretched out. Everyone seems to have upped their drinking lately, and it seems Sheree is no exception. Neither am I, to be fair.

"So, I can take advantage of you?" I say.

Sheree giggles and gives me that mischievous look of hers, pulling me closer.

"Belinda's asleep. We have to be quiet... but I'm not sure if that's possible," she whispers in my ear as she slaps my bum before pulling me inside her husband's lavish penthouse. Sheree, with her blinged-up fingers, exquisite diamond stud earrings and the best fake tan money can buy, is always asserting her dominance over me in subtle little ways like the bum slap. She likes to think that she owns me. And I'm okay with that. I take a seat on the couch as Sheree hands me a glass of white wine. It's been a few hours between drinks and I'm keen to refuel the tank and go again, so I down the vino and we chat as she dries off my hair with a towel and unbuttons my shirt.

"You need to get out of these wet clothes," she says before leaning in, kissing my chest and licking my nipples. She loves doing this. They're sensitive as fuck and I don't mind the feeling either.

It's not long before I'm lying on Sheree's bed, beads of sweat on both our brows, and half-drunk glasses of wine on each bedside table. Sheree stares at the ceiling with a slight smile and look of contentment. I'm absolutely spent. But still restless. Why am I always so goddamn restless? I check the time on my phone in as subtle a way as possible.

"Oh, no you don't," warns Sheree. Damnit, not subtle enough. "Every time we hook up, the window of time between sex and you leaving narrows."

"It's a school night."

"So?"

"I have to work in the morning. Don't you have to get Belinda to school?"

"She gets herself up. She's very independent, you know."

"By choice or necessity?"

"What's that supposed to mean? Are you questioning my parenting?"

"Only because I care. If I didn't give a shit, I wouldn't bother."

Sheree's eyes narrow on me. "Oh, that's so sweet of you, but I know you're full of shit," she says as she rolls over onto her side, leaning on her elbow. She strokes my hair. "Why don't you just go straight to work from here?"

"You know I can't do that." I knew this was coming. She tries it on me all the time.

"Why not? You got your work clothes. You can have a shower. With me. I'll make sure you're polished clean, every inch of you," Sheree says as she kisses me. She can be very persuasive. I take the kiss, but without passion, trying to resist the temptation. But, as usual, blood rushes to my loins at lightning speed. I have no control over that. I mean, does any man?

"I have a very specific morning..."

"Routine," she finishes my sentence. "Yeah, heard it before, but does it involve a blow job?" she says as she grabs hold of my cock, which instantly grows in response.

"I can't focus on work..."

"Without it, yeah, yeah, blah, blah. Go on then, you buzz-kill," she says as she pushes herself away. I get out of bed, feeling my hard-on soften, and gather my clothes. While I dress, I think of things I can say to pacify Sheree. I don't like leaving on a bad note.

"Where were you earlier?" Sheree asks.

"With another woman."

"You're such an arsehole."

"At least I'm honest."

"I'll give you that. And it's what I love about you. Unlike my husband, that patho-fucking-logical lying, sociopathic cunt."

This happens every time we hook up too – Sheree will unload her resentments about her husband onto me, and I let her. After all, Charles, or "Chuck" as he's known in the industry, is a massive fuck-stain. I have no problem letting Sheree unload on me. I actually find it rather entertaining. But this time, she used the L-word, which is new.

"Hey, I thought we agreed not to use the 'l' word?" I say as I lean in for a kiss goodbye.

"Relax, I know you're incapable of love."

"What's that supposed to mean?"

"The only way you connect with women is through your dick, Archie Flynn," Sheree replies as she kisses me back. She pulls away, smiling but in a facetious way. "But that's okay. Suits me."

Ouch.

At roughly four a.m., I finally entered my own apartment, my mind racing about what Sheree had said to me before I left. I had been thinking it over the whole ride back home across the harbour. The only thing that quieted my thoughts was entering my bedroom and flicking on the light switch to reveal a girl in my bed. This is Gemma, twenty-two years old, bouffant black hair, and slightly on the chubby side. She lays across the bed wearing black lingerie and suspenders. She brandishes a whip with tassels, the kind you get from a dominatrix store. Fuck me. Guess I'm not getting shut-eye anytime soon. I wonder how long she's been holding this pose for, waiting for me to come home. Gemma was definitely *not* scheduled in tonight.

"You're in so much trouble," Gemma says, surprising me. I jump in fright.

"Jesus Christ, scared the shit outta me," I say, eyes bulging. "What are you doing here!?"

"Thought I'd surprise you. Been waiting all night. Where have you been, naughty boy?" Gemma swings the whip across my arse. Hard. It stings yet slightly arouses me at the same time.

"Oww! Fuck, man. Gemma, I am absolutely routed."

"Literally?"

I nod yes, trying to remember that honesty is usually the best policy.

"I can smell the sex on you from here. Who is she?"

"Does it matter?" I say as I hang my suit jacket up in the closet. I take my vape from on top of my book *The Easy Way to Quit Smoking* by Allen Carr. He doesn't recommend vaping, by the way. I take a pull and close my eyes as I half-blow, half-sigh a thick plume of smoke into the room. Is this really happening? All I wanna do is shower and sleep.

"No, it doesn't. I know you fuck other women and I don't care."

I take another deep pull on the vape. I know there's no way out of this. Hang on a minute... "Gemma, how the hell did you get in here?"

"You gave me a spare key," Gemma finally says with a deadpan expression. My eyes narrow on her.

Gemma is a client of mine, one of the youngest on my books. As such, I have a deep respect for her. She is a real hustler. Firstly, she's indigenous, which is a disadvantage in itself. She comes from the other side of town, Western Sydney. A "westie", as Sydney's elite are wont to say. She comes from a suburb called Blacktown. Yes, really. It seems that Sydney's early settlers were both racist and lazy when it came to naming towns. Gemma grew up in a housing commission, or "housos" in Aussie slang, living a somewhat disadvantaged life compared to my own more privileged, middle-class upbringing. She was prostituting herself at eighteen, but unlike most of her peers who spent their hard-earned cash on alcohol and drugs, Gemma saved hers. Well, besides buying the occasional whip.

Secondly, Gemma is an entrepreneur. But not your tech start-up kind. She's an interesting cat, to say the least. She figured she could do what her employer – the brothel – did, only better. She networked and grew a list of working girls, promising less commission taken from their earnings, as well as the personal contacts of all her clients she slept with. By age nineteen, she left the brothel and linked up her clients with her girls through her mobile phone, clipping the ticket on every order. And she's younger than any of the working girls on her books! I found this both impressive and extraordinary.

By age twenty, she went above-board and created her own website. An "air-brothel", so to speak. Without physical premises, she saved a ton of money on capital by providing an outcall escort service only. And now she was working on an app. She has effectively brought sex work into the digital age. And by twenty-one, she was a self-made millionaire. This was when she came to Bryce & Co. for advice. I became her financial advisor and within a year had increased her investments by over fifty percent. Of course, the insane tech-stock bull run during the pandemic helped. But Gemma didn't care. She thought I was a genius. Soon, we were sleeping together, which strictly went against company policy. Which is why my boss, the "Bryce" in Bryce & Co., doesn't know. And hopefully never will, as far as I'm concerned.

"Are you sure?" I say, my bullshit detector running hot as I take another pull on the vape. "I don't remember doing that." I know how smart she is. A little *too* street-smart for my liking. I'm sure she knows how to pick a lock or hotwire a car.

"You telling me the king of stamina hasn't got it in him?" Gemma delivers the line while popping a boob out of her bra. I stare at her large, erect nipple. She knows my Arch-illes heel.

"I'm telling you I have to work in three hours, and King Stamina needs to rest."

"I thought you like a workout before work."

"Nice try."

"You know that one minute of sex is the equivalent of running a kilometre?"

"Really, is that true?"

Gemma won't give up on getting what she wants, and she knows the right strings to pull.

"For whoever's doing all the work, it is," she says as she rolls onto her backside, opening her legs slightly, "but if you're the starfish, there's not gonna be many fitness benefits. Guess I'll be the starfish. Get to work, boy."

"Honestly, I'm about to collapse into a deep sleep, and the only way this is gonna happen is if I starfish—"

Gemma cuts me off by grabbing my crotch. "I got something that can assist with that," she says as she pulls out a small vial of white powder. Gemma is also a bad influence on me, but what am I supposed to do – she's a valuable client. I gotta take one for the team, right? She reminds me of a David Attenborough documentary I once watched on the hyena and the wildebeest. The hyena has great stamina and chases the wildebeest until it is all out of gas, ready for the taking. Right now, I feel like the worn-out wildebeest, condemned to surrender to Gemma, the predatory hyena. I'm too tired to kick her out. She's got me cornered.

I share a bump of coke with her, the drug hitting the back of my sinuses. Coke isn't really my thing, despite the rampant use of it in my industry, and the general obsession Sydney-siders have with it. But right now, it provides a well-needed and instant pick-me-up. I feel a slight movement in my loins soon after. All cocaine does for me is make me horny and want to fuck, basically. And Gemma knows this.

"Ooh, doesn't feel like *he's* too exhausted," she observes, unzipping my fly.

"I can't think straight right now."

"Well..." Gemma says as she stares down at my cock hardening in her hand, "*he's* certainly thinking straight."

I start to protest but Gemma places a finger on my lips. She follows this by going down my body.

"Ah shit," is all I say as Gemma takes me in her mouth. I pull on the vape, close my eyes and exhale. And here we go again. I won't disgust you with the rest of the kinky shit that followed. At some point, my eyes definitely closed.

But not for long, as the faint glow of the morning sun struggled to penetrate the rain clouds outside my bedroom window. I see that Gemma is leaving. "Thanks again, Archie," she says as she exits.

I stir, remembering something as a matter of personal security. "Hey, you got my key?" But the only answer I receive is the sound of the front door shutting. "She's still got my key," I say to myself before closing my eyes.

I drift off to sleep just as Siri sounds the alarm, a gentle violin rousing me awake again. I try to ignore her. But Siri is not done.

"Good morning, and happy birthday Archie. Today it's overcast with an eighty percent chance of showers. You have a meeting with Bryce at ten a.m."

"Siri?" I say with his eyes still closed.

"Yes, Archie?"

"Fuck off!"

Chapter 3
Archie Flynn

I was born Archibald Ignatius Flynn in 1991. Yes, Ignatius is my middle name. And yeah, it's embarrassing. I didn't have to divulge that. But I did it to gain a little sympathy, build a little rapport, you know. That said, don't you dare tell anyone. The only people who know my middle name are my best friend, Bryce, who also happens to be my boss (more on that later), and my father, Robert Flynn. Oh, almost forgot the other half of my gene pool – Pamela Flynn – but she doesn't really count because she isn't a part of my life anyway. I'm unsure if she goes by that name now. You see, she upped and left when I was seven years old. Haven't seen or heard from her since. Mother of the century, right? You should probably know that. My old man, Robert, or Rob as he's keenly known, blamed it on Pamela, insisting there was another man, of course. But I suspect there's more to the story. And guess what – there is! But let's not delve into that just yet. Some background first.

You see, Pamela came from Sydney's Upper North Shore, a leafy and affluent area of the city. Some would say stuck up or snobby. She was a private schoolgirl-type, attending a place where you pay tens of thousands a year for a "quality" education. Her family had what they call "old money", and they never approved of her marrying Pops, Mr. Robert Flynn.

Robert's family was working-class, across the harbour in Balmain in the city's Inner West. It was a pretty rough area back then, even a little dangerous. Just pub fights and shit. Not today though. With its proximity to the city and harbour views, it's fancy as fuck. Even more so than where Pam's stuck-up family were from. The irony, right?

Another way to look at it is when Pamela's family were watching the Wallabies play rugby union, Dad's were watching the Balmain Tigers in the rugby league. Now, this kind of cross-pollination of a couple hooking up from opposite sides of the harbour is rare even today, but back then, in the sixties and seventies, you can bet your bottom dollar it was practically unheard of. No wonder the marriage didn't last. But did she have to up and fuck off? I mean, *what kind of a mother does that to her son!?* I think about it at least once a day, and it does my head in.

But not usually while I'm staring at red streaks on my bare buttocks in the bathroom mirror after going on a sex bender with three different women and barely getting any sleep. Gemma certainly whipped my arse good. And I notice a hickey, where someone's bitten and sucked my neck like a vampire in a blood bank. But I can't remember who. Was it Gemma, Sheree, or... Vanessa! That's her name. Fuck, I knew it would come back to me. My money's on Gemma. I try to rub it off, hoping it's lipstick. No go, so I apply some foundation to hide it somewhat, after which I check my ever-so-slightly receding hairline and apply some eye drops before I step into the shower.

As I feel the soothing hot water washing away my sins, I consider that I might have deep psychological issues. When you have a birthday that ends in a zero, it's a good time for self-reflection, and what better place than the shower for that? Additionally, if it wasn't for Siri, my AI companion and the closest thing to a meaningful relationship I have, I wouldn't have even realised. I wonder if anyone else will remember. Will I get a "happy birthday" today? I'm in my dirty thirties now, on the freeway to forty. All my friends are already married with kids. Is it time to grow up and do the same? Nobody likes a thirty-something man-whore, do they? I brush my teeth and tongue with toothpaste, and take stock of my life.

I need help.

Some of my best thinking is done in the shower. But not this morning. I'm feeling intense shame over my man-whoring ways. Plus, I'm in survival mode, just to make it back to the office. Can you believe it? After years of working from home, my boss wants us back. And for what? It makes no difference. And of all the mornings for a return to the office, I pull an all-nighter. At least with a Zoom meeting I can turn the camera off, hiding my shabby, hungover appearance.

My boss didn't cope so well with the whole working-from-home thing, you see. Claims it's not good for his marriage. I believe this is why he wants everyone back. To get away from his wife, although he'd never admit it. But if I can do my job from home, maybe I can do it from anywhere. I do kinda miss the social element, but that's the only con against an extensive list of pros.

I still feel slightly drunk. I really gotta get my shit together.

Chapter 4

West Rocks

British convicts, AKA criminals but mostly petty, first settled and started building the city here where I live in The Rocks. Much of the old town remains. Narrow cobblestone laneways, charming sandstone ruins and historic, heritage-listed pubs that I drink at. Surprisingly, I enjoy the walk to work, through the old Argyle Cut beneath the freeway and the Harbour Bridge that the convicts hand-cut through sandstone rock. The tunnel connects the two sides, The Rocks with West Rocks, which is the side I live on.

West Rocks is full of the original sandstone cottages and classic terrace houses lined up next to each other, that might not look out of place in England. On the harbour's edge, one of the four original piers, known as Walsh Bay Wharves, juts out. Originally a part of Sydney's port infrastructure, they have now been converted into multi-million-dollar apartments, hotels, theatres, restaurants and other shops. What was once the roughest part of the city is now the swankiest – textbook gentrification.

Looming over West Rocks now is a new casino, Sydney's tallest skyscraper, standing erect like some kind of futuristic giant penis. I could only guess that the billionaires behind the development needed to make a statement, compensating for their own short-comings. And just to rub salt into the wound, they built it on historically and culturally significant land, the indigenous-named Barangaroo. Go figure.

My home is in Argyle Street, roughly halfway between the harbour and the Argyle Tunnel cut beneath the bridge. I attempted to live in other districts of Sydney, but always found my way back. I grew up here, it's home. I love the history and character of the place. The sense of stories past. A natural harbour full of indigenous tribes living in harmony with nature and (somewhat) with each other, before the fateful day in 1788 when it was transformed forever after British convicts were Shanghaied and shipped to the other side of the world. Must have been brutal, cramped inside filthy spaces below deck with barely enough room to lie down to sleep. Many didn't make it, poor fellows.

That's the other reason I never leave the Rocks – my roots run deep here. You see, luckily for me, a few of my ancestors survived the punishing journey and were rewarded with the promised land. I often wonder if the sun was shining and the harbour was glistening when Colin Flynn arrived in Circular Quay. Coming from cold, rainy and dirty London, Sydney Harbour must have looked pretty fucking sweet. Especially after being cooped up on a ship for months on end, dealing with disease and sleeping in your own piss and shit.

I like to imagine Colin Flynn emerging from under deck, taking in the surroundings and proclaiming in a thick Cockney accent, "Well, chain me up and lash me nut-sack, you call this a fooking punishment? Ha!"

She may have looked like paradise, but it was definitely not all sunshine and rainbows. The Rocks was rough as guts in its early days. Building the colonial outpost was no easy feat. Food and water were scarce and the labour was brutal. Sewerage lay in the cobblestone roads until the rain washed it into the harbour. There were hardly any women so sexual frustration was through the roof, with such suppressed energy usually channelled towards violence. There's no information on what Colin Flynn was charged with. All we know is that he served in the British Military. The rest remains a mystery.

Dorothy Roberts arrived on the female convict fleet, the infamous *Lady Penrhyn*. Charged with the crime of poverty. Yeah, that was an actual offence in those days, can you believe it? But the real reason these women were sent down under was to tame the sex-starved male convict colony. And as you can imagine, this was like throwing a lamb to a pack of wolves. The combination of years of working brutal conditions with no female company, and a shipload of rum "generously" thrown in by the government, meant the party escalated fast, to say the least. It doesn't surprise me that my great, great, great, great-grandmother Dorothy Roberts found herself in trouble.

Luckily, drawing upon his hand-to-hand combat skills from his time serving the army, Colin Flynn pulled three men off Dorothy Roberts and beat the living shit outta them. What a fucking hero. I wouldn't even exist if he hadn't pulled that move. They were together ever since. And so, my Australian family tree began. Yep, I came from full-blood convicts, and I'm proud as fuck. I like to think I inherited Colin and Dorothy's tenacity and pure grit. But not their pugnaciousness. I'm a lover, not a fighter, remember?

Today, Colin and Dorothy's original cottage they earned once pardoned has been built over by a giant backpackers youth hostel, which I walk past on my way to work. To think my own home is only a few blocks away from where my ancestors lived. It's a two-story, three-bedroom original terrace home. Perhaps too big for a single man living alone, although it's one helluva bachelor pad. The house was part of a former housing commission, but as the area grew to become some of the most coveted real estate in Sydney, the government realised its value and kicked out all the tenants so they could sell the homes for a shitload of dough.

I grew up in one of these housos. And Dad was one such unfortunate tenant to get kicked out. But he can't complain really (although he still does) because for so many years we had it so good, living in an apartment in this weird-arse-looking building I'm walking past right now – The Rocks' infamous Sirius Complex. This eye-catching building in the so-called Brutalist style was built during the seventies and looks like individual boxes stacked on top of each other. People either loved or hated it.

Still, it has some of the best views in Sydney, which its tenants paid piss-all rent for, including Dad. The government was set to demolish the building until the local community, us included, protested and campaigned for it to be saved. The community won, and Sirius was now being redesigned into a futuristic Japanese Metabolist boutique hotel or some shit. It's my mission to buy one of the apartments. Just like Colin and Dorothy overcame adversity to build a life and future family tree at the end of the Earth, I wanna come full circle and reclaim a home for Dad in his beloved Sirius Complex.

Growing up in the housing commission in The Rocks, I never wanted to be poor again. Perhaps this was the catalyst for my fascination with finance and is what drives me to make money. I'll be honest with you – I fucking love money, I won't lie about that. And I already rent one of the former housing commission homes turned prime real estate original sandstone cottages. It is a bitter-sweet victory, but it's not enough. I aim to buy that one day too. It'll cost several millions, but I will get there. I'm gonna be made. I owe it to Colin. I owe it to Dad.

But most of all, I owe it to myself.

Chapter 5

Bryce Hitler

I work in Bridge Street in the financial district of Sydney's CBD. I guess you could describe it as a watered-down version of Manhattan's Wall Street, with about as many financial cunts per capita – perhaps even more. But despite appearances, I am not one of them, I swear.

It only takes me roughly fifteen minutes to walk from home, door to door. Convenient, huh? Most poor shmucks in Sydney waste precious time and money commuting to work in the god-awful traffic, which can take you sometimes take half an hour to go one kilometre during peak hour, I shit you not. This is also why so many people have been enjoying working from home.

Bryce & Co. is on the thirty-eighth floor of Chifley Tower, the tenth most expensive skyscraper in the world. The offices of Bryce & Co. occupy half the floor, facing west into the city. I occupy the second-best office in the firm, a corner office facing south-west back into the dense concrete jungle of high-rise hotels and office buildings. Okay, it's not a view of the harbour, bridge and Opera House, but not bad for a twenty-nine-year-old, huh? Fuck, sorry, thirty. My boss takes up the other corner office, which faces north-west and gets some of the fancier views.

As I exit the elevator doors every morning, I greet Jess, the young receptionist. She flashes me a toothpaste-commercial-worthy bright white smile. "Good morning, Mr. Flynn."

"Please Jess, call me Archie," I say as I pass towards my corner office.

"Sorry, Archie," Jess replies, her cheeks slightly flushing.

In case you're wondering, I haven't slept with Jess... yet.

My office at Bryce & Co., an asset management firm, consists of multiple computer monitors lined up across an American-imported mahogany-oak-wood desk. I know, what a wanker. Wasn't my choice – my boss, who I'm sure you'll meet any minute now, gifted it as part of my promotion to the corner office. He says it will make me feel powerful, and I have to say, he's right. The thing weighs a ton, so it's not going anywhere soon. One day I hope to make partner.

All the digital screens are used to monitor the day's stock prices, graphs and flow charts. This enables me to capitalise on opportunities playing the stock market, as well as observe long-term trends for my clients' funds. Although I'd never admit it out loud, the recent COVID 2.0 crash turned out to be an absolute cracker – the firm's best year to date.

But the first thing I check isn't graphs or flow charts, but my personal finance blog – *The Bear of Bridge Street*. Yep, another schmuck writing a finance blog. But this one's got a twist, I'm just not sure what it is yet. I'm not aiming to be a "finfluencer" or anything. I started writing it during lockdown as a hobby when there was an insane bull-run in the stock market and crypto that was totally unsustainable, which I also cashed in on. Sounds kinda fucked up to say this, but the global pandemic offered the best years of my life, capital-wise.

But I don't have much of a clue about writing blogs, and even less of an idea of how to market them. I'm a numbers man, but I'm enjoying putting these words on the page and sharing my thoughts with anyone who'd care to listen. Which, at current subscriber level, is a whopping 49. Ooh, look out, two new subscribers today. That's cracked half a century, a cause for celebration.

I perform a little victory dance while sitting at my desk just as my boss, Bryce Hitler, pops his head around the office door.

"Seen the numbers too, hey mate?"

I instinctively minimise my blog screen and nod in agreement, having no clue as to which numbers he's referring to. Bryce still looks at me a beat with his head sticking out, "Welcome back, bud," before busting into the room. This is his signature entrance. Head first, body follows.

First things first, I know what you're thinking and he's no relation to Adolf. Still, I often wonder why he doesn't change his goddamn name – I'm sick of having to explain this to people. I've even asked him several times. But what baffles me even more is that Bryce's father enrolled him into school under his mother's maiden name, but as soon as

Bryce grew up and learnt what his father's name was, the one on his birth certificate, he changed back to Hitler. Why would anyone want to be called Hitler? Bryce claims it's a good conversation-starter and has helped him make connections and build important business relationships. I would beg to differ, were it not for the fact Bryce has built one of the most successful financial advisory and investment firms in Australia.

He's eccentric, to say the least. His outrageously expensive suits make me look like I shop at Lowes. His bright, colourful neckties are louder than a cockatoo on meth. He's more old-school like that. Myself, I opt for no tie, like most modern men nowadays. But Bryce, he even ties them with a perfect, fat and proud Windsor knot. A Windsor knot! Who does that? I tried once, took me nearly fifteen minutes before I gave up. You need a college degree to tie a Windsor knot. Don't have time for that. But Bryce has the Windsor down pat and can tie one in under fifteen seconds, which is pretty impressive.

Besides the neckties, Bryce is defined by his honey-blond hair, slightly receding but combed into a parting, and impressive range of designer specs – I'm sure he has a pair for each day of the week. Bryce also wears suspenders that were last in fashion in the eighties, popularised by Gordon Gekko in *Wall Street* or Patrick Bateman in *American Psycho*.

But what really makes Bryce distinctly Bryce is his use of worry beads. He carries them around whenever he's working, constantly twirling them in his hands. Stress management. Fair enough, I don't blame him with over a billion dollars of funds under management. Some people meditate, others jog or do hot yoga – Bryce carries around worry beads. Whatever works, I guess. And the beads must be working because Bryce is the most talented investor I know. He takes big risks, which takes massive balls, and they pay off more than not. I suspect these big bets probably keep him awake at night, and the worry beads are a necessity.

Despite his eccentricities, Bryce and I have grown pretty close over the years, to the point where the relationship is becoming confusing. He's something of a mentor, having taught me a lot and played a massive role in me being the investor I am today. But the thing that bugs me is that he's a married man with two young children, yet he loves to, not-so-subtly, live vicariously through me.

"Good morning."

"What do you think of this one?" he asks, referring to his tie while checking himself in my full-length mirror on the rear wall. It's a red tie with purple peace symbols all over it. "I think it's a particularly powerful tie myself." He stands facing me now. "You think it's powerful?" Before I can answer, Bryce properly takes me in for the first time, and declares, "Look at you. Been at it again haven't ya, you dirty dog?"

And here we go. "Not this morning please, Bryce," I respond.

"I know, I can tell. You've hardly slept, have ya?" he says as he sits on the edge of my desk, readying himself for the juicy details.

I lean back and let out a telling sigh. I know what's coming.

"Come on, dish it up, old fella. Spill the beans," he says rubbing his hands together. "Who was she? Where'd you meet? Brazilian wax?"

"Please, not today."

"Come on, man," Bryce says as he leans towards me and sniffs, his nostrils flaring. "I can smell vagina."

"Really?"

Bryce nods enthusiastically. I smell my armpit.

"Oh, you must have *really* got down and dirty last night. Come on, was she a freak in the sheets or what?"

"More like, *they*."

Bryce loses it. Clenches his fist around his worry beads, his eyes bulging. "Get the fuck out. You were with *two* women last night?"

"No." I let it linger for dramatic effect as Bryce's face turns from excited to confused. I hold up three fingers, just to see his reaction, which is priceless.

"Fuck. Off!" Bryce is beyond excited now. "You slept with *three* women last night. Like, separately, or all at once?"

"Shh, keep your voice down."

"Oh my God," he says as he crosses to close my office door.

"Separately, and it wasn't intentional."

"You *accidentally* slept with three women last night!? Oh, you are the fucking master, man," Bryce says in a high-pitched voice.

"It's not all it's made up to be, trust me." I attempt to shift the subject from myself. "How's *your* sex life, Bryce?"

"I'm married," replies Bryce, as if this explains enough. "I haven't had sex with Karen in, like, four months."

"Jesus. Four months, really?"

"*Four* months," Bryce says as he leans in close to me, looks me straight in the eyes and says with dead-set conviction, "You see? I *need* this, man. Give me something, anything," he pleads.

"I was thinking that maybe it's time for me to settle down."

"No! Are you crazy? Do *not* settle. You're fucking with me right now, right? Why would you even say such a thing?"

"You don't recommend the whole wife and kids thing?" I goad him.

"No. Don't go there. Just. Don't do it, okay. Your life, as you know it, will be over. Hey, that reminds me. That Halcyon Funeral Homes stock you added to the fund – genius move, killing it! Literally, ha!" Bryce jumps up in excitement.

The only thing that gets Bryce more aroused than my sex life is making money.

"Have you read the latest quarterlies, is that what you were victory-dancing over? The pandemic got the death rate up, and now flu season is kicking in, it's like a double-whammy. They're calling it flu-rona season. But you know what I'm calling it? Fucking cha-ching season, man. Let's check the latest numbers." Bryce excitedly grabs a TV remote control from my desk, and switches on the TV mounted on the wall above the mirror. The ABC News programme is on.

"Finance isn't on for another half hour," I tell him, hoping he will leave and come back.

"I'm not after the finance figures, bud. I'm looking for the daily..." Bryce squints his eyes at the screen. "2453 national deaths. That's a fucking record!" he says, all too enthusiastically.

"You need some psychological help, boss."

"Come on, everyone knows I'm a psychopath. Why do you think I'm so successful? How close are we to market open?" Bryce says, looking at his vintage Rolex Oyster watch. "Ooh, we're close, baby. Numbers are gonna be punchy this morning. Time to shift some digits," he says, heading for the door. "Lunch, Archie. You are telling me every filthy detail about last night," he says before disappearing and then reappearing at the door. "Oh, and don't forget Jeremy and Sandra's wedding this Saturday."

I look up. "This weekend?"

"They moved it forward as soon as the wedding guest allowance was raised. They sent a digital invite. Jeez man, I knew you wouldn't check your email, so I RSVP'd for you. I got your back."

"Where is it?"

"Palm Beach!" he calls out, exiting the office.

My mind kicks into overdrive. I open my desk drawer and pull out a dexamphetamine tablet, pop it in my mouth, crunch it between my teeth and let it dissolve beneath my tongue for maximum impact. My phone beeps, and I see a message from Dad.

Happy birthday, son. Hope you're having a better one than me. They got me on all kinds of shit here and my brain's all muddled. Love Dad.

As I take a piss at the urinal in the restroom, I smile at the thought of Dad remembering my birthday, before remembering that I'd completely forgotten about my friend's wedding. I was supposed to organise a plus-one but haven't found anyone. The groom, Jeremy, is the last remaining friend of mine to get married. Which now makes me the last man standing. And I don't even have a date to bring to the wedding. How pathetic. How lonely.

I feel an irritation again and look down, noticing something on my manhood. "Well... hello stranger?" The slight abnormality on the end of my penis seems to have grown since earlier this morning. Nothing more than a pimple, I hope. Is that normal, a pimple on your dick?

A work colleague enters the restroom and takes up position right next to me. Shit, it's Kevin from IT, and he always glances at my willy whenever we're at the urinal. I quickly finish my business and zip up.

"Hey Arch, how's it hanging?" asks Kevin.

"It's hanging fine, why?" I answer a little too defensively as I splash my hands with water and hurry out of the restroom.

Chapter 6

Textbook Wedding

The weather-gods turned it on for Jeremy and Sandra's wedding. It was a bloody cracker of a day. Sun was finally out, and Palm Beach looked stunning – everything lush and green from the never-ending rain-bomb.

Palm Beach is a completely different side of the city to The Rocks. In fact, it's hard to believe it's a part of Sydney at all. It's the most northern beach, end of the line; a green peninsula bordered by Pittwater harbour on one side, and the vast blue Pacific Ocean on the other. Once a holiday getaway for Sydney-siders, it's now one of the most prestigious suburbs in the entire metropolitan area. We're talking some serious dough up this end of town.

Palm Beach is also a popular spot for weddings. Whereas The Rocks epitomises inner-city urbanisation, this end of town is a nature lover's paradise. At the very end of the peninsula, the beach stretches narrow to the point where Pittwater is on one side, and the ocean is roughly one hundred metres away on the other side. The beach finishes with a large, rocky headland called Barrenjoey Head, jutting out with its only man-made structure, a lighthouse, towering over the two beaches. If the sea level significantly rose, Barrenjoey would become an island. In fact, it probably will be before too long. It's no wonder people like to get married here. I'd probably get married here if I were that way inclined – and I'm currently trying to figure out whether I am or not.

On the Pittwater side sits The Boathouse, a restaurant and bar built out over the water alongside a wharf, and the venue for the wedding reception. I won't bore you with the wedding details. It was a traditional ceremony inside an old sandstone church. Till death do us part and all that crap. No one objected. It's the reception where the real fun begins. Everyone loosens up, bridesmaids get a little tipsy, love is in the air and pheromones are emitting all over.

At the reception, I'm standing amongst a group of attractive men and women, who I don't really know or how I came to be socialising with them. I'm looking for an out and subtly scanning the crowd for Bryce while pretending to be interested in the conversation which is dominated by an alpha-male who I'm fairly certain is on the cola. Despite my little bump with Gemma the other night, I'm not much of a fan of cocaine. Especially in social situations. Where most men use it to help their game, I find it a hindrance. The only drug I need is women.

Speaking of which, as I'm scanning the over-water deck of wedding guests for Bryce and Karen, I lock eyes with a lovely-looking lass across the party. I had noticed her during the wedding ceremony in a nearby church, where we also exchanged a glance. She looks fit. Very tidy. An athlete's body, but without the flat chest. Her boobs are spectacular. And she's maybe taller than me, which can intimidate most men, but not me. I love the challenge. But perhaps her most appealing feature is her charisma. She has a bunch of men surrounding her, mostly tattooed and looking deadly in their tuxes, completely infatuated with her and whatever it is she's talking about. She exudes, I dunno, a star quality or something. She stands out from the rest of the women here. Even taking the shine off Sandra, the bride, but without making an effort to. Who is she and where is she from? I knew right then that I had to talk to her.

Luckily, Bryce and Karen suddenly appear and snap me out of my reverie, just as my gaze started bordering on creepy. But of course Bryce picks up on my radar, which is always on.

"G'day mate? Who you got your eye on?" he asks, following my gaze.

"Yeah, who's the sorry-arse victim?" Karen adds.

Karen Hitler, Bryce's wife, isn't a fan of my bachelor lifestyle. What's worse, she thinks I'm a bad influence on Bryce. She's always having a dig at my singledom, but it's mostly playful. However, she discourages Bryce from going for after-work drinks with me. Of course, this was a major pain-point for Bryce, as he would be my wingman any day. Instead, whenever we do have a drink after work, as far as Karen knows, it's all business meetings. I couldn't help but notice how well she was looking.

"Wow, you scrubbed up all right, Kaz," I say, complimenting her.

"Don't try it on me, Archie-nova. I'm immune to your charms," Karen retorts.

"I'm not," adds Bryce with a smile and a slightly disconcerting wink.

"Oh, really? Well, why don't you two share the first dance together?" Karen says.

"Maybe we will," Bryce adds before turning his attention back on me or – more precisely – who has caught my interest. "So, who is she?"

"Who's who?" I ask, playing dumb.

"Come on," Bryce says as he follows my gaze. "Oh… Ooohh, yeah," he adds in a kinda creepy tone as he spots the mystery woman across the deck. Karen slaps Bryce's arm as he ogles her. "I think I see, yeah, that's the BOG right there," he observes.

"The BOG?" Karen asks.

"Best On Ground," Bryce replies matter-of-factly.

"Fuck you. *I* am your BOG, you hear me?"

"Of course, baby. I mean, besides you of course, she is the BOG."

Karen narrows her eyes at him.

The woman notices me, distracted and mesmerised once again, staring at her from across the deck. She raises her eyebrows at me and mouths, "What the fuck?"

My cheeks flush red. I instinctively slap Bryce's arm.

"Jeez, Bryce, be a gentleman. Don't stare."

"What are you talking about?" Bryce asks. "And why am I getting slapped from all sides?"

"Because you're a fucking dipshit, Bryce," Karen offers.

"Thanks, honey. Why did you marry me then?"

"Because you're successful and you got a nice dick."

"Fair enough." Bryce seems genuinely satisfied with Karen's reasoning.

We all share a laugh and a drink before the Master of Ceremonies, a young blonde woman who has overdone the fake tan, announces, "Thank you all you beautiful people for being such gorgeous guests. We are now ready to serve the first course. If you could please take a seat at your allocated table. All seats are labelled by name. Happy hunting!" She finishes off her speech by blowing a big kiss to the crowd.

Inside The Boathouse, all painted white timber with a nautical theme, I find my name tag and take a seat at a large round table mostly filled with other couples, and a few singles. I breathe a sigh of relief as I see Bryce and Karen are seated at the same table, almost directly opposite. A young couple sit to the left of me, briefly greeting me. Dreading the thought of being sandwiched in between two couples, I check the name-plate to the right of me. *Jezebel Ekas*, it reads. Another middle-aged couple sit to the other side of my single-serving, mystery neighbour for the next three hours.

Jezebel Ekas. Sweet. At least I've got a single woman next to me. Let's hope she's half-decent.

With that, Jezebel Ekas sits down next to me. I do a double-take. It's the mystery woman from across the room. Jezebel recognises me as the man staring at her only moments before.

"Oh, you, the starer," she says in an American accent.

Stammering slightly, I quickly scramble for an excuse. "Oh, uh, no, not really I... was just, you know, admiring the artwork on the wall behind you. It's, uh, quite abstract and captivating." Fuck me, what did I just say?

She raises an eyebrow, clearly not buying it. "The artwork? You mean the life-preserver? I'd hardly call that art, let alone abstract."

My cheeks flush with embarrassment, and I chuckle nervously, trying to recover. "Right, right! Silly me. Umm, I meant the unique pattern of the, ah, wallpaper! It's like a work of art in itself, and I was just... lost in thought, you know?"

She looks outside to where she was standing. "The wallpaper? I can see from here, it's just a plain white wall." She turns back, gives me a sceptical look, but I keep digging, continuing on with my flimsy excuse.

"And there was this curious resemblance to a cloud formation above you. I think it was a cumulonimbus, but it looked just like Godzilla ... I must have zoned out for a moment."

Her expression softens a bit, and she seems to be holding back a smile. "Alright," she glances down at my nameplate, "Archie Flynn. You just keep your head out of the clouds from now on, okay?"

And just like that, this woman changed my core belief in love at first sight. Love in general, to be fair.

I nod, feeling relieved that I had somehow dodged a bullet. "Absolutely, no more wall-watching and, umm..."

"Cumulonimbus?"

"Right. Cloud appreciation... stuff." I am tongue-tied – a first for me.

She rolls her eyes playfully. "Good. I'll hold you to that."

A slightly awkward silence falls between us as I read her name tag again.

"Jezebel Ekas..."

"Oh, you can read? That's a plus."

"That's quite a name. And vaguely familiar. Have we met?"

"Is that the best you've got?" Jezebel replies before snapping her head around towards a bowl of pistachios on the table, her gorgeous, long locks whipping me across the face.

"No, really. I feel like I've seen you somewhere before."

"I don't think so," she says as she cracks open a pistachio and throws the nut inside her mouth, catching and crunching almost simultaneously. Insanely hot.

The situation calls for one of my winning lines that has a ninety-seven-percent success rate. I take an ice cube from my drink. Jezebel observes with vague curiosity as I drop the ice at my feet and crush it with the heel of my Christian Louboutin loafers.

"You okay?" she asks.

"I am now, just needed to..."

"Break the ice," Jezebel says, cutting me off and staring at me deadpan as she cracks open another pistachio, throws the nut in her mouth and crunches it loudly between her perfect white teeth. "Heard it before," she says before turning away.

Across the table Karen catches my eye and mouths, "Ouch." I deflate, sinking into my seat. Jezebel begins a conversation with the older couple next to her other side and the couple beside me are engaged in another conversation. I'm sweating with embarrassment, and I hate this wedding already and want to leave.

A young fellow with a designer moustache sitting next to Bryce notices his name tag. "Your name's Hitler?" he asks.

Bryce, who is more than used to this, turns and sighs. "Yep," he replies. "No relation, if that's what you're gonna ask."

"Wow. Never met a Hitler before. Didn't know they still exist!" Moustache says, having a laugh.

"Well, you do now," Bryce says, his body turning towards Karen to signal the conversation is over. But Moustache is not done. He's one of those slightly tipsy, over-confident

Aussies, arguably worse than a coked-up Sydney-sider. He spots Karen's nameplate.

"*Karen* Hitler?" he says, eyebrows arched, "Wow, that's like a double whammy!"

Several people at the table laugh. But not me. And certainly not Bryce and Karen. The joke refers to the "Karen effect" – a middle-aged white woman and the type that requests to speak to the manager when things don't go their way. Thus, whenever someone meets a Karen now, instant judgment arises, even if the Karen is not even a *Karen*. It seems Karen Hitler, and her husband, are oblivious to the Karen effect. As close friends of mine, I had considered, but chosen not to, ever raise the subject.

Right now, I wish I had broached it.

"What is that supposed to mean?" Karen asks Moustache.

"You've a problem with my wife's name?" Bryce adds.

"No. It's a joke. You know, a *Karen*..." Moustache attempts to explain but only receives blank expressions from the Hitlers. I feel the tension building. From personal experience, I know Bryce's temper can go off quicker than a bride's nightgown, so I attempt to defuse the situation.

"A 'Karen' is the name used for someone who feels self-entitled and likely to complain. Don't worry, Karen, it's nothing personal. I'll explain it to you later," I chime in, before addressing Moustache. "Hey, you should be grateful we have a Karen at our table. If the food is shit, she'll complain to the manager."

This elicits raucous laughter from almost the entire table, especially Moustache. Also finding it incredibly funny is the gorgeous woman sitting to my right – Jezebel Ekas. Although she's trying to contain herself, she can't stop giggling. And I can't stop noticing.

I'm back in the game!

Bryce winks at me from across the table, indicating that he agrees. Of course he's observing every moment and every interaction between us. My confidence soars like a sea eagle catching a breeze, gliding effortlessly over an ocean of ego.

After some amusing table conversation about the Karen effect, the food comes and drinks flow. The vibe is merry, full of love and laughter, just like a jolly-good wedding should be. Jezebel keeps up with me on the drinks, and more than holds her own. Respect.

Everything is going swimmingly until the conversation at my table is dominated by a posh elderly lady named Anne, who might actually be the real *Karen* of the table. She has been asking about the different couples around the room, giving them her approval. She's from another, much more conservative, generation. She finishes up her prying with the couple seated next to me. I keep my head down, focusing on my food and avoiding contact with Anne, praying she doesn't speak to me.

"Oh, well how lovely. I wish you all the best with your upcoming nuptials." Anne smiles before turning her attention towards me. "And how long have you two been together?"

I look up, mouth full of too much food. Jezebel and I then glance at each other. Jezebel, mouth also full of food, shakes her head in a definite *no*.

"We're not together," she says covering her mouth.

"Actually, we just met," I explain to Anne talking with my mouth full. Jezebel, still chewing, nods in agreement.

"Oh..." Anne muses. "So, you're not married?"

"Yep," I offer as I take a generous sip of my Semillon Sauvignon Blanc and attempt to make small talk with Jezebel to avoid a conversation with Anne but she persists.

"That's interesting. How old are you, if you don't mind me asking?" she pries further.

"I just turned thirty this week." I received a few "happy birthdays" from around the table, including from Jezebel next to me. Bryce, across the table, realises he forgot, and I see him silently curse himself followed by Karen asking him what's the matter. Anne, unfortunately, continues.

"Well, you know what that means? Time to start thinking about marriage and family."

I let out a laugh, spraying wine across the table. Some guests are disgusted. "Sorry! Shit, I'm so sorry." Jezebel can't help but have a little chuckle. "Caught me a little off guard there, Anne. Thing is, you see, I'm not interested in marriage."

It feels like the entire Boathouse goes silent. Anne looks like she'd just been denied entry to the pearly gates of heaven. "How on earth can you not be interested in marriage?"

"Yeah, why is that Archie?" Bryce adds fuel to the fire, with a shit-eating grin.

"You are thirty, for goodness sake. You don't find it a tad peculiar?" Anne presses.

"I don't have a strict policy on marriage." It's true, I don't.

"A strict policy? It's not a business transaction!" Anne retorts.

"It is a contract, though, isn't it?"

"Well… yes, there is a contract. But I don't think that makes it a *transaction*."

The entire table now is totally engrossed in the exchange between me and Anne. I decide to capitalise on the opportunity.

"Your words, Anne, not mine. But let's look at it more from an investment perspective. By the way, I've got nothing against marriage. Each to their own. However you wanna live your life – married, single, gay, straight, tran-tastic, non-binary, whatever. Knock yourself out. But I'm a numbers guy. And the numbers tell me that fifty percent of marriages in the US end in divorce. Now, that goes up to seventy-five percent for second marriages. Australia's trending in a similar direction. So, let's say half of those who stay together are happy, and I think I'm being generous here. This is evidenced by the rise in infidelity over the past twenty years, which increased by forty percent for women alone. You just need to look at the success of such dating apps as Ashley Madison. Now, if just half of the couples that stay married are happy, that leaves a twenty-five percent success rate. And again, I'm being generous… you just gotta do the numbers."

If I thought the room was quiet before, now I swear I could actually hear crickets outside. Anne looks beyond speechless, like she might be on the verge of going into cardiac arrest, which I don't want. I'm not evil, so, to soften the blow, I add, "I just don't find it necessary for two people to have to sign a contract to prove their love and devotion to each other. But there are assets and finances involved so, in a way, that is business." I resume my eating, hoping the matter is over.

Bryce starts slow clapping, genuinely in awe at my speech. But Anne isn't done.

"But what about children? Surely you must have a purpose to pro-create?" Anne pushes.

I was really hoping to leave it there. But she brought the kids argument into it; she had just brought a knife to a gunfight. And I'll be honest, at this point, I was kinda hoping she would.

"I don't want kids."

Anne gasps, incredulous. The rest of the table are loving the interaction, none more so than Jezebel, Bryce and Karen.

"You don't want children?" Anne retorts. "Who on earth doesn't want to have children?"

"Me," I answer as I attempt to continue my meal. But every time I try to take a bite, Anne barks another question at me.

"Why not?"

"Umm…" I decide to really push her buttons now, "I just don't see them as a worthwhile ROI."

This response prompts some knowing chuckles from around the table, and a few gasps. Anne looks confused. Finally, her partner, Rupert, speaks up and explains, "Return on investment, dear."

"I know what ROI stands for!" Anne snaps back. "Don't man-splain me!"

Rupert is swiftly put back in his place. I feel sorry for him.

The repellent old witch continues, "And I find that incredibly selfish."

This is the straw that finally breaks the camel's back, as indicated by my carefully placing down my knife and fork. I have given up on finishing my meal. This one's for Rupert.

"Well, that's interesting. I see it differently. You see, I think there's too many people on this planet. So many that it's no longer sustainable. We're destroying it, as the climate emergency has shown us. Truth is, I'd love to have children. But I've chosen not to out of love for our Mother Earth. I guess you could say I'm taking one for the team. I'm sacrificing my desire to have children. Which, I believe, is the very definition of selflessness. Sometimes, it breaks my heart that I won't get little rugrats, just so selfish people like you who, let's be honest, probably shouldn't be breeding, can."

The whole table is stunned silent. Except for Jezebel, who is trying her best to contain a laugh but failing. Meanwhile, Anne's jaw has hit the floor, while Rupert grins, nods, and starts clapping. Anne belts him across the chest. There are bursts of relieved laughter. I feel great.

The second and third courses arrive, the wine flows and the conversation resumes between me and the intriguing woman with the American accent next to me. That is, until we all finish our desserts – a delicious souffle – and Jeremy, the groom, begins his speech.

"It was my dream to get married ever since I was a little tacker. Mum, you'll remember this – seven years old and I said, 'Mum, one day I'm going to marry the girl of my dreams',"

Jeremy says proudly to "awwws" and a few claps. Not from me. I throw up some souffle in my mouth. And feel Jezebel's stare.

"And you know what?" Jeremy asks the crowd. "Today, that dream came true."

Another round of "awwws" comes from the crowd – mainly the female contingent, of course.

"You okay there, mister?" Jezebel asks in a hushed tone.

"Fine. Went down the wrong way."

Jezebel nods, staring, seemingly unconvinced.

"It's just... All this effort, time and money to make everything so *perfect*. And if it's not then..."

I can't find the words to finish my sentence. But that's okay, Jezebel Ekas does it for me.

"Bridezilla emerges."

Her comment catches me off guard. I look her in the eye, taking in the description she used. "Yes... Bridezilla."

Jezebel nods. "Could explain your Godzilla in the clouds," she casually says as she sips her wine. I follow suit, nodding in agreement.

"Makes sense."

"Whenever the bishop, celebrant, whatever asks if anyone objects to the marriage, I always secretly hope someone will. A bit of drama, you know?" Jezebel says, keeping our conversation hushed.

Again, her comment surprises me. We lock eyes and I offer a simple, "Same," and I'm not lying. I secretly always wanted to see someone object to a marriage, just for the pure spectacle of it.

"Spice things up," she adds.

"I've never openly admitted this extremely selfish desire to anyone."

"Well, aren't I special."

The first round of semi-funny speeches wraps up after dragging on a little too long, and we settle into more wine and conversation. Now, we're cooking with gas.

"It's refreshing to see someone be real for a change," Jezebel says, complimenting me.

"You mean the whole marriage and kids thing?"

"Yeah. Most people would've just told her what she wanted to hear."

I nod, appreciating the compliment after our previous awkward encounters. "Guess I'm not most people." I regret saying this cliché as soon as it leaves my mouth, and quickly change the subject. "You're American or Canadian? I'm not gonna guess because I always guess wrong and end up unintentionally offending the recipient."

"American."

"Which part?"

"California."

"Nice. Never been, but I hear it's pretty wild."

"Wild? How?"

"You know…" For some lame-arse reason, I attempt to sing the 2Pac song, "California… knows how to party," complete with a little shimmy. The beers and wine have kicked in.

Jezebel offers that deadpan stare again, yet I detect she's holding back a smile.

"Yeah… wild."

I quickly change the subject. "What brings you out here?"

"Work."

"Which is?" I say as I fork some leftover beef bourguignon into my gob.

"MMA?"

I stop chewing. "MMA? As in, mixed martial arts?"

"Yup."

I do my best to act nonchalant, and continue maneuvering food around my plate with my knife and fork absentmindedly. "You… you're a professional MMA fighter?"

"Uh huh," she says all too casually, taking some stew from my plate with the grace of royalty at finishing school.

"Like… you beat people up for a living?"

"It's a sport. It's tactical. But, yeah, more or less."

"Your fights on TV?"

"Some, mostly pay-per-view. I'm gaining traction. I'm down here to train, focus, away from distractions back home."

I am impressed as I am curious/cautious. I suddenly feel emasculated knowing that this goddess I'm trying to hit on could beat the living shit outta me. "I've never met a professional fighter before."

"First time for everything," Jezebel says.

"Sure is…" I imagine her dominating me in the bedroom. Flipping me over her shoulder, Kung-Fu style, onto the bed and then doing a somersault in the air and landing on top, straddling and pinning me down at the same time. She slaps me hard across the face and says, *who's my bitch?*

Luckily, I snap out of it as the MC takes hold of the microphone again. "And now for the newly married couple's first dance. Bring it on Sandra and Jeremy – woo hoo!" With that, the theme music from *Dirty Dancing* comes on.

"You gotta be shitting me," I think out loud, which elicits a laugh from Jezebel.

Along with the song comes the *Dirty Dancing* dance moves from Jeremy – not quite as sharp and smooth as Patrick Swayze's, though.

"No Jeremy, please don't do it," I plead to myself. But Jeremy *is* doing it, and then some, taking the dance extremely seriously, flicking back his non-existent hair between dance moves. Eventually Sandra joins in, Jennifer Grey-style – but with a fraction of her grace and poise. However, this doesn't deter the crowd who clap and cheer them on in encouragement. Predictably, a bridesmaid and her corresponding groomsman step onto the dance floor to join Sandra and Jeremy, leading the rest of the wedding party in a choreographed dance. Then, much to my despair, other couples step up to the dance floor. It's getting dangerously close and I silently pray to God that Jezebel doesn't ask me to dance. I can be a smooth operator, but a fucking hopeless dancer.

And right then it happens, almost in slow motion. I feel Jezebel turning towards me, and hear her say, "I need a dance partner."

I'm looking away, pretending not to hear her.

"Hey, Mr. Flynn – you hear me?"

I have no choice but to turn and face her. "Who? Me?"

"You heard me."

"Oh, you see, here's the thing – I don't dance."

"What do you mean you don't dance? Everybody dances."

"I pulled my hammy while training last week. I don't think it's a good idea. As an athlete, I'm sure you understand."

"We'll take it slow. I'll lead."

Jezebel grabs my arm and yanks me up out of the chair. The strength of her, Jesus. I don't know whether to feel turned on or inferior. We hit the dance floor and, yes, I feel awkward AF dancing. I'm not drunk enough. To make matters worse, Jezebel's got some serious rhythm. I do my best to follow her lead. Luckily for me, most of the attention is still on Jeremy and Sandra's routine. The climax of the song comes and the dance floor naturally parts to make way for the final move – the lift.

As the song reaches its climax, Sandra strips off the bottom half of her pristine wedding gown and throws it away. Shit's getting real, it's business time. Jeremy positions himself at the edge of the dance floor for the final lift. Sweeps back his non-existent hair, steadies himself. Sandra runs towards him. Jezebel and I have stopped dancing now (thank God) and people are cheering and clapping the newlyweds on. Sandra picks up quite a pace, perhaps too much as she is a fast runner – a former high school one-hundred-metre sprint champion and all. She over-launches for the lift, catching a slightly drunk Jeremy off balance as he catches her, accidentally launching her over his head. She flies through the air and belly-flops onto one of the tables closest to the dance floor. She lands hard on top of plates and glasses still yet to be cleared by the caterers. At the same time, Jeremy loses his footing and flips backwards, landing on his back and hitting his head on the wooden dance floor. The sound of cheering quickly turns to screaming as the bridesmaids rush towards Sandra, while a few people attend to Jeremy, who is now out cold.

"Somebody call 000!" someone yells.

Jezebel and I watch the whole incredible dance sequence failure together, and while we clearly both want to laugh, we realise it is probably too inappropriate.

After Jeremy is cleared from the dance floor, the DJ tries to revive the mood. Jezebel and I resume dancing, still rather awkward on my part, contrasting to Jezebel's natural rhythm. She is clearly in control of the situation and there's nothing I can do about it. I don't like it.

But then "Nutbush City Limits" by the legendary Tina Turner blares on the speakers and those who can perform the line dance stick around. One such Nutbush groover is yours truly, learned during my days as a part-time wedding DJ while studying applied finance at university. For some unknown reason, Aussies, including city folk, could not get enough of this line dance at weddings. I silently thank the gods for delivering perhaps the one song that I might be able to impress Jezebel with. And impress I do.

Although I haven't danced the routine in at least ten years, I've still got it. I nail every kick, switch and swivel. So much so, that other wedding guests fall in behind and next to me, letting me lead the dance. They're all attempting to mimic my moves, including Jezebel, who's having an absolute ball and laughing. I'm not sure if she's laughing *at* me or *with* me, but I don't care. As long as she's laughing and having a great time. I feel like a fucking rockstar.

The song finishes and I receive a round of applause. Then the MC kills the mood by announcing that both Sandra and Jeremy are in need of medical care, and unfortunately the wedding reception will be cut short. Goddamnit, just when I was getting my groove on.

Outside, we watch as paramedics carry Sandra and Jeremy into waiting ambulances. They are both in neck braces and lift their hands waving to a clapping and cheering crowd. Someone yells out, "If you can survive this, you can survive a marriage!" followed by laughter.

Bryce and Karen come outside. Karen has her arm around his waist, supporting him as he hobbles out. "What happened to you?" I ask.

"Think I pulled a hammy on the dance floor," Bryce says with a grimace.

"Does everyone pull their hammy around here?" Jezebel asks. I laugh nervously.

"No, why?" Karen replies.

I quickly change the subject. "How'd you manage that?"

"It's your fault. He was copying your Nutbush and kicked out too hard like he was some fucking ninja."

Jezebel laughs, as do I.

"Yeah, yeah, laugh it up," Bryce adds.

"Your hammy looked okay out there, kicking up a storm," Jezebel says to me, a slight twinkle in her eye that hints she knows my hamstring injury story was total bullshit. I change the subject again.

"Ah, Bryce, Karen, this is Jezebel. Jezebel, this is my boss, Bryce, and his wife, Karen."

"The infamous Hitlers, I remember. Nice to meet you." Jezebel smiles politely.

"You don't have to introduce me as your boss, Arch. We're mates too," Bryce says, looking slightly hurt, and not just from the hamstring.

"Jezebel, these are my friends."

"Nice to meet you, Jezebel," Karen says, "but I'm afraid it must be a meet, greet and goodbye. I need to get this klutz home." With that, she carries Bryce away.

"See you at the office, bud!" Bryce says over his shoulder while hobbling away. I turn to Jezebel who is sipping from a glass of champagne, watching the ambulances leave.

"Poor things. What a tragic wedding."

"Isn't it just," I muse.

There is a slightly awkward silence, but Jezebel handles it by taking in her surroundings. "It's beautiful here," she says, gazing up towards the lighthouse on top of Barrenjoey Headland.

"First time in Palm Beach?"

"Yeah. Feels a world away from downtown."

"That's Barrenjoey Lighthouse," I say, sensing an opportunity.

"Oh right, I love lighthouses. Is it still functioning?" she says staring up at the old structure. It's time to stick my neck out.

"Sure is, wanna take a look?"

I have a little Dutch courage from a few wines by this point. Jezebel, who's been keeping up on the drink, shoots me a look, sizing me up. Like a professional fighter sizes up their opponent. I start to wonder whether this is a good idea.

"The lighthouse? Now?" she asks.

"Sure, why not? I know the trail. It's moderate to easy."

"It's not the difficulty of the trail I'm concerned about."

"Oh, I see. I get it. But seriously, we both know you could kick my ass."

Jezebel laughs at this, which eases the tension. But she still doesn't commit. Not yet.

"I don't know."

"Come on, the wedding's been cut short. The sun hasn't set... yet." I'm pulling out my best game now. "But from up there, the sunset over Pittwater..." I pause for dramatic effect. "*It's like a Van Gogh painting.*" I couldn't tell you the name of one Van Gogh painting, but it doesn't seem to matter.

"Van Gogh's my favourite artist," Jezebel says, smiling slightly, seemingly coming around to the idea. She gazes back up to the lighthouse. I expertly spot an unopened bottle of champagne in an ice bucket and make a beeline for it. Checking for any of the catering staff around, I swipe the bottle and present it to Jezebel just as she turns back around.

"Hopefully, this gets you over the line." Jezebel laughs. I go in for the kill. "Lighthouse. Sunset. And a bottle of Moët, whaddya reckon?"

"Okay, you got me," Jezebel relents. "But as soon as it starts to get dark, we're back down."

"Of course."

"And there aren't any snakes, are there?" Jezebel asks with a serious expression. "Because I hate snakes, and I know your country's full of them."

"There's no snakes in Palm Beach," I lie. "Relax, you're safe with me. Spent plenty of time in the outback," playing up the macho Crocodile Dundee cliché role, sometimes works like a charm with the American chicks. On other occasions, it backfires.

"Yeah, whatever," Jezebel replies. That's a backfire, in case you were wondering.

We walk down onto the beach where Jezebel takes off her heels.

"I'm serious, better be no snakes."

"No snakes in Palm Beach," I lie again.

We walk along the beach a couple of hundred metres until we reach a beachfront sandstone boatman's cottage at the foot of the rocky, gum tree-strewed island-like headland. To the left, the trail begins but forks off in two directions. The left sign reads *Access Trail*, which leads to a steadily sloping and ascending concrete path. The right one reads *Smugglers Trail*, which climbs straight up on a much more natural route with steps made from natural sandstone, and disappears behind a massive rock.

"Okay, the left trail is longer but easier, and the right trail is faster but steeper."

"Faster but steeper," Jezebel says immediately and assuredly.

I lead her up the steep sandstone steps into between two massive rocks. We are barely five metres in when I hear from behind...

"Oh my God."

I turn around to see Jezebel stopped in her tracks, eyes wide and mouth agape, staring off the path ahead of me. 'It's a fucking snake!" she says.

Thinking she's taking the piss, I follow her glare but it's hard to make out any snakes amongst the subtropical forest floor. "There's no snake."

Jezebel has turned back towards the start of the path now. Is she for real?

"It's there, to the right of you."

She genuinely looks freaked out. If she is having me on, she deserves an Oscar. I turn my gaze again into the shrub, and notice what looks like a large branch lying on the forest floor. I'm slightly tipsy and the light is fading so my eyes are not at their best.

"That's just a stick," I declare with a chuckle.

"That's no stick. Look again."

I look again, trying to adjust my eyesight. The big stick moves. Holy shit, she's right – it's a fucking snake! The sun comes out from behind a cloud now and illuminates the reptile with filtered sunlight through the trees. It's roughly seven metres up and to the right of me, and it's a good two metres in length. It has a gorgeous green, yellow and black pattern – the kind that would make a nice pair of boots. A python. Possibly Eastern diamondback. Nonvenomous.

"Okay yeah, that's a snake."

Jezebel immediately hikes her dress up and begins descending the steps towards the front of the path.

"Hang on a second. It's just a python, nonvenomous."

"I don't give a shit. I ain't walking up there." She's standing at the entrance to the trail now, vigilantly glancing this way and that for any other nasty surprises. "I'm heading back."

I cannot believe it. I've seen a few snakes in my time, but hardly any in Sydney. And just after I had reassured her that there are no snakes here. I mean, really, what are the fucking chances? This goddamn snake was gonna cock-block me. I needed to change my tactics.

"You ever feel fear before you step into the ring?"

"Of course."

"But you step inside anyway, right? You face the fear."

She says nothing, just looks back in the direction of The Boathouse, then up towards the lighthouse. I press on.

"This is good training to overcome that fear. Channel that fear into positive energy. Feel the fear and do it anyway." Pretty sure that's the name of a self-help book I read, but it's all I got. I look back at the snake. It's slithering over a log now in a direction away from the path. "The python has almost gone now. As long as I stamp my feet as I walk, any snakes will steer clear, I promise. Besides, what are the chances of seeing another one, really?"

And thank God, it works.

"If I see anything else that moves, I am tapping the fuck out," Jezebel says as she agrees to push on with the hike. I start trekking, stamping my feet heavily on the ground as I lead the way through the giant boulders where the trail levels out. It follows a ridgeline with thick, subtropical forest and coastal scrub down below, with the vast blue Pacific Ocean as a beautiful backdrop. The path weaves through more massive rocks and levels out into scrubland. I start to tire a bit when steps climb the headland towards the lighthouse above, which has a view back over the peninsula. The ocean beach is on the left and Pittwater Beach on the right. The sun is getting low over The Boathouse below, with guests filing outside, waiting for taxis.

"It's beautiful," Jezebel says.

"Isn't it," I agree, panting heavily. I notice Jezebel's breathing is normal, and she hasn't even broken a sweat.

"Come on, we're almost there," she says, taking the lead in front of me.

All the stamping and walking uphill has got me puffed. But now I get to see the absurdity of the situation: Jezebel walking in front, with the most perfect and shapely booty mind you, bushwalking in a glamorous dress, while clutching her high heels. And me in a tux, bow tie loosened, sleeves rolled up and jacket over the shoulder in the middle of the bush. Just two strangers going for a hike in black-tie on a Saturday. As you do.

We continue up the trail, and the path eventually breaks out to a grassy area in front of an old lighthouse keeper's cottage. We follow another path up the side of the cottage where we reach the peak of the headland with the sandstone lighthouse before us. It rises roughly thirty metres high. I'm puffing and panting, wiping sweat dripping off my brow. Jezebel casually takes in the lighthouse, as well as the panoramic views of the ocean, Lion Island and the Central Coast north of Sydney, as I catch my breath.

"Wow, it's incredible," she says, hands on her hips as I hunch over, taking a breath. I seek support, leaning up against an old stone sundial. I pop the cork of the champagne bottle which shoots skyward before gravity draws it back down into the scrub in front of us.

"Don't worry, I'll retrieve that."

"Good, I hate litter-bugs," Jezebel says, smiling as she joins me at the sundial. She grabs the champagne bottle from me and takes a swig before handing it back. Although the only thing I crave right now is water, I take a swig of the sparkling bubbly.

"You need to work on your fitness, boy," she observes.

"It's all right for you, you get paid to keep fit. I work my ass off sitting at a desk all day."

"Excuses," Jezebel teases before taking the bottle back, swigging from it. "Besides, you really need a desk to do your work?"

This comment hits a nerve. She was right. Most of the time I'm free to be on my feet, taking calls on my AirPods while glancing at my multiple iMac monitors like a proper wanker. I really had no excuses.

The sun sets over Pittwater as we finish the bottle of champagne and get to know each other. A few distant rain clouds out west make for a brilliant orange, pinkish hue as the sun sets. Despite my claims of a beautiful sunset from up here, this is the time I've seen it. But the gods are my wingman tonight, and Jezebel is seriously impressed. The colours in the sky bouncing off the water below set the scene for a perfect first kiss.

"This is perfect," I say, thinking out loud. My comment compels Jezebel to look at me, who was still staring out at the multi-coloured sky. I feel her gaze and look her directly in the eyes. And yes, we have a *moment*. You know, the one right before the lean-in. The mutual, silent communication that it's on. It's one of my favourite moments – what life is all about. Jezebel is both receptive and vulnerable, and we share a short but tender, and incredible, kiss. Slight pull back. More eye contact.

This time Jezebel leans in, and we kiss more passionately. I flick the tip of my tongue inside her mouth. I feel her tongue meet mine. This encourages me to stroke her hair away from her forehead and then grab hold of the back of her head as we massage each other's tongues. Jezebel grabs a hold of my shoulders and the passion escalates fast, intensifying by the second. I honestly cannot remember the last time a first kiss felt so good. So electrifying. Engulfing. A wave of lust washes over us as I pull her towards me. I reach down and place one hand on the side of her left thigh and the other on her gorgeous right breast, which fits perfectly in the cup of my hand. But Jezebel pulls back.

"Easy tiger," she says.

"I'm sorry. This is just so incredible."

"It is, so don't ruin it."

We get back into it. Jezebel sits atop the sundial while I stand up in front and position myself between her legs. Never did I imagine this would happen today when I woke up this morning. Out here, in nature, under the sunset, with the most gorgeous woman at the wedding. I can't help myself as carnality takes hold of me and I wrap Jezebel's legs around my body, pushing my now-hard manhood up against her crotch.

Jezebel's reaction – more like a reflex – is swift as she pushes me away and administers a short but quick and brutal jab to my nose. I hear a slight crunch beneath Jezebel's fist. It all happens so fast. I flinch, stepping backwards. A few seconds of silence as I process what just occurred. My eyes fill with water and the pain is immediate as I taste blood that has dripped into my mouth.

"Ah fuck," Jezebel says, the reality of the punch sinking in. "Fuck, I'm sorry," she offers, "but I'm not that kind of woman. What did you think, I was going to fuck you on the sundial after just meeting you!?"

"Aw man, this hurts," I say pathetically, clutching my schnoz, blood now dripping down my white shirt. "It really hurts." My eyes are watering; in fact, I'm practically crying.

"I'm sorry but I'm no slut," is all Jezebel says. She hands me a tissue, grabs her high heels and marches away towards the trail, leaving me speechless and wounded. And not just my nose – my ego is shot to shit.

The sun is disappearing fast now, and more rain clouds are hovering above. Suddenly everything feels surreal. In the middle of nature, blood oozing from my nose, still slightly drunk despite being smacked hard in the face with a brutal dose of reality. *Is this really happening?* It takes me twice as long to get back down the trail as it took us to get up. And by the time I reach the beach, it's almost dark and has started to rain.

When I reach The Boathouse, Jezebel is nowhere to be seen.

My eyes open. I'm at home in bed. And I'm in pain. Alcohol pain. Broken nose pain.

And, the worst, the soon-to-be-reliving-last-night's-events pain. I blink and squint at the ceiling. Recall. Oh, here it comes. *Crinnnngggee*.

"Aw, fuck me."

Chapter 7

Stage 1: Denial

I 'm in Dr. Singh's clinic, who holds my face in the palm of his hands, observing my nose beneath his spectacles hanging over his scrunched expression. "Well, the good news is it's just a fracture, Archie, which means it doesn't need realignment. Meaning, there's no need to re-break it."

"Okay, that's a positive, I guess."

"It will heal itself. But you will need plaster."

"Heal itself? What about..." I catch myself, not wanting to sound too vain, "my face?" Fail.

"You mean, will it affect your pretty-boy looks?" The doc knows me too well. After all, he's been treating me since I was a whipper-snapper.

I massage my brow. "My nose, doc, how's it gonna look if we just let it *heal itself*? Please, be honest. Am I gonna look like one of those front-row forwards with an S-bend in their schnoz?"

"Have I ever been dishonest with you?"

He was right. If there's one thing that I could give Dr. Singh credit for, it was his brutal honesty.

"Here's the brutal truth..."

Christ, here it comes...

"I think it will be an improvement," he says.

Jesus. I hang my head to hide my smile, since I want to look angry, not amused.

The doc continues, "I don't much about front-row forwards, but you know the late actor, Marlon Brando? He got a broken nose early in his career. Instead of getting it fixed, he decided to keep it. Thought it gave him character. Then, he went on to play such masculine roles as the Godfather. The rest, as they say, Archie, is history," Dr. Singh explains as he prepares gauze tape and a rhinoplasty splint immobiliser. "Looking at you now, and don't take this the wrong way, but I think your broken nose gives you more character. This could be your Marlon Brando moment."

I have to hand it to him – the Marlon Brando comparison did make me feel instantly better. "Thanks," I say as Dr. Singh applies the splint to my nose. "Oww."

"Man up, boy. Almost done."

Despite the pain, I manage another smile. I like Dr. Singh. He's one of the few doctors I've met who is sensitive to my problems. He cares. Or, at least, pretends to care.

"It was a woman, wasn't it?"

I knew this was inevitable. "Yes."

"Ahh, I thought so. You know, you could have her reported on an assault charge. The police take punches to the face very seriously these days. Ever since the coward punches that forced the lockouts."

"No, it's okay... I deserved it."

"Oh, you didn't assault her, did you?"

"No, of course not. You know I wouldn't do nothing like that." At least, I didn't think so. What constitutes sexual assault nowadays? Ever since the Me-Too movement, the lines have become increasingly blurred. "I think I just moved too fast is all."

Suddenly, I remember getting a slight pain when I had gotten hard and pressed my dick up against Jezebel, right before she snapped off the short but brutal jab. That pimple-looking thing on my penis.

The doctor finishes taping my nose, and steps back to admire his work.

"You are done, my boy. Now, just keep the tape on for two weeks, and we'll schedule an appointment for then, okay?"

"No worries..."

As I said, Dr. Singh knows me well, and he must sense something else is on my mind.

"Is there anything else you wish to address?"

I search for the right words, "Is it normal to get a pimple on the end of your penis?"

Dr. Singh simply stares into my eyes, as if searching for the subtext of what I'm really asking. "Well, that depends on, firstly, whether it is a pimple. And secondly, how big... the apparent pimple is..." This is followed by an extremely awkward silence. Although

Singh has been my general practitioner for decades, I've never had a reason to show him my nether regions. This is taking the doctor-patient relationship to a whole new level.

"Umm…" is all I can manage before the doctor takes professional control of the situation.

"Stand up," he says, almost too casually, "and drop your pants." Singh takes a pair of surgical gloves, and pulls them on. Still feeling awkward as fuck, I drop my dacks. Dr. Singh glances up, his eyes meeting mine. It's weird, to say the least. "I'm not going to pull them down for you."

I yank down my undies, cheeks flushing red. I cannot help but notice Dr. Singh frown as he checks my package. "Well, hello stranger. Got yourself in a bit of a pickle, hey boy?"

"Umm… what do you mean by 'pickle', doc?"

"Hmm… most unusual," he says as he shifts his head from side to side with a magnifying glass, getting different angles on the lump on the end of my schlong.

"Unusual how? It's not a pimple? Talk to me, doc."

"Definitely not a pimple… most unusual, though. I've never seen this variety of STD before." I stare down distraught at my old fella. Dr. Singh nods sympathetically as he stands up straight, clutching his magnifying glass. "You can pull your pants up," he says as he turns away. "I have to ask you, Archie – have you had unprotected sex lately?"

I feel like replying, does the Pope shit in the woods? "Well… maybe," I reply as I pull up my undies and pants, zipping up my fly in record time.

"You might want to get in touch with her."

I halt momentarily as I buckle up my belt. "Get in touch with her…" I say, thinking out loud. Singh picks up on it. He's intelligent. He knows *some* of my devious behaviour, but not all, thank God. But well enough to know that I could well be sleeping with multiple women.

"How many?" he asks.

I think. Seriously think. Think really, really hard that it strains my brain and I even feel a little sting in my nose after I do the math.

Dr. Singh loses his patience. "You don't know, do you?"

I sit back down. Defeated. Ashamed. Disgusted at myself. "No…" I have no idea. I've never had a sexually transmitted infection before, but always suspected my promiscuous ways would catch up to me. And now they have, I'm in a state of shock. "It's been, um, you know, complicated. This whole COVID lockdown thing hasn't treated me kindly," I justify myself pathetically.

"It hasn't treated anyone kindly. But engaging in risky behaviour is not going to help."

I feel like a child being lectured by my schoolteacher.

"I... went a little crazy after it lifted... I live alone. The isolation, you know? There's only so much porn one can watch..."

"I'd consider this a wake-up call, Archie."

I wanted to leave right then. But I need Dr. Singh now more than ever. This is a code-red emergency. I need my penis to be fully functioning for the sake of my mental health.

"Well, what now? Don't you have any drugs to make it go away – a cream, ointment or something? Anything?"

"I'm afraid not. If I don't know what it is, I don't know how to treat it. And it is against health regulations to prescribe medicine when we are yet to determine the efficacy of it."

"So, *what* then? We're just gonna leave it there!?"

"Research. First I have to take some photos. To officially log this... phenomenon."

"Please do not call it a phenomenon." Dr. Singh is oblivious to my concerns as he readies a professional DSLR camera with an enormous lens.

"New camera," he says smiling down at the equipment, adjusting the focus. "I've been waiting for a worthwhile moment to practice my photography skills."

I shoot daggers at him. What did I say about the doctor caring? I take it back.

"Now, just hold steady please," he says while readying the camera.

"Doc, what exactly do you mean by *phenomenon*?" I ask, my patience wearing thin as I drop my pants again as Dr. Singh zooms in. "That's quite a lens. You sure you need a lens that big?" I observe.

"This could be an entirely new sexually transmitted disease, and needs to be officially recorded," Singh says a little too excitedly.

"Oh, that's great. I'm so happy this is such a pivotal moment in your career."

"I'm sorry, Archie. I've worked in the medical profession for over thirty years. It has been a dream of mine to discover a new disease. Never did I ever expect it to be an

STD, but lo and behold, here we are." Singh finishes off his speech with a snap of the camera. He immediately repositions for another angle, looking up at the light. "Need more backlight," Singh says as he crosses to a lamp. "Hold this please," he says, passing the desk lamp to me. "Angle down."

"Christ. I think you're wrong, by the way. I don't think it is an STD," I say while shining the light which only accentuates the lump's hideousness.

Dr. Singh snaps another photo. "It's natural you feel like this – you have some grieving to do. You are clearly in denial."

"Grieving? Denial? What are you talking about?"

"Denial, the first of the five stages of grief. Eventually you will transition to anger. Then bargaining, followed by depression..."

"Grieving what?" I ask, cutting him off.

"The loss of your manhood."

"Don't say that. Please, doc, do not say that."

"Relax, eventually you will reach the fifth and final stage of grief – acceptance."

"I don't want to accept this!"

"Relax, Archie, this will only be temporary... hopefully. But for now, your sex life is over as you know it. You simply cannot continue like this." The doc turns away, communicating with his body language that the session is over. "You must refrain from all types of physical intimacy until we discover what this is."

Dr. Singh's final blow hits me deep in the solar plexus. I'm utterly speechless. Can only stare, dumbfounded. Shocked. Paralysed in fear...

In denial.

Chapter 8

Old Mate Pops

Sydney Adventist Private Hospital is on the leafy Upper North Shore. Out of nowhere appears the semi-high-rise hospital building jutting out of the eucalyptus tree woodland of Lane Cove National Park. The hospital is nestled amongst nature and old Federation-style mansions on humongous blocks. When I end up on my deathbed, this is the place I'd like to be. Which is why I chose it (and paid for it) for Dad. I want him to get the best treatment in the most serene environment. He has his own private room with views over the national park and the CBD beyond. The astronomical fees are worth it for that alone.

Dad has prostate cancer. I never considered what a cunt cancer is until my old man got it. Diagnosed at late stage too, already aggressive as fuck.

The other reason I'm rather fond of this hospital is the abundance of cute nurses who fill the corridors and attend to Dad. Even some of the female doctors are great eye-candy. As such, I always carry a bunch of flowers as I cross into the hospital entrance. Even though the flowers are meant to be for Pops, they're not really – he hates flowers. Well, not entirely true, he just hates cut flowers. Thinks they should be left in the ground where they belong. Fair enough. But the nurses think it's sweet, me bringing him flowers every week. Whenever they spot me walking through the hospital wards with a big fluffy bunch of Lilly Pilly, Bottlebrush and Grevillea, I love being on the receiving end of the subtle smiles that creep onto their face. I even got a few of their numbers already and dated one briefly, but I think she got transferred to another hospital or something.

"Hey Dad," I say as I enter my father's private hospital room. Robert Flynn is propped up on the bed, intravenous drip in the arm, and TV remote in hand. He is watching reserve-grade rugby league on the TV.

"These regional guys play better than the Tigers, I tell you," Dad says, not taking his eyes off the screen.

There is a cute nurse in the room (see, told you). She notices the flowers I brought. "Oh, let me get you a jug of water," she says with some brand of African accent, smiling at the flowers and then giving me that *how sweet* look I always get.

"Why, thank you. I think they could use a drink; I know I could," I say suggestively.

The nurse smiles and leaves. Dad watches the nurse exit with the flowers, one of his dark bushy eyebrows raising. He then stares at my plastered nose.

"What's wrong with your face?"

"I'm good thanks, Dad, and you?"

"It was a woman, wasn't it?"

"What are ya watching?"

"It was a woman," Dad says, nodding his head, turning his focus back to the rugby. "Why do you always bring me flowers? You know I hate flowers!"

"You love flowers, you tended to them in the garden more than you tended to me."

"That's not true. But yeah, I like flowers. In the garden where they belong. Alive! Not decapitated. Now, they're just flowers living out a slow death, just like me."

"You're not dying, Dad."

"I mean, really. Who brings his old man on his death bed a bunch of flowers so he can watch them slowly wither away? Whataya trying to do, speed up the process?"

"Come on, you're not on your deathbed." Then, more quietly, "You're gonna get through this. You're a fighter. A survivor."

"Oh, come on Archie. We both know I haven't lived a healthy lifestyle. Not since..."

"Mind over matter, Pops – you're gonna survive this. You'll see. You just need to switch that neg-head brain of yours." The nurse returns, holding a jug full of water and the flowers and places it by the window.

"Oh, perfect, thank you," I say. She shoots me a quick glance and smiles, which I reciprocate, and then stare at her arse as she leaves the room. Dad clocks it all, of course.

"Oh, *now* I get it. I see why you bring me flowers," he says shaking his head. "There you go, thinking with your dick again. Not about your pops. You know, someday, your insatiable dick is gonna get you in serious trouble."

"Huh... funny you say that..."

"Oh, shit, what? You slept with someone's wife and they beat the crap outta you?"

"No... just a little STD scare."

"I knew it, herpes!"

"Unidentified, actually."

"Unidentified!? What the hell are you talking about?" Dad looks genuinely concerned.

"They don't know what it is yet, so nothing's confirmed. Relax."

"Shit, Archie. If any penis could discover an alien disease, it would be yours. Your cock's gonna drop off one day."

"Thanks for the support, Dad."

"I'm just saying, son – you gotta stop fucking around. I mean, you're thirty now. Sorry about not getting you a birthday present by the way. It's the meds these guys have me on. I'm forgetting shit, you know."

"It's okay. Just wishing me happy birthday was enough."

"No, it's not okay, Archie. It's your thirtieth. That's a big one. I shoulda got you a present. I *will* get you a present. You're officially over the hill now. It's all downhill from here. Enjoy the peak as much as you can, because it's one fast downhill slope."

"Well, that's positive."

I sometimes wonder why Pops says such things. Thirty is hardly over the hill. Hell, forty wasn't even considered over the hill these days. Fifty? Maybe. But then it struck me. Dad was thirty years old when my mum left him. Everything was downhill from there for Robert Flynn. I don't say anything, only stare, feeling pity for him that life has made him this way and he's still holding onto this resentment, adding to his cynicism and bitterness. But Dad has a way of reading my mind.

"Your mother left me when I was thirty."

"Yeah, I remember."

"For that no-good cheese-dick real estate agent. I think that's why you're such a womaniser. Afraid to commit 'cause your mother walked out."

An interesting point, though not one I hadn't considered before. Not that I feel this way consciously, but perhaps buried in my subconscious, is there a deep-rooted fear of abandonment? Is that why I never allow myself to get too close or intimate with women? I should talk to a therapist about it. I make a mental note to book a session with one.

"You should go see a psychologist," Dad says.

"I'm not a womaniser. I just love women so much that I love a lotta them."

"You realise you can't fuck around now, Archie. Not until they sort this alien dick-flu you got. I'm serious, son. *No fucking around*. Is that why she busted your nose, 'cause you passed this shit onto her?"

I make a vow to Dad to remain abstinent until the minor issue is sorted. He makes me promise and all, so I do. And I mean it. If I really do have some kind of highly contagious STD, then the last thing I want is to spread that shit around. Dad seems satisfied with my vow of abstinence, and at that point, I get up to leave.

"Hang on, I haven't given you your thirtieth birthday present yet."

"You don't have one."

"I know I wasn't the best father. I know I wasn't around much. And that you had to do all the chores after your bitch-mother left. No. I need to say this. I've never been good at expressing love, Archie. Especially after she abandoned us. I didn't know how to. I stopped loving... And I don't want the same to happen to you, son. Bitterness, resentment, vindictive thinking, it's what got me here. It's all up here, son,' Dad says while tapping his head. "You are what you think. You don't let love into ya heart, bad things will happen, you understand. Do not lose sight of love, no matter what happens. Promise me?"

"That's the second promise I'm making you today. Stretching the relationship."

"Promise me, Arch."

"I promise... Is that my birthday present?"

"No."

I sigh, rudely checking my Apple Watch for the time.

"There's something that I never said to you. That I've always found hard to say..."

"I'm adopted?"

"No!' Dad blurts out. He's clearly uncomfortable with what he's about to say. "I love you, son."

This hits me for six. My old man is right; I hadn't heard it before. At least, not for as long as I can remember. I agree whole-heartedly with my father – whether it was because he grew up male in the boomer generation, taught to bottle up and suppress his feelings, or the fact his wife and love of his life had left him for a better-looking, more successful man, I was the collateral damage, starved of the love of my father. Or maybe it was there all along – he just didn't know how to express or give it. One thing is certain, this was the first time I had ever heard that beautiful sequence of words from him. *I love you, son.*

It takes me a while to process and reply. "Thanks... I love you too, Dad." It feels weird, but ultimately good to say.

Not much is said after that, and I leave the hospital, oblivious to any of the cute nurses on the way out. I'm inside my head. In the rideshare on the way home, I stare ahead through the front windscreen. A tear rolls down my cheek.

As we drive through the bushland towards the city, I reflect on my visit to Dad. I repeat his words in his head – *never give up on love*. Had I given up on love? Have I ever even been in love? Like, real, love? I always got love and lust mixed up, especially in my earlier years. These days, it leans more towards lust. I think as I've gotten older that I may have become more emotionally detached. I do need a psychologist – there's some deep shit festering beneath that I can't quite put my finger on. But I don't even wanna face it right now. I need a distraction. Alcohol, sex, anything.

"Hey Siri, play messages," I command my phone.

She immediately obeys with, "You have six new messages. First message from Veronica Venezuela: 'Hey handsome, you wanna come around tonight? I've been a mucho naughty girl.'"

I would love nothing more than to booty-call Veronica tonight but I just made a vow to my old man. Siri asks, "Would you like to reply?"

"No."

"Next message is from Claire Tinder: 'Just want to say I had an amazing night the other night and would love to do it again... like... now if you're free?'"

"Aw man," I say to myself as I catch the rideshare driver glance at me in his mirror. I adjust my pants as I feel myself getting a hard-on. There's that familiar sting on my dick again.

"Would you like to reply?" Siri asks.

"No," I say.

"Next message is from Mary Instagram," Siri announces. "'Babe, I wanna lick your balls. Call me.'"

I can't believe what I'm hearing from Siri. Neither can the driver, locking eyes with me in the rear-vision mirror again. "Man, what is your secret?"

I have dating chat with the driver all the way back to West Rocks. After he drops me off and thanks me for what he considers to be my "pearls of wisdom", I head inside and immediately get to work cutting ties with all the women in my life. This may sound harsh but I blocked all my current booty-call contacts in my phone, and on socials. It was for their own good. If it makes you feel any better, I messaged them the following before blocking them:

I'm sorry, I have to ghost you for your own protection. Also, get yourself checked for STDs. All the best, Arch.

This took me the good part of two hours. Next up, I had to delete all the dating apps on my phone. This included your Tinder, Bumble, Hinge, Plenty of Fish, OkCupid, Happn, Zoosk, Badoo and eHarmony. Then there was the more niche variety such as Adult Matchmaker, Ashley Maddison, Woo Plus, AfroCupid, IndoCupid, ThaiCupid, Wild, 3Fun, Fetish and Straight-to-the-date... Don't ask.

Deleting them felt strangely liberating. My phone seemed to appreciate the clean-up too, as it instantly functioned faster once the apps were uninstalled. But I also felt incredibly horny, as if cutting ties with all these contacts for sexual gratification had ignited the desire for a good old-fashioned flogging. Well, porn isn't off the cards is it? In fact, porn is all I've got now. At least for the foreseeable future, until this god-awful thing on my penis is gone.

I open a private browser tab and navigate to Pornhub, my new best friend. I watch the first video I find – "Ebony Mum Seduces Stepson". That'll do. What is with the obsession with step-siblings, sons and daughters in porn? Anyway, I don't think about that too much – I am that horny.

I watch the porn and begin playing with myself, but as I stroke harder I let out a massive cry.

"Aaaarrrrgggghhhhhh!"

The pain is instant and paralysing. I leap up and rush to the bathroom.

"Fuck me!" I yell as I look down at my penis. I don't like what I see. The lump has grown and turned an orange-purple colour. I grimace and slump up against the wall of the bathroom, clutching my crotch and moaning as I slowly slide down the wall and curl up into the foetal position. I haven't sobbed like this in years.

My life, as I knew it, was fucking over.

Chapter 9
The Rain Run

Jezebel putting me to shame when hiking up Barrenjoey Head inspired me to order a new set of Adidas jogging sneakers, running shorts and a sweatshirt. They just arrived and I'm using my new attire to get back on the exercise horse. But it's raining outside and the fat little devil on my shoulder is telling me to use it as an excuse not to go for a jog. Because, you know, rainwater being so deadly and all. I try my best to ignore the little devil bastard as I emerge from my front door, but water pours over from the balcony above. The lazy fucker on my shoulder whispers in my ear that I shouldn't ruin my new clothes because that's what rainwater does, right?

So, I turn back but instead of envisioning the little devil, I have a strange confrontation with an imaginary David Goggins standing in my doorway. He's staring at me with that look he does, shaking his head and saying, *Don't even fucking think about it. Remove that pathetic-ass excuse from your mind. Now. Fucking. Now.* I read one of his books months ago, also as an excuse to get off my arse, but hadn't done anything about it till now. Bryce put me onto him. He swears by David Goggins.

But Goggins is right. It's just a bit of rain, I tell myself. Nothing like a good run in the rain. Without another thought I step back outside, shut the door and jog across the street to a set of old sandstone stairs leading up to Observatory Hill; the old, circular park that overlooks West Rocks and across the harbour to Balmain.

By the time I reach the top of the park, not even a few minutes later, I'm absolutely rooted. I bend over, gasping for air. A shadow encroaches and I look up to see imaginary Goggins in front of me, arms crossed, shaking his head again.

"Fuck off, Goggins," I say out loud as I double over to catch my breath.

Imaginary Goggins reminds me of the embarrassment of climbing Barrenjoey Head with Jezebel when she barely broke a sweat. *Jezebel, who broke my nose.* The thought angers me, which I channel into energy to push on.

I continue jogging the path along the top of the park through some giant, hundred-year-old fig trees. It's not long before I'm catching my breath again. I stop and notice a couple working out in the Observatory Hill Rotunda, keeping out of the rain – it looks to be a woman and a male personal trainer. The personal trainer holds up boxing pads as the woman punches away. But not in an exercise routine kind of way. No. This woman moves fast, and punches with force, making the trainer struggle to maintain his footing. She punches like... well, a professional.

Holy shit, is that... Jezebel Ekas!?

I stop in my tracks and consider turning back and hiding behind the fig tree, but it's too late. As if somehow sensing my presence, Jezebel stops punching and looks in my direction. The personal trainer follows her gaze and glares, shifting his stance and playing the hero, ready to protect his client from the strange man lurking nearby. He is lean and muscular with hair tied back into a short ponytail, with a bushy beard and arm-sleeve tattoos. I'd best describe him as some kind of hipster athlete.

"Archie, is that you?" Jezebel asks.

"Jezebel?"

"You know this guy?" Hipster Athlete asks, overly surprised.

Jezebel nods slightly, takes in my face. Or, more specifically, my plaster-taped snoz. I can see the past weekend's events flooding back for her – the wedding, the reception, Jeremy and Sandra's failed *Dirty Dancing* manoeuvre, the walk up to the lighthouse, the snake, the first kiss and, unfortunately, my lasciviousness and subsequent punch in the nose.

"What are you doing here?" she asks.

"Rain run," I reply, not really knowing what that is.

"Rain run?"

"I like running in the rain. I find it, ah, cleansing." Of all the parks in all the world, she walks into mine. What are the chances? I mean, really.

Hipster Athlete looks unimpressed, shifts his body language, facing away from me, ready to resume training, "Come on," he says to Jezebel, trying to get her attention back, "let's not break momentum. It's fight night Friday."

But Jezebel ignores him, and continues staring at me. "Your nose... is it broken?" she asks.

"Oh that. Yeah, just a fracture. But it's cool. I deserved it."

"Deserved what? Did this guy hurt you?" Hipster Athlete asks.

"No. Just give me a second," Jezebel says to him as she takes off her gloves and steps down the rotunda stairs, joining me in the pouring rain. We seek shelter under an oak tree, which offers some respite from the rain, and takes us out of earshot of Hipster Athlete, who watches on like a hawk watches its prey.

"What are the chances, huh?" I say, attempting to break the ice. "City of six million people and you train in the park next to my home?"

"I live downtown," she says avoiding eye contact, looking out at the normally panoramic view over the harbour, but which now is just grey clouds and rain. "Listen, I'm sorry I broke your nose. That was wrong."

"I deserved it."

"No. You didn't," she says, finally meeting my eyes. "I mean, treating me like one of your sluts is not cool, but violence isn't the answer."

"Interesting coming from someone who beats people up for a living."

"I was triggered. There are things that have happened that, umm, I'm not going to go into right now."

"Okay." Now I'm the one to admire the non-existent view. "I don't think you are a slut. I just, I... there's no excuse for my behaviour... I'm sorry."

"I'm sorry I broke your nose."

"It's okay, I'm glad you did it."

"Come on."

"No, really. I think it's gonna add to my character."

A hint of a smile creases Jezebel's eyes. A slightly cheeky glint. "Really? Like an improvement?" she says with her slightly mocking smile, which I can't help but find incredibly charming.

"Maybe, yeah." I smile myself, feeling the mood lighten.

"A bit of ruggedness, maybe?"

"Exactly, like, Marlon Brando, you know?" The reference seems lost on her. "He broke his nose too and..."

"Yeah, I get it," she says cutting me short. "I'm sure the ladies will love it."

I'm not sure what to say to that, and there's an extended silence. Slightly awkward. I'm the one to break it.

"Anyway, I just wanted to apologise."

Jezebel waits for it. I glance over to Hipster Athlete who stares back with a steely glare. I turn my attention back to Jezebel.

Jezebel nods. "Apology accepted. Look, I better get back to work."

"Yeah, I don't think your trainer likes me too much."

"Oh, Steve. Don't worry about him. He's just anxious about my upcoming fight."

"You sure can pack a punch. Surprised you didn't knock me the fuck out."

Jezebel laughs as she walks away. Even sweating in her activewear, she is so smoking hot.

"Thanks for, ah..." *Now just what am I thanking her for?*

"Improving your looks?"

I laugh. "Yeah. Good luck in the fight, Jezebel Ekas. I'll be rooting for you."

"Rooting for me?" she asks, not getting the Aussie slang.

"Ah, cheering for you," I explain as I back away. "Australian slang. You'll get used to it." Jezebel smiles. As do I. I smile and wave goodbye to Hipster Athlete Steve, who doesn't reciprocate. "Maybe I'll see you around," I say with a wave, this time directed at Jezebel. I'm about to resume my rain run as Jezebel looks over to Steve, who shrugs impatiently.

"Hey, wait!"

I stop in my tracks.

"I got a couple of spare tickets..." Jezebel says, stopping me in my tracks, "to the fight," she adds. "It's at the Entertainment Centre this—"

"Friday night," I say finishing her sentence, "I heard." I glance at Steve, who appears severely unimpressed by the invitation.

"There will be two tickets at the door under your name, Archie Flynn."

I grin from ear to ear. I haven't felt this happy since I lost my virginity in the eighth grade. Jezebel returns to the rotunda. I smile again at Steve, give him the thumbs up. If looks could kill...

I head straight back down Observatory Hill and enter my home dripping wet. So much for the exercise. Hey, progress, not perfection, I tell myself before Goggins reappears. I hurriedly push off my sneakers, pull off my wet socks and carry them to the laundry. I throw the socks into the washing machine and rip off my t-shirt, shorts and underwear, and throw them in too. I then grab a towel and wrap myself in it as I make my way to the kitchen, open the fridge, and grab a bottle of white wine. I've earned it. In the living room I plonk myself on the couch, switch on the TV and pour myself a well-earned vino blanco.

I open the browser on my phone and type Jezebel's name. Instagram comes up at the top of the search results, and I click the link. I spit half a mouthful of Clare Valley Riesling over myself as I notice she has over 100k followers. I sit up straight, and flick through her photos. Pics of her training, posing and real fight action shots. In every shot she looks stunning. Even when dripping with sweat or straining during an intense workout. I immediately feel aroused but know the pain that brings on, so I imagine eating a piece of dog shit to reverse the blood rushing down there.

"Holy shit," I say out loud, "chick's the real deal."

I sip my wine, press the "follow" button and spend the next few hours scrolling through her Instagram feed, liking a pic every now and then. But not so many as to come off like a creep.

What were the chances of seeing Jezebel Ekas again? I mean, it's not like we live in a small city. There are six million people in greater Sydney. I'm not overly spiritual, but is this what they call a gift from God, or the universe, or whatever you wanna call it? Is it a sign that I happened to bump into her again, not even a week after we first met at the wedding? Or is it just a plain existential coincidence? I am an atheist, after all.

I just turned thirty, and have been thinking about cleaning up my act, and my philandering ways. And it's perfect timing because, since I'm abstinent, I can't sleep with her anyway.

What if Jezebel is the one who can fix me?

Chapter 10

Friday Night Fight

Qudos Bank Arena is in the middle of the Sydney Olympic Park further up the harbour where it narrows and turns into the Parramatta River. The arena hosts the Sydney Kings NBL team as well as concerts. I hardly go here. It's too far west, even though it's only a thirty-minute ferry ride up-harbour.

It must have been at least ten years ago I was here. A Kylie Minogue concert, the first one I ever went to. I never tell anyone that. A girl had invited me. We dropped ecstasy together and grooved along to "Spinning Around" and "I Should Be So Lucky". And consider *yourself* lucky because I'll take that information to the grave. Damn, what was her name? I think hard but for the life of me I can't recall it. In my defence, I was only nineteen. Did I sleep with her? How many women have I slept with since? Hundreds? Over a thousand? God only knows. All I know is I lost count a long time ago.

This reminds me of the unfortunate passenger on my penis. Is this God's punishment for my promiscuity? Have the sins of the past finally caught up with me? Hopefully, it's just a warning. If God almighty really wanted to punish my penis, he'd have given me much more than a larger-than-average pimple-looking thing on the head of my schlong. What I am thinking – I don't even believe in God! I'm doing serious head-miles over this. I just want to take a scalpel and go to town on it, but that probably wouldn't help matters.

"What are you thinking, man? Snap out of it," Bryce says next to me in the arena, who to this point had been lapping up the atmosphere, even though the arena is nowhere near full capacity. Bryce turns his attention back to the lack of spectators while squirting tomato sauce over his Four'N Twenty meat pie, which contrasts with his two-hundred-dollar Ralph Lauren shirt.

"Pretty pathetic turnout," he says before taking a much-too-large bite of pie. The sauce now drops down onto his one-thousand-dollar Canali suit pants. "Aw man, shit! This is my favourite Friday night attire. And why does it always happen to the new clothes? And white shirts!?" he complains as he wipes the sauce from his pants. "It's like a rite of passage for me with new outfits; they must be stained within a week. Karen's gonna fucking kill me."

Karen *will* kill him. Myself, I find it amusing.

"What are you laughing at, Mr. Hugo Boss seven days a week?"

"Not everyone can afford a new suit for every day of the week, boss."

"Don't insult me, man," Bryce says, looking genuinely hurt. "I own a suit for every day of the year."

"Don't lie."

"Okay, maybe not *every* day, but I'm working on it. I'm up to a hundred and seventy-eight."

"You own a hundred and seventy-eight suits?" I ask, genuinely impressed. I've only got three suits, and tonight I'm wearing my best – a light grey Heritage Hugo Boss, slim-fit virgin-wool serge. It's tailor-made and fits like a glove. I'm hoping it will impress the shit out of Jezebel, while driving her trainer to hate me even more. That's if I get to see her post-fight. But it's not just about the look. The suit gives me confidence, makes me feel James Bond-ish, of the Daniel Craig variety – my favourite Bond by a long shot, even though I'm brunette.

"It's not a poor turnout. The main card is hours from now. It'll fill up."

"Ah, yes, of course. That explains it," Bryce observes again, scoffing down his meat pie. "Hey, if it is a sell-out, that means this chick must really dig you."

"How so?"

For some reason this makes Bryce laugh, so much so that a piece of beef mince springs forth from his mouth to several rows in front. Lucky they're empty.

"Ah shit, bud, you really crack me up," he says as he stuffs the last of the meat pie in his mouth. He attempts to clean his hands and mouth up with a little serviette, without much success. He looks for somewhere to wipe his sauce-covered hands, before he resorts to licking them. I can't stand to watch, so I pass him a small packet of tissues. He gratefully cleans himself, and his clothes, up.

"Hey bud, where's your head at? It's Friday fight night!" Bryce says as he mock-shadow boxes, ducks and weaves, followed by a sip of something from a hipflask he pulls from his inside jacket pocket. "Best way to save dough on drinks at a sporting event," he says holding out the hipflask to me. Bryce is as tight as he is wealthy. Perhaps he's wealthy *because* he is such a tight-arse.

"What's in it?" I ask, referring to the hip-flask thrust in front of my face.

"Does it really matter?"

I take the flask and sip. Gasp. Almost dry retch. "The fuck is that?"

"Green Fairy. Absinthe. And not the phoney kind. This shit's illegal in Australia. Ordered on the dark web, imported from Amsterdam via Switzerland. Three-hundred and eighty bucks a bottle. Drink enough and you'll hallucinate."

"What are you bringing absinthe to a sporting event for?"

"This is our first live MMA fight, man. I'm pumped! Plus, it's not often I get a hall-pass from the wife," Bryce says, just as his phone rings. He checks it. "Ah shit, she must have heard me. How does she do that?" Bryce gives me the quiet signal as he answers his phone. "Hey honey... what noise... oh, that's Archie's TV... we *are* having a business meeting... he has a TV in his office too... to keep up with the financial news ... the business paid for it, yes." Bryce rolls his eyes as I listen with a mixture of bewilderment and bemusement. He continues, "Why are we watching TV during a business meeting? Well, honey, the evening finance reports, of course... I'm not lying, baby... Oh, it's coming on now, I gotta go... bye, bye." Bryce massages his forehead, then quietly, into the phone, says, "Love you too, sugar plum," and hangs up.

"Sugar plum?"

"Don't even." Bryce takes a large swig on his absinthe that makes him gasp.

"Lying to your wife again, sugar plum?"

"I can't tell her I'm at the MMA," he croaks out, thumping his chest with his fist as if to force the absinthe down. "Karen thinks you're a bad influence on me. She thinks you're a... womaniser."

Initially, I'm speechless. I've always known Karen Hitler was not the biggest fan of me. But a womaniser? I never had somebody call me that before. Well, actually, that's a lie. Still, it takes me a while to process, and just when I'm about to probe Bryce for more info, the announcer, well, announces the next fight.

"Okay ladies and gentlemen, the fight you've all been waiting for tonight..."

"To be continued," I tell him. I watch him smile to himself, quietly stoked he's been saved by the bell.

The announcer is in his element.

"Introducing the Mongrel from the Jungle..." he sings out to the audience with a sweeping gesture to the changing rooms.

"Who the hell is the Mongrel from the Jungle?" I say aloud to nobody in particular. I'm not liking this already. Bryce, conversely, seems to be getting even more psyched.

"Mongrel from the Jungle, ha!" he bursts out with excitement.

I am yet to lay eyes on the recipient of such a nickname, but I know two things. The first is that I do not like the nickname. The second is, I know this nickname could not possibly belong to Jezebel, so I am unsure if it's a positive or a negative at this point.

The announcer continues, "Current Brazilian national MMA flyweight champion, Bruna Gonzalez!" The few cheers from the crowd are drowned out by the home crowd. It's comforting to know that most here are supporting Jezebel. But then Bruna Gonzalez enters the octagon. She is stocky, wide-shouldered with enormous muscles. Her hair is in cornrows, giving her an extra-menacing look. In short, she looks brutal. She looks like the Mongrel from the Jungle. And this is a big, fat negative. A cold shiver goes down my spine. Bryce doesn't help my sudden onset of anxiety.

"Your girlfriend is fighting *that*?" he asks wide-eyed.

"Boss, please. Can we remain positive here?"

Bryce eyeballs me. "Shit mate, you're really clamming up. You okay? More absinthe?"

I ignore him. The announcer turns it up a notch. "And further up the Americas, from the sunny state of California..." The crowd cheers. "We have the undefeated, current poster girl of the MMA..."

Bryce nudges me. "You hear that? Poster girl of the MMA, mate. She makes the octagon the hot-agon. See what I did there?"

The news does settle my nerves somewhat. The announcer continues, "Jezebel... Ekaaaaaaasssss!"

The crowd erupts in applause as Jezebel makes her way to the stage to the strains of "California" by 2Pac. The very song I had lamely sung to her upon our first meeting! She looks fit in her fight shorts and sports bra, her toned physique on full display. Jezebel's hair is tied back into a tightly woven ponytail. She nudges her boxing gloves together as she enters the octagon. She is significantly taller than Bruna Gonzalez, yet nowhere near as stocky. You can easily see where the even weight is distributed between the two – Jezebel in height, the Mongrel from the Jungle in width. I am nervous again because while Jezebel is super fit, she looks like a runway model standing next to the Brazilian.

Nonetheless, I am in awe. As is Bryce, equally impressed. "She looks super fit, bro," he says, taking another sip of his rocket fuel.

I observe Jezebel's trainer, Hipster Athlete Steve, follow Jezebel along with the rest of her entourage and take a seat ringside. The referee steps in between the two modern-day warriors. "Now remember, no strikes to the groin, eye gouging, biting, throat striking, hair pulling, head butting or finger breaking. And always listen to me and comply." Both fighters nod in agreement. I can feel my pulse beating.

"That's it? Everything else goes?" I ask.

"Have you ever watched an MMA fight?" Bryce asks. "It's pretty brutal. And the women, even more so."

Now my pulse really quickens as I find myself nervous on Jezebel's behalf. It's an odd feeling. Alien. I can't quite pinpoint it but it seems like I genuinely care about this woman who I still barely know.

The bell rings. The referee lets go of their fists and steps back. The warrior women circle each other before Bruna Gonzalez moves in low and fast, like a young, female version of Mike Tyson. Jezebel retreats, copping blows mostly to the gloves, but a few to the abdomen. I start sweating now as Bruna keeps up on her, pinning Jezebel up against the cage. She defends with her arms and gloves in front of her chest and face. Bruna lays into her but Jezebel seizes her moment and short jabs Bruna in the face before tackling her to the ground.

"Yeeahhhh!" I'm on the edge of my seat already.

"Holy shit!" Bryce adds. "You go girl!"

They now engage in a game of Brazilian jiu-jitsu, wrestling on the floor. Each fighter anticipates two or three moves ahead, like a game of chess. It's as fascinating to watch as it is panic-inducing. I can't believe what I'm witnessing. My hands grip the program I have rolled up and twisted so much that the ink is beginning to smudge. But my concern turns to joy when Jezebel manoeuvres Bruna into an arm-bar, trying to force her into submission. Bruna somehow breaks free and grapples with Jezebel, picking her up and slamming her on the floor.

I stand up in my seat, gasping, "That can't be allowed!"

"Hooolllllyyyy shhiiiiiittttz!" Bryce screams, shoving some popcorn in his mouth. I cannot believe he finds this entertaining.

Jezebel is getting belted in the face by Bruna's fist as she straddles her. Blood squirts from Jezebel's nose. Fuck me. I sit back down, stare at the floor, unable to watch. Unknowingly, I have clasped onto Bryce's arm without realising. Bryce stares down at my tight grip on his forearm, slowly piling a small handful of popcorn into his gob while looking me in the eye.

Jezebel arches her back and knees Bruna in the arse. Bruna flies forward, smashing her face into the floor. Jezebel takes the opportunity to flip Bruna over and lands an absolute belter into her face which prompts a cheer from the crowd, including me. Bruna lands back against the floor, limp.

I instinctively jump up and yell at the top of my lungs, "ONYA JEZ!"

Jezebel hears, recognises and subtly acknowledges my war cry, and subsequently grabs Bruna in a chokehold and puts her to sleep. The referee calls game over. I'm pretty sure I notice Steve glance in my direction before rushing the stage to congratulate Jezebel.

I jump up and down cheering. Bryce joins me and we are jumping, hugging and high-fiving each other and anyone around us within reach.

Jezebel gets up and holds a fist out to the crowd in triumph.

I wipe my brow, pretty sure I'm sweating more than both of the women in the ring put together. Bryce stops cheering and gives me a look that I can't quite read. Like he's never seen me like this before, or something.

"You gonna congratulate her or what?"

"I can't go down there now."

"Not *now*. But she gave you VIP tickets," says Bryce.

"VIP, how?"

"You see this right here?" Bryce holds up my pass hanging around my neck. "That's your backstage pass."

I wait until the initial post-fight press interview is done and then I'm flashing my pass to a heavy-set security guard at the entrance to the changing rooms. The bouncer, playing God, nods his head back down the corridor without making eye contact. What a douche, I think as I head down the dark hallway and find a door with nameplate reading *Jezebel Ekas*. I can hear excited voices inside. I knock. My pulse picks back up. Sweat beads form again.

"Who is it?" a male voice booms from inside.

"Archie."

The door opens. It's Hipster Athlete. He greets me with disdain. "Oh, *you*?"

"Steve, don't be so rude – I invited him," Jezebel says from behind. Yeah, Steve, don't be so rude, I think. Jezebel has trainers and other various people that make up her entourage surrounding her. Some apply ice packs to various parts of her body. Others wipe away some blood from her nose, while another massages her shoulders. And they all lavish her with praise. Steve motions with his head, much like the bouncer before him. I smile and step inside.

"I won't hold you up. Just wanted to say thanks and congratulations," I offer.

"I'm sorry it didn't last longer," Jezebel replies.

"I'm not."

Jezebel smiles. "Ha... well, thanks for your support," she says, wiping sweat from her forehead with a towel. "It's my fans that get me through."

"Well, you definitely have a new fan in me," I say. "Your nose okay?"

"Just a small break, nothing to write home about," she says before winking at me. "Call it karma." The young blonde female medico patching up Jezebel's nose glances at my own taped-up nose. I see her mind turning it over.

"You break your nose in the ring too?" she asks.

Before I can answer, Hipster Athlete Steve does me the courtesy. "Oh, please. He's not a fighter. Look at him," he says mockingly.

"Steve, please," Jezebel cautions. Steve stops laughing, put back in his place. I clock the power dynamic in the relationship. Jezebel can fire his ass anytime, I realise. And from the way Steve feels threatened by my presence, I sense his feelings towards Jezebel go beyond just "professional". And Jezebel knows it.

"I'm a lover, not a fighter," I say, ignoring Steve. "Not that I have anything against the sport. I have a lot of respect for what you do, but I have to admit, I find it hard to watch." I see an opportunity open up to communicate that I'm still interested, in case she doesn't know it already. I've only got a few seconds before overthinking it will close the window of opportunity forever. Fuck it. Fuck Steve. "Or I just find it hard to watch *you* fight."

The room seems to go dead quiet for a few beats. A few of the entourage glance up at me, but my eyes remain fixed on Jezebel, who meets my eye. I hear Steve scoff under his breath. This pleases me, and my pulse settles. My work here is done.

"Okay, well, I'll let you enjoy your post-match celebrations. Thank you once again, Jezebel."

"And thank you for coming, Archie."

Steve happily ushers me towards the door.

"Listen, ah, we're gonna celebrate the win with a few drinks at the pub if you wanna tag along?" Jezebel asks. Steve sighs. I grin.

"I accept your invite," I reply.

"I gotta have an ice bath. Freshen up. Probably be, what, one hour? If you wanna meet us at the ferry."

An hour later, having said goodbye to Bryce who seemed disappointed not to be joining me, we are on the ferry from Olympic Park down Parramatta River towards the harbour. There's a bar on the ferry and Jezebel shouts her entourage, including me, drinks for the journey back into the city. I'm impressed with her generosity and wonder how much her prize money is. Her entourage continue to surround her, with Steve sticking to her like a fly to shit. I just hang back, enjoying the cool night-time breeze and views. It's not often I travel up-harbour. Christ, it's not often I make it past West Rocks.

I turn my attention back on Jezebel and her post-fight get-up. I've never really been into leopard print, but Jezebel, in her mini skirt, pulls it off like no other. She pairs this with a black lace top that hugs her perfect boobs. Without realising, I'm staring at said boobs until Jezebel who, like all women, has an uncanny sense of when a man's eyes are preying, stares straight back at me. And it takes a few beats before I snap out of my boob-trance, locking eyes with her. I feel the blood immediately rush to my face as I flush red. Fuck! Jezebel, however, smiles as she continues the conversation with one of her entourage. This puts me at ease a bit, except for the fact that Steve seems to have busted my boob-trance too, and stares wide-eyed at me. Then, he does the strangest thing and squints at me, like, all suspicious. I read his look as, *I'm onto you*. He definitely witnessed me boob-trancing-out, and the whole moment seems surreal, so I turn my attention back to the harbour views.

But then another one of Jezebel's entourage, who must feel pity for my lonesome self, joins me at the balustrade. I think it's the woman who was massaging Jezebel post-fight in the changing room. She's blonde, a bit plump yet still fit-looking. And she talks with a sporty-bogan accent. True-blue ocker.

"So what degree are you?" she says as she leans against the balustrade next to me, beer in hand. I realise it's not actually the masseuse, but the blonde medico who was patching up Jezebel's nose.

"Degree?" I ask.

"Six degrees of separation?"

I tilt my head, forehead creasing.

"How do you fit in?" she explains.

"Oh, I get it. I met Jezebel at a wedding last weekend."

"You only know each other a week?"

"Yeah."

"And she invited you tonight? Wow, okay."

She sips on her can of seltzer, and I can see her mind processing the information as she glances back at Jezebel. I know exactly what she's thinking, but I don't say anything, waiting for her to speak first.

"I'm Larissa. Jezebel's medic," Larissa says as she raises her hand for a fist-bump.

"Oh, one of those, are you?" I say as I fist-bump her.

"Fist-bump's the new handshake."

"Fair dinkum?"

"Fair dinkum."

I chatted with Larissa all the way back into Circular Quay, gaining some intel and insight on Jezebel. She's been here roughly six months to train away from distractions back home in California. Exactly what those distractions are, I am unsure – but I do remember Jezebel mentioning in Observatory Park that there are some things I don't know about her past. Larissa mentions she came out of a long-term relationship and I suspect this has something to do with it. I catch Jezebel's eye a few times from across the deck, and I'm pretty sure she's aware that we are talking about her. That woman is switched on or psychic or something.

We depart the ferry at Circular Quay which is always a hive of activity on Friday night. Human traffic strolls past professional buskers singing, dancing or performing stunts. There's a light show beamed onto the Opera House and hordes of tourists gathering around to watch. We all walk west into the Rocks to a bar called the Harbour View, a classic old pub sitting beneath the Harbour Bridge. One of Sydney's oldest pubs, the venue spans four levels, each offering a different kind of atmosphere and music.

Two burly bouncers man the door, but Jezebel is waved right through with her entourage, and I tag along from the back. For some reason I hold up my backstage fight pass to the bouncers who react in confusion. I'm clearly not thinking straight and feel like an outsider compared to Jezebel's groupies. We all head up to the third level where there is a bunch of seating booths, a round bar and a small dance floor. The place is filling up with it now being after ten p.m. The atmosphere is dark and moody with low lighting, a black and brown colour scheme and a slightly musky smell of burnt tobacco.

Inside the bar, I stand back again, observing Jezebel and her entourage from the outskirts of the group. I feel slightly uncomfortable and consider calling it a night. A DJ mixes old-school nineties hip hop from his booth in the corner. It is clear how much these people adore Jezebel. Not that I can hear what they are saying, but their body language says it all. There may as well be a spotlight on Jezebel as her friends, trainer, manager, promoter, fans, and whoever else surrounds the charismatic American. Jezebel looks magnificent, and she does give off a certain aura.

I remember the natural high after a hard-fought win in rugby back in my high school days. Even if you were bruised and sore as fuck, you were still on cloud nine. And that's exactly where Jezebel's at.

Suddenly Jezebel makes a beeline for me. "Hate to break up your little party but it's shots time," she says while staring straight at the barman. "Ten rounds of tequila," she demands, "and some lemon and salt for the softies." She nudges and winks at me cheekily, with her perfectly applied eyeliner and mascara. Not too much, not too little. The perfect amount of make-up. I feel slightly emasculated.

"Lemon and salt with tequila? What is that, an American thing? We drink it straight up down under," I declare a little too seriously.

"Oh, you drink tequila here?" she says, smiling and showing her pearly whites.

"You kidding? I bathe in it," I reply.

"I'm a softie; I'm defo gonna need lemon and salt," Larissa adds, appearing next to us at the bar.

The barman lines up eight shot glasses side by side and runs the bottle along, filling them up with tequila.

"On the tab, thanks," said Jezebel.

"Let me get this round," I offer.

"Don't be ridiculous."

I was impressed. Most of the women I dated in Sydney insisted on splitting the bill, but here was this incredible woman insisting on shouting drinks for everyone. Her generosity was highly attractive; I couldn't stand tight-asses, aside from Bryce of course. I couldn't help but wonder about her prize money and whether her entourage were freeloaders, as I glanced across the group lining up for free shots. My thoughts were interrupted when I noticed Steve staring at me again. Bet Steve's a tight ass.

Jezebel handed me a shot of tequila, and the barman placed some lemon and salt on the bar. Larissa wasted no time and got stuck into them.

"Cheers, cunt," Jezebel said as she clinked glasses with me, who was honestly a little taken aback with her use of the word *cunt*. "Sorry, just know how much you Aussies love to say that. It's practically an illegal word in the States."

I laughed and held my glass up towards Steve. "Cheers, cunt," before downing the shot. Steve followed suit, slamming the shot glass upside down on the bar top, letting out a loud sigh, and staring at me wide-eyed. It was getting weird.

"All right. Now..." Jezebel poked me in the chest, "... you're coming to dance."

"I don't dance."

"Oh yeah, I remember – the hammy, right?" Before I could answer, she followed up with, "Get your ass on the dance floor," as she grabbed my hand and dragged me past a livid Steve, whose glare followed us as we made our way to the stairs leading up to the rooftop.

The pub's rooftop bar area and dance space featured the massive sandstone pylons of Sydney Harbour Bridge towering above. Chinese lanterns of various colours hung overhead, making for a picturesque scene. Slow, groovy tunes played by the DJ set a romantic atmosphere that suited me perfectly. As I held Jezebel close, her hip pressed firmly against mine, her fragrance – jasmine – stimulated my senses. Everything felt right, and there was something about this woman that just clicked with me. We were in perfect harmony, riding the same wave since we first met, despite the broken nose incident. There was almost a serendipity to it all.

"Who would've thought, huh..." Jezebel said, her eyes glinting mischievously, "you and I dancing again."

"Under a starry sky... two broken noses, so romantic," I added with a smirk, attempting to match her playful tone. She laughed, her sense of humour never failing to enchant me. Even with her taped-up nose, she looked captivating.

"It *is* kind of romantic," she said, gazing at the dark clouds above. "But not so starry. What is with all the rain? I thought it was meant to be scorched earth down under."

"It can get hot down under," I teased.

"Is that right?" Jezebel's expression shifted to a more serious tone. "Because all I see are ominous-looking clouds – a bit like your eyes, the window to your soul."

"Are you saying I have a gloomy soul?"

"Don't get me wrong, you're fucking hot. You have these cute dimples, and the most beautiful eyes; one of the things that first attracted me to you. But I'm just not sure what's behind them."

"Oh, I got no soul now!?"

"I think it's there somewhere. Deep down. Hiding. Afraid to expose itself to the light."

"What if I like the dark side…"

"Okay, Darth Archie."

"Darth Archie… I kinda like that."

Star Wars jokes aside, Jezebel's comment lingered in my mind as I pondered my past philandering and relationships with women. The truth is, I haven't ever had a purely platonic relationship with a chick. I just don't see the point. Or is it something deeper than that?

"Wow. Where'd you just go? More introspection?" Jezebel said, bringing me back to the present. I smile and nod. Her ability to read me never ceases to amaze me.

There's no way I can have a platonic relationship with this woman. But then I am reminded of my affliction on my precious manhood and realise that, even if I wanted something more than friendship with Jezebel, I couldn't. I have a duty to protect her. These things are called sexually transmitted infections for a reason – they're highly contagious. And I cannot be honest with her about it either. If I exposed her to it, it could turn her off completely. A deal-breaker. And not just because of the hideous physical aspect of the STD; she would know the truth about my promiscuity. I'd lose her forever. Plus, I made a pact with the old man – I promised not to fuck around until this thing is well and truly gone. So, I have no choice but to pursue a platonic relationship with Jezebel Ekas, an absolute first for me.

"I have my own personal reasons for a platonic relationship," I say. Jezebel continues to stare, as if trying to solve a complicated equation reflected in my eyes. Or are we having another moment? Do I go for the lean-in? My pulse quickens. But the whole mood is instantly ruined when Steve appears suddenly on the dance floor with Larissa. They start slow-dancing next to us, although Steve seems more interested in Jezebel than me. I cringe.

"I think Steve wants this dance," I whisper in Jezebel's ear.

"Have you got a problem with that?" she says quietly back.

"I think Steve has a problem with *me*," I reply. "And has a serious hard-on for you."

"Gross. It's not all about sex, you know."

"Okay, I think he's…" I don't want to say the L-word. "…got a crush."

As we move slowly and closely together, Jezebel decides it's a good time to pry. "You're a fuck-boy, huh?" The directness of the question takes me by surprise.

"What? No, what makes you say that?"

"Come on, sure you are. I know a player when I see one."

"You clearly don't, because I'm not."

"That old quickie-at-the-wedding move? Didn't seem like your first rodeo."

"Nup. Not my style. In fact, it was extremely out of character for me," I lie. "I think it was all the pent-up sexual energy."

"I don't. Tell me about this pent-up sexual energy."

"Well... It's been a while."

"Bullshit."

"I was in a desperate state that night."

"Oh please," Jezebel says, reading my mind again.

Just then, the DJ speeds up the beat with the next tune, which seems to delight Steve, who breaks away from Larissa and starts shifting and sliding his feet, Michael Jackson-style. I shit you not. I am astonished, looking at Jezebel to ask whether he's taking the piss or is for real.

"Oh boy, here we go," Jezebel says, rolling her eyes, seemingly having witnessed this show before.

"Woo hoo, yeah! Go Steve!" Larissa encourages him, the tequila having gone straight to her head.

"Wow. This is the real deal, Steve's really going for it, huh?" I say, bemused.

Steve, determined to steal the spotlight, busts out some sharp dance moves. A circle forms around him and Jezebel now breaks away from me and joins in clapping Steve on, but in a way that suggests she feels obligated to. I cringe, but not wanting to look like a sour-puss, reluctantly join in, cheering on the dance maestro. To my amazement (and amusement), some of Steve's dance moves involve him flexing his pecs, which bob up and down through his tight, sleeveless shirt. But the ultimate flex is his final robotic dance sequence which finishes with his elbow held up in the air while his forearm dangles back and forth. He signs this off with a click of the fingers and points directly at me. Is that a challenge? Surely he's not calling me out for a dance-off? I hope not, because I'll lose. Steve receives a small round of applause as he struts off the dance floor, throwing a smirk my way as the dance prodigy makes his dramatic exit. I silently thank the gods that there's no dance-off.

"Another drink?" Jezebel asks me.

"As many as it takes to erase that from my memory forever," I reply. Jezebel laughs.

We made our way to the bar, where we continue celebrating as Jezebel's entourage slowly fall away one by one. Except for Steve, of course. I was fairly certain Jezebel wanted to leave with me, but not wanting to overstay my welcome, I casually mention that I lived close by and was planning to call it a night. To my delight, Jezebel objected with a slightly slurred voice.

"Oh, come on, stay for one more," she insisted. "I'm not done celebrating yet."

Steve chimes in, reminding Jezebel of their recovery session the next day, checking his watch, and emphasising that it was getting late. I couldn't help but wonder who this dude thought he was – her father?

"My recovery will be sleeping in," Jezebel retorts, taking another swig of seltzer.

"You didn't even have your ice bath," Steve points out, which Jezebel waved off.

"Don't worry about me, Steve. I'll have a cold shower in the morning."

"How are you getting home?"

"Archie's going to walk me home."

Her request caught me by surprise, but I tried my best not to show it. "I'll make sure she gets home safe."

Steve's stone-cold expression was priceless as his eyes darted between Jezebel and me. The tension in the air was palpable. But Jezebel quickly defused it by standing between us, placing her hands on Steve's shoulders.

"We did good tonight. Thank you for everything," she said to him quietly before giving him a warm hug. Steve responded with something I couldn't quite make out amidst the noise of the bar, but which sounded an awful lot like, "*Really, this fucker from down under?*"

Jezebel reassured him, "I'll be fine. Seriously. I'll catch you tomorrow."

Finally, Steve got the message and left the bar, shooting a glare back at me as he raised two fingers to his eyes and then pointed them directly at me. I slightly tilted my head, giving him a small frown before he smirked and exited. Hilarious.

After one last drink, Jezebel and I decided to leave the bar before we were completely intoxicated. As we strolled through the narrow, wet cobblestone laneways of The Rocks, the midnight hour had quieted the usually bustling nightlife of the inner city. A few distant conversations could be heard from hidden whiskey and wine bars, but the rain had dampened the energy of the night.

In a tipsy, light-hearted state, we laughed together, reminiscing about Steve's comical dance moves. Jezebel's infectious personality made me laugh even harder. At one point, she laughed so hard that she fell over, clutching her jaw in mock pain. As the laughter subsided, I helped her up, and we shared a heartfelt embrace.

At that moment, I felt a spark of connection, but our inebriation made me hesitate to take it further. The old me would have seized the opportunity, but now I knew better. Instead, I suggested I walk her home, and Jezebel playfully agreed, asserting that she wouldn't walk alone through "downtown" as the Americans call it.

As we approached her high-rise apartment building, our arms interlinked for support, I thanked her for the tickets to the event. I mentioned Bryce, who she briefly met at the wedding, and Jezebel playfully referred to him as "Bryce Hitler" followed by a laugh. I explained that Bryce was both my boss and a friend, and our relationship was complicated. She agreed.

After finding her keys, she teased me with a suggestive look, but I respectfully declined her invitation to come up to her apartment. I knew where it would lead, and I didn't want to risk anything in our drunken state. I thanked her for the night and mentioned that I was content to leave it there. A first for me.

Jezebel seemed surprised by my decision but accepted it with good humour. Expecting at least a kiss goodbye, instead I offered my hand for a handshake. She stared at my hand a few beats, as if unsure what to do with it. Finally, she accepted my handshake, playfully referring to our interaction as "doing business" and nodding as if completing a formal transaction.

I smiled and bid her goodnight, leaving with a sense of restraint, relief and pride. This was progress. Both for myself and for building a potentially meaningful relationship with this fascinating woman.

"Thank you for walking me home!" she called out after me.

"Anytime!"

Chapter 11

Stage 2: Anger

I'm busy bashing away at my keyboard in the office, each key suffering my wrath as if I'm crafting the angriest email in history. But, of course, I'm not. It's just a mundane stock analysis report. Yet, I despise it. Work feels like a shit sandwich today. The office, an unwanted presence. Or maybe there's something else brewing beneath the surface? Of course, there's something else brewing beneath the surface.

In walks Bryce, holding a steaming cup of coffee like it's a precious elixir. "Got a bone to pick with your keyboard, mate?"

He seems way too chipper for me and my foul mood. I don't even bother to look up, my fingers continuing their percussive dance on the keys.

"You're not firing off another email to Sharon from accounts, are you? Last thing we need is another HR complaint about you, mate," Bryce adds, settling into my office as comfortably as if it were his own, sipping his cappuccino while gazing out at the view. A routine he's made a habit of.

"Duncan McTaggart, the cop from Brisbane, wants his portfolio adjusted," I finally respond.

"Constable McTaggart? How much is he playing with?"

"A hundred K, give or take."

"Decent sum for a copper."

"Inheritance."

"Ah, righto. We making him dough?"

"Not much. He jumped on board before the market's recovering. We're not back in black just yet," I explain, fully aware that this isn't the real reason Bryce is visiting. I wish he'd just quit the foreplay and get to the point. "Is that why you've graced me with your company this morning, boss? To talk finances?"

"Have a serious conversation about work? Heaven forbid," Bryce retorts, turning to face me. "You know why I'm here."

"Can't say I'm in the mood this morning."

"You're never in the mood anymore. Just throw me a bone. Did you at least get a goodnight peck or a little touchy-feel?"

My irritation bubbles up, breaching the surface. "I said I'm not in the mood, Bryce!"

Naturally, Bryce is taken aback. "Whoa there, someone woke up on the wrong side of the bed this morning."

I should have left it at that, apologised and removed myself from the situation. But my impulse to deflect often overshadows my emotional intelligence. "How's everything on the home front, boss?"

"Kindly drop the 'boss', mate," Bryce retorts, pondering the question. "And what do you mean? Things are fine. Why?"

"How're things in the bedroom with Karen? Is the fire still burning?"

"It's there, but you know how it goes after a few years of marriage. What are you getting at?"

"If you're living vicariously through me, maybe things aren't all sunshine and rainbows at home?"

"Right. And what's your point?"

"You're clearly not getting your fair share. And if that's not putting a grin on your face, why stick around? You taught me yourself – you've got three choices in these circumstances: alter the situation, extract yourself or embrace the status quo. None of these involve me playing therapist for your lacklustre sex life."

Bryce rises from his seat, and almost looks hurt. "Remember, I'm your superior, you arsehole," he grumbles before making his exit.

I lower my head in shame, the weight of my words sinking in. I've stirred up a mess, and it's clear that I need to address it quickly before it costs me my job.

I locate Bryce in his corner office, his gaze fixed on the million-dollar spectacle of the harbour and Opera House. "I'm sorry," I say, leaning against the doorframe. Bryce barely acknowledges me, offering a dismissive wave of his hand. "Seriously, there's something eating at me lately."

"Forget about it," Bryce mumbles as he takes a seat at his desk, shuffling papers and avoiding my eye. It's clear that I've managed to really rattle him this time. I decide to join him, taking a seat opposite.

"I projected my frustrations onto you. I was in the wrong, and I apologise. As your employee, I was way out of line."

"I said let it go."

"I've been dealing with a lot of built-up frustration. Truth is, I haven't had sex in over a month myself."

Bryce merely nods, his focus shifting to his computer as he moves the mouse around.

"I can't even relieve myself. It's like my balls are about to explode."

Bryce finally engages. "What, have you taken a vow of celibacy or something?"

"Are you nuts? No. It's this issue down there."

This piques Bryce's interest. "What's going on?"

"That's the messed-up part – the doctor doesn't even know."

"What do you mean, an STD?"

I nod. I become paranoid about other colleagues hearing so I quickly rise, shutting the office door. I continue in a hushed tone, "The doc has never seen anything like it."

"Wow, that's something. Who gave it to you?"

"I don't even know who it's from."

"Doesn't surprise me. Bound to happen sooner or later. Surprised you didn't catch something earlier."

"That's not helpful."

"And regarding the blue balls, you really need to deal with that. I've done my research, it's a real thing. You could have an imploding orgasm, which is not the nice kind. No wonder you're on edge."

"Imploding orgasm... what the fuck is that?"

"You don't wanna know. Just find a way to rub one out."

"It fucking stings!"

"Listen, it's not worth stressing over. It'll probably go away on its own. They usually do, don't they?"

"This thing is just getting worse – bigger, uglier and more painful by the day."

"Yikes…"

"And you know the worst part?"

"It gets worse than that?"

"I think I'm falling for Jezebel. Girl of my dreams. She's the best, and I can't even be with her!"

"Well… Archie Flynn finally meets his match, huh?" Bryce remarks, a hint of amusement in his tone. I offer a slight nod, and a half-hearted shrug.

"Look, this could be a gift wrapped in shit."

"Sorry, what?"

"A gift wrapped in shit. You know, a silver lining. If not for this… issue, you would've already slept with Jezebel and then she'd just be what? Another conquest. This situation could be good for you, giving you time to really get to know her before taking things to the next level. They say things happen for a reason, yeah?"

I ponder Bryce's words, and surprisingly, they ease my mind about the situation. What if my condition is actually helping the burgeoning relationship, not sabotaging it? I have to admit, Bryce's perspective impresses me.

"A blessing wrapped in shit, huh?"

"A gift wrapped in shit," Bryce confirms with a knowing nod and a friendly smile. "Now, go shift some digits."

Chapter 12

Jezebel Ekas

I find myself gazing at an unsent message to Jezebel, my finger hovering over the send button. Maybe I should call instead... no, wait. Phone down. I fixate on my phone, resting on the kitchen counter. A strong yearning to see Jezebel again grips me, yet I'm determined not to make it sound like an invitation for a date. Dating her isn't an option. What's the use if I can't take things to the next level? But I remind myself, it's a gift wrapped in shit as Bryce would say, and that means I have to play this slow. Stretch it out, like the old-fashioned art of courtship.

"Just dinner," I murmur aloud to myself. "Just a casual thank-you dinner... Hey Siri, call Jezebel Ekas," I request. The phone emits a dial tone, and my heart starts to race. But as soon as I hear her voice, a wave of calm washes over me. The conversation is short and to the point. Dinner is on. My place.

Five hours later, I'm busy in the kitchen. This translates into me deciphering the instructions of a meal kit I ordered from a company that we have holdings in at work. The company's success skyrocketed when the pandemic struck. Bryce was positively thrilled and heaped praise on me for my foresight in investing in the company. While their performance might have waned a bit since then, they did make good profits for our clients. Now, I'm expressing my gratitude for those profits by continuing to patronise them even as people venture out for food once again. Well that, and the fact that I'm an abysmal cook. Plus, Jezebel is en route, and I need to make a lasting impression.

Of course, Jezebel won't suspect that I'm relying on a meal kit. I'll simply present this Mediterranean-style salmon dish with lemon, sweet potato and broccoli as if it's part of my expansive culinary repertoire. I strategically place a few bits of food debris on the cutting board alongside a generously sized knife to convey the illusion that I've been diligently toiling away in the kitchen.

Now, onto the wine. I've deduced that Jezebel is quite the wine enthusiast, and this happens to be a domain where I'm relatively competent. Meat dish equals red; seafood equals white. Actually, that's the breadth of my wine knowledge. So, I choose a Clare Valley Riesling to harmonise with the salmon. I pour myself a glass and savour a healthy gulp, because let's be honest, wine is an essential co-chef while tackling meal prep.

But first things first, I remember to extract some financial magazines from the drawer of my coffee table and neatly lay them on its surface. This manoeuvre is meant to convey that I'm not only profoundly devoted to my work, but also that my financial game is on point. Should she consider this alpha male as a mating partner, she knows her future is secure.

Then, I discreetly stow away my vape and my quitting smoking guide in the same drawer, out of sight. Carrying my Riesling with me, I enter the bathroom and lift the toilet lid, inspecting its cleanliness. Not satisfactory. Donning my dishwashing gloves, armed with toilet cleaner, I attack the toilet bowl with fervour. I then scrub myself with vigour in the shower, taking a moment to perform some manscaping before I'm reminded of the unwelcome passenger on my nether regions.

Back in the kitchen, I appear fresh and put-together, yet somewhat disheartened. The plan is simple: a cosy homemade dinner, good wine, a touch of romance. Thank her for the evening and that's it. You've got this.

It isn't long before the doorbell chimes, announcing Jezebel's arrival. I halt in the middle of the kitchen, eyeing the oven and then the stovetop. I cross over, turning the knob on the gas burner to reheat the pre-cooked salmon in the pan. The stove fan whirs to life as I slip on an apron, neatly tying its belt. The apron boldly proclaims, KING of THE KITCHEN.

Rushing down the hallway, I reach the front door and swing it open to reveal a breathtaking Jezebel. Wearing a cute, half-sleeve, beige dress and her long, naturally curly hair out, she's a vision. Subtle makeup accentuates her eyes with precision, showcasing her sharp features. Frankly, she looks stunning beyond words, rendering me momentarily speechless.

"Everything alright, King of The Kitchen?" Jezebel's voice cuts through the quiet.

"Sorry, uh, come in. You look... you look sensational," I say, managing to regain my composure.

"Thanks," Jezebel responds as she enters. I notice her taking in my living space. Her eyes sweep across the entrance – the door, the floor, the walls – all in a matter of seconds.

"Please," I gesture, inviting her to proceed down the hallway. As she goes, Jezebel sneakily peeks up at the staircase.

"Wow, lovely place," she comments, her tone warm. "Mmm, I recognise that smell."

"You do?" I ask as we step into the lounge room adjoining the kitchen.

"Salmon, sweet potatoes and greens. Easy Eats meal kit, right?"

I freeze, my face betraying me by turning a bright shade of crimson. Jezebel's eyes shift from the words on my apron then back to meet my gaze, accompanied by a playful wink and a smile. She proceeds to explore the living and dining areas, leaving me torn between feeling embarrassed and undeniably charmed. Never before has a woman not only exposed my deception, but also playfully mocked it with such casual cheekiness. Like a fascinated zombie, I shuffle to the stove and turn it off. The salmon is already cooked.

"They offer quality produce, and the instructions are straightforward," I say, attempting to justify my actions.

"Recipes."

"Pardon?"

Jezebel, absorbed in my bookshelf, corrects me with a smile. "They're recipes, not instructions."

"Right. The recipes are simple to follow, though?"

"Yep, just as they say," Jezebel responds, winking at me again, before selecting a book from the shelf and inspecting its cover. My admiration for this woman grows exponentially.

"I, uh... We actually have shares in that company at work. Made significant gains for my clients."

Jezebel remains engrossed in reading the back cover of a book. I can't discern the title, but I'm desperately hoping it's not *American Psycho* or *The Wolf of Wall Street*. I realise she might be curious about my reading choices. "What book you got there?"

"Oh, fan of David Goggins, huh?"

"Oh, uh, not really, to be honest, I find him a bit intimidating."

"You've met him?"

Realising how that statement might be misinterpreted, and at the risk of sounding crazy by revealing my David Goggins-like imaginary personal trainer, I backtrack. "No, but I imagine he would be, you know. Does that sound weird?"

"Not really. I know what you mean. But I like him," Jezebel responds.

"Can I get you a glass of wine?"

Jezebel lowers the book, her gaze still lingering on its cover. "And how's that exercise working out for you? Yes, please."

"I go through phases. I was quite active up until recently. Red or white?"

It's true. I'd been indulging in plenty of "sexercise" until a certain unwelcome guest entered the picture.

"*Vino tinto, por favor*," she says, running her eyes over the rest of my book collection.

"Excuse me?"

"Red wine, please."

"You speak Spanish?"

"*Un poco*. It's practically a second language in Southern California. I see you have a lot of business and self-help books here," she remarks, casually pulling out another book on quitting smoking that I had forgotten about. Fuck!

"I believe in Kaizen," I offer as I pour two glasses of rich McLaren Vale Shiraz.

Jezebel examines the back cover of *The Easy Way to Stop Smoking* by Allen Carr.

"You familiar with the concept?" I ask, expecting to have to explain the term, which roughly translates to continuous improvement.

Instead of seeking clarification, Jezebel turns her shoulder around, tugging at the collar of her t-shirt. On her upper back, I spot a tattoo of the Japanese characters for Kaizen. Although not typically drawn to tattoos, I find this one incredibly alluring.

"I'm beyond impressed," I manage to murmur, genuinely in awe, before bringing the wine over to join her.

"I've always believed you can learn a lot about a person from their book collection," Jezebel muses as I hand her the glass.

"I was just thinking the same thing," I respond, offering a smile as I raise my own glass. "Cheers."

"What are we toasting to?" she asks.

"To exquisite wine, delightful company and stories of broken noses."

Her laughter fills the room as our glasses clink together. "To broken noses."

We take a sip. Jezebel nods her approval of the wine. "Nice. Syrah?" Her insights continue to amaze me.

I nod. "Perfect for winter, absolutely freezing outside. Oh, that reminds me," I say, retrieving a box of oversized matches, displaying them and giving them a light shake. I then make my way to a shadowed fireplace, which Jezebel hadn't previously noticed.

"Oh my God!" she exclaims with delight, her eyes lighting up.

"Yes, it's the original cottage fireplace, and it's still functional, which is quite rare," I explain, crouching down in front. Extracting a match from the box, I strike it against the rough surface and lower the burning match into the fireplace. The flames catch onto the scrunched newspaper, gradually igniting the thinner wood and moving their way upward to the logs. Entranced by the process, both Jezebel and I watch the flames dance and flicker. A soothing silence envelops us, the crackling of the fire intermingling with the patter of rain against the windows. We share a tranquil moment, captivated by the warmth and glow of the fire. The combination of the rain outside with the crackling of the fire makes for a perfect date-night in.

"Do you know how old this fireplace is?" I ask, breaking the silence.

"No," Jezebel answers, trying to play down her being in awe of the fire, though her fascination is evident.

"Neither do I," I reply, rising to my feet. "But the cottage is an original, over a century and a half old. That's super old, for Australia anyway."

"It's beautiful," Jezebel observes, her gaze still fixed on the mesmerising flames. The gusts of wind and the sound of raindrops add to the cosy ambience. With another sip of wine, we share a wordless understanding that the evening is off to a promising start.

"Hungry?"

We settle across from each other at the dining table, conveniently placed between the kitchen and the inviting lounge area with its crackling fireplace. The scent of burning wood fills the air. The culinary creation from Easy Eats is plated and ready. I'm pleased to note that she seems to enjoy it already. Her affirmation comes after her first bite of the salmon and sweet potato mash.

"Hmm, nicely heated," she remarks with that playful glint in her eyes, once again indulging in a bit of teasing. This woman is quickly becoming my fascination, and I can feel myself falling for her – hard.

"So, you're in finance?" she inquires, taking a small mouthful.

"Finance?" I reply, raising an eyebrow playfully. "I own and manage an investment fund, if that's what you mean."

"Yeah, a finance guy."

"You don't sound all that convinced."

"I don't exactly dislike that world," she responds, looking up as she searches for the right words. "But I have to admit, when I think of finance guys, I often picture Wall Street types, the whole douche-bag persona."

I chuckle at this, unsurprised by her perspective. "You're judging me."

"No... well, maybe just a little."

"Allow me to challenge your perception of the 'finance guy'," I suggest with a grin. It's a common stereotype that I often encounter, especially from the opposite gender. "My work is nothing like *The Wolf of Wall Street* or any of that. I actually help people for a living."

"Really? How?"

"I help them make money, assist in managing and safeguarding their wealth," I elaborate, taking a bite of broccoli. "I work towards securing their future, their retirement. But beyond the surface, what I provide is peace of mind. It's the assurance that, no matter what happens, things will be okay."

Jezebel nods thoughtfully while chewing, absorbing the information. "And how exactly do you do that?"

"People hire me to invest their money. I select a range of companies, or stocks, that I believe, after thorough research, will bring them substantial returns. Essentially, I seek out smaller companies, mostly in the tech sector, that might not be profitable yet but show promise and are undervalued. I group these stocks into exchange-traded funds, or ETFs, which I then manage for a nominal fee from our clients."

Jezebel continues to nod slowly as she savours a piece of salmon.

I continue, "One of my funds, Pennywise, has yielded considerable profits for my clients, particularly in recent times. Most of these clients have families and aren't wealthy. They lack the knowledge on how to make their money work for them, so I do it on their behalf. In return, I receive a commission, while they gain more options in life and a sense of security. It's a win-win scenario." I finish my explanation before forking a generous portion of salmon into my mouth.

"You derive your income from commissions based on managing other people's investments? That's quite smart."

"I also reinvest my earnings into many of these same companies."

"So your interests align with your clients."

"Absolutely. You're more intelligent than I initially thought."

"Well, that's a backhanded compliment if I've heard one!"

"Sorry, I didn't mean it like that."

"Because I fight people for a living, right?"

"That may have had something to do with it."

"So, you judged me because of what I do for a living?"

She got me. "Maybe... A little."

We share a smile. I'm both impressed and humbled by Jezebel's genuine curiosity about my profession. Most women tend to lose interest at the mere mention of finance-related matters. They often stereotype me as just another wannabe Jordan Belfort, something I've come to accept. Yet, here's a woman – stunning, sharp, and intriguing – asking the right questions to understand my work, which in turn leads to a deeper understanding of me. No woman has taken the time to comprehend my business before. In fairness, I've never shown much interest in theirs either... until now.

"That's my guiding principle – aligning my clients' interests with my own. And it seems to work."

Now it's Jezebel's turn to be impressed. "And here I was, thinking of you as just another Gordon Gekko."

"I'd never insider trade, I'm not a criminal." This wasn't entirely true as I had been known to buy the rumour before. "But that's a great movie," I reply with a smile. "And besides, I judged your profession too."

"Really, in what way?"

"There's a certain type of – how should I say it – *image* associated with MMA fighters."

"And what would that be?"

"Bunch of mugs. Grubs."

"Grubs?"

"Muscles, tattoos, a tough-guy demeanour. Your trainer, Steve, is the embodiment of that stereotype."

Jezebel's laughter fills the room. "And how about the women?"

"They're similar – just female counterparts, really. You're an exception, of course. You look outta place, but in a good way."

"Not all of us are like that," she says, her gaze unfocused as she looks past me towards the fire. "But I can't deny that the sport attracts its share of rough characters." She takes a sip of her wine. She seems to be enjoying my company. A comfortable silence envelops us as she continues to gaze towards the dancing flames.

It's not long before we finish up dinner and are sitting on the sofa in front of the fire, with about a foot's distance between us. I look directly at the fire, staring into the flames while holding a glass of red. Jezebel sits sideways, her feet almost tucked beneath her bum. She also clutches a glass of red. We talk dating and she tries to think of the last time she'd been on a date, like a proper date. It occurs to her that this is the first date she had been on in almost two years. After she ended her relationship with an arsehole domestic abuser – she won't even say his name – she had put all her energy into her sporting career. It was a messy ending, dating a fellow MMA fighter. He had hit her bad, several times. After the asshole broke an AVO, he was finally locked up, convicted and sentenced to eight months in prison. Lousy eight months for repeatedly bashing the woman he supposedly loved. What a joke. And what a fucking coward. It goes without saying that I've always thought men who bash their women are the lowest of the low.

But Jezebel just gets on with it. It's what she does. It's not the first time she's been knocked down and certainly won't be the last, she tells me, physically and emotionally. She's accepted that's a part of life. And, as one of her favourite movie characters of all time once said, "*It's not about how hard you hit. It's about how hard you can get hit and keep moving forward.*"

Jezebel had been fending for herself ever since growing up in Santa Monica, Los Angeles. Coming from a mixed-race family, she found herself bullied on all fronts. So, she developed a thick skin early on, and learnt how to administer punishment too, having taught a few girls a lesson or two. Of course, this resulted in much stress for her parents, who had to pull her out of multiple schools – if she hadn't been pushed out first.

The African-American community found itself gentrified out of Santa Monica, and even though Jezebel's family knew the beach was no longer a place for them, they stayed. Today, her parents are much more accepted as a couple, with American society slowly but surely coming around to the idea of interracial relationships. Jezebel tells me that's what she loves most about Australia – a country where interracial dating doesn't seem to be an issue.

Different history, different brand of racism, I think to myself.

She first came here to distance herself from the fuck-stain ex, which turned out to be an excellent move. She had the wife-beater to thank for a rapid advancement in her career. After the nasty break-up, court cases and his subsequent jailing, Jezebel buried herself in her work as a coping mechanism. She trained like never before.

She tells me her routine – wake up, prayer and meditation. Stretching. Light breakfast. Gym. Eat. Fight in the gym with her trainer. Sparring in the ring. Eat. Sometimes nap. Jog, at least ten kilometres a day, while listening to motivational audiobooks and podcasts. Her current favourite being David Goggins', of course. I consider telling her that he's my imaginary personal trainer but I refrain.

She studied the greats – Ronda Rousey and Holly Holm, among others. She refined her jiu-jitsu down to a fine art with the help of a Brazilian ex-pro. Sometimes she found herself working, training and studying up to twelve hours a day. She mastered the art of visualisation. And when she stepped in the ring, she imagined she was fighting the arsehole-ex, much to the regret of her female opponents. Since the break-up, her record was 11-0 with eight knockouts... *thanks asshole.*

Jezebel had planned on putting herself back on the dating scene after a year and a half of being single and moving up the MMA ranks. Then COVID-19 hit, and suddenly she wasn't allowed to go out, unless for essential purposes.

Then, unfortunately, it was my turn in the spotlight.

"I don't get it," Jezebel says, taking a sip of wine. "How are you still single?"

I'm accustomed to this question, and I've rehearsed my answers countless times – all of them mostly lies. "I was waiting for it."

"What?" Jezebel inquires. "The question?"

"It always comes up eventually. I don't know. It's not like I planned on being single at thirty. It's just how life unfolded."

Jezebel remains silent, nodding in agreement. Her life hasn't quite gone as she envisioned either. "Have you ever had a serious relationship?" she asks.

"Yeah, sure. I came close to marriage."

"She turned you down?"

"No, it's not that. I didn't actually propose. I chose not to."

"Why? What was the issue?"

"Remember what I said at the wedding?"

"Oh, yeah... that."

Jezebel looks away, sipping her wine, nodding as if accepting my explanation. We both notice the sound of the rain pelting down heavily now outside. I use it as an escape route.

"Looks like it's pouring again," I say, turning my gaze to the open window. As I glance back at Jezebel, her face is unexpectedly close to mine. Here it is, that moment I both desire and dread. Her perfume reaches my senses, sending a shiver down my spine. The hairs on my neck stand on end. She places her drink down, and I follow suit. We lean in and kiss, a beautiful and electrifying moment. It's passionate and intense, throwing me off balance in a way I haven't felt in a long time.

We finally break away, our eyes locked. The kiss was clearly mutual, an incredible experience for both of us. But there's a hint of fear in my eyes.

"Friends don't do this," I blurt out.

"No, they don't," Jezebel says, leaning in for a second kiss, even more intense than the first. Her hair carries the scent of gardenias. The temperature rises, sensations deepen, and I kiss her neck below her left ear. She inhales deeply, a soft moan escaping her lips. She pushes me back onto the couch and straddles me. Heat courses through my veins, but then there's a sharp pang of now-familiar pain down below.

"Hold on, wait a moment," I say, gently lifting her off and settling her back onto the couch beside me.

"What's wrong?"

"We're friends."

"Oh, come on. You're still playing that card?"

"I thought that's what we decided…"

"Are you serious? Friends?"

I'm at a loss for words. Of course this is more than friendship. I didn't invite her over for dinner just to be *friends*. But I can't let this go any further. I have to protect her from the ugly condition plaguing me. And I can't let her see it – I will lose her forever. I need to think fast. I pull out the classic line that a conservative woman says to a guy when his hormones are running hot. "I think we should take things slow," I manage to say.

"Take things slow?" Jezebel questions, puzzled.

I nod. She slumps back on the couch, turning away. I realise I need to support my stance. "I've always been too impulsive," I begin, feeling encouraged by my reasoning. "And I don't want to be that guy anymore, especially not with you. I want to do this right."

"But you said you're not a player."

"And I'm not. But it seems every time I rush into things, they don't work out in the long run. Maybe if I take it slow for once, it'll have a better chance of lasting." Yes, I think, I've hit the nail on the head.

Jezebel finally makes eye contact, a smile playing on her lips. "So, you're saying you want something lasting?"

I nod, my internal victory dance in full swing. "Absolutely," I answer, triumphant.

The smile spreads across Jezebel's face. She leans in close. "I can respect that," she says before giving me a peck on the lips. "Just know that I haven't had sex in over a year."

Fuck me. I can't take this any longer and need to call it a night already. But Jezebel seems okay with that too. I see her to the front door, a mix of emotions running through me.

"Thank you. Tonight was… different. But in a good way."

I smile. The moment lingers. She wants a lean-in. But I know my willpower cannot handle that right now. Way too risky. But it's Jezebel who unexpectedly extends her hand for a handshake. I stare at her, puzzled.

"I'm just fucking with you," Jezebel chuckles. "Your reaction is priceless."

She laughs again and then pulls me in for another kiss. I'm caught off guard once more. Beneath her strong, determined exterior, this woman reveals herself to be laid-back, playful and genuine. It's another one of those incredible kisses, worthy of a Hollywood romance. The world seems to fade as we share that electric moment. Finally, our lips part.

"Goodbye," she murmurs softly.

"Goodbye," I manage to whisper under my breath, feeling a bit lightheaded. I stand there, watching her leave, unable to shake off the daze that she's left me in.

I shut the door, resting my head against it for a moment. Slowly, I turn and head upstairs. As I step into my bedroom, I'm faced with my bed – a reminder of what could have been with Jezebel. An image of us together, intimately entwined, flashes in my mind. But that's not happening – because of this damn issue with my penis.

Then I lose it. "Damn you!" I shout at my own crotch, my frustration boiling over. "You don't belong here! You're not welcome!" Grabbing one of the pillows from the bed, I slam it against the wall, my anger fuelling every punch.

"You miserable, cock-blocking bastard!"

I continue to vent my frustration, slamming the pillow against the wall until it rips open, feathers scattering in the air. My rage doesn't subside; I move on to the next pillow, my fists pounding against it, unleashing all the pent-up sexual tension I feel. Feathers fly as I thrash the pillow around the room.

The room is soon filled with a cloud of feathers, a surreal but strangely beautiful manifestation of my anger.

Chapter 13

Honeymooning

And so, it continued for weeks. I'd never felt such a strong desire to be with a woman, yet each time we were together, the prospect of intimacy felt like torment. It was a dating experience unlike any I'd had before. I was caught in a strange tug-of-war, pulled between opposing forces at either end of the rope.

After the home-cooked dinner at my place, we went on a date to Luna Park across the harbour in North Sydney. It felt like I was living out a scene from a cheesy American rom-com, with the clichéd theme-park setting. We held hands! She screamed and gripped my hand on the big dipper! We even won a stuffed toy at one of the carnival games!

I considered myself a decent shot, hitting six out of ten targets, until Jezebel took her turn and effortlessly shot the shit out of all ten. Americans sure know how to shoot, hey. It's like second nature to them. I asked if she owned a gun which she did back home and was bummed she couldn't bring here, which I thought was kinda strange but decided not to get into the whole gun-control debate.

The day was fantastic, and I particularly cherished the moment when Jezebel kissed me on the roller coaster, right before the big dip when she screamed and gripped my leg like a vice. On the ferry ride back to Circular Quay, we braved the elements on the front deck, the boat bouncing over the harbour's swells. Even when a wave splashed over the bow, soaking both of us, we managed to laugh it off and seal the moment with a kiss. I felt more alive than ever.

Our next date took us to the movies. I intentionally planned these outings around public spaces, ensuring no opportunity for things to get hotter and heavier. I was actively pursuing a different approach than I had before. More importantly, I was thoroughly enjoying Jezebel's company. It was genuinely fascinating to get to know her before doing the deed.

One of the most memorable days we had was when we decided to take the ferry over to Manly, a picturesque beachside village near the entrance of the harbour. Manly is nestled between the ocean on one side and the harbour on the other. I showed her both the expansive ocean beach and a couple of my favourite harbour beaches. But the one that held a special place in my heart was Shelly Beach.

We strolled along the oceanfront boardwalk that led from Manly Beach around the headland to little Shelly, about half a kilometre away. Shelly Beach was a gem, small and sheltered, an aquatic reserve surrounded by a nature sanctuary. My goal was to introduce her to a hidden spot atop a cliff that offered a stunning view of the ocean. Jezebel hesitated but followed me onto the bushwalk, seeking reassurance about the presence of snakes again. I promised her that we were unlikely to encounter any again.

However, irony had other plans.

I shit you not – barely ten meters into the bushwalk, I heard a gasp behind me. I turned around to see Jezebel retreating, her hand covering her mouth. She was pointing to my left. When I followed her gaze, there it was – a snake about two meters long, and brown, gliding over a log. To say I was surprised would be an understatement. This was no python – it was an eastern brown snake, deadly as fuck. But I didn't tell her that. I said it was a harmless brown tree snake, of course. But apparently, that fact didn't matter to an American suffering from ophidiophobia. So much for our bushwalk and the romantic cliffside ocean vista I had planned. To be honest, I was glad to get out of there myself.

Soon I had exhausted all my options for date venues – theme parks, cinemas, markets, even a footy match, despite my lack of interest in the sport. I did, however, buy a Sydney Swans scarf to pretend I was a fan. It was clear that I needed something unique, something that wasn't the usual run-of-the-mill date. That's when I came up with the idea of a salsa dancing class. Big mistake. Little did I know that salsa class would prove to be my undoing.

In fact, this class turned out to be the straw that broke the camel's back for Jezebel. The rhythm of the dance, the closeness of our bodies, and the way I held her in my arms – it all got to her. With our bodies pressed against each other, I could feel her against my thigh, and as I responded to the intensity of the moment, it became too much for her to handle. Things took a turn when I tried to part ways again that night, attempting to maintain our slow pace of intimacy.

"Okay, you win. You've proved yourself. You are capable of a platonic relationship with a woman. Congratulations, now come and claim your prize," she says outside the dance hall. She looks sexy as fuck wearing a red dress that came high up her thighs to allow maximum movement for the dance routines.

I am so fucking horny I can hardly think straight, but press on. "But you have a fight coming up."

"Oh my God, what is wrong with you? I have *never* had to ask a man for sex. *Ever*!"

"I'm looking out for you. I thought athletes didn't have sexy-time before the big game."

"Don't pull that shit on me."

"I'm sure Steve would agree." Jezebel's shoulders slump as she lets out a hard and fast sigh. "I'm just thinking of you, babe," I say as I grab a hold of her shoulders. "I really wanna support you in your career. And all this pent-up energy is only gonna serve you well."

I was getting good at this. It used to be that I'd say whatever was needed just to get inside a woman's pants. Now, I'm saying whatever was needed to stay *out* of her pants. Same skill, opposite outcome. Nonetheless, Jezebel's eyes still narrowed, reading me. Studying me.

"Okay," Jezebel softens as she embraces me. "But if I win, I want to be rewarded." She kisses me on the lips. "Deal?"

"Deal," I say, a whole new conundrum just dropped on my plate.

She must lose.

I find myself sitting ringside in the VIP section. I've opted for my best pair of blue jeans sitting over my brown suede high-cut boots, a crisp white shirt with a tan leather jacket that fits perfectly over my broad shoulders. I look damn good, and confidence emanates from within me. Still, there's an undercurrent of frustration, a hint of anger bubbling beneath the surface.

As I watch Jezebel in the ring, my emotions ride on every punch she throws, every combination she lands.

"Yeeeaahhh babe, kick her fucking aaasssss!" I can't help but yell, my enthusiasm drawing glances from fellow spectators. I don't pay them any mind, though. In this moment, all that matters is the fight before me.

The intensity is electrifying as Jezebel corners her opponent, relentless with her one-two body blows. The woman she's up against is a solid, blonde-haired Russian fighter. She tries to manoeuvre along the ropes, attempting to escape Jezebel's onslaught, but there's no reprieve from the relentless assault. Then, it happens. The Russian drops her guard for a fraction of a second, and Jezebel seizes the opening. With a combination that's part hook and part uppercut, she lands a crushing blow to the Russian's jaw. The impact is devastating, and she crumples to the canvas, knocked out cold.

I erupt with exhilaration, my voice practically hitting the stadium roof. "Fuck yeeeaaaahhhh! Yeeaah, babe! Fuck yeeaahh!" In that moment, I'm purely caught up in the adrenaline and the victory.

Jezebel notices my reaction, and she turns toward me with a cheeky glance that seems to say, "You're next."

Suddenly, the weight of her words sinks in, and my excitement is swiftly replaced by a creeping fear. "Holy shit," I mutter under my breath, realising the gravity of my situation.

We celebrate Jezebel's victory at a bar in Darling Harbour on the west side of the CDB. It's busy and Jezebel is dressed to the nines, wearing a black skirt paired with a tight leopard-print top that exposes her midriff and accentuates her perfect boobs. She looks smoking hot and turns heads as we enter the bar. It's an upmarket joint full of mostly affluent North Shore and Eastern Suburbs twenty-somethings.

Jezebel's entourage has once again tagged along, including Steve. It's clear by now that Jezebel and I are dating, and it's even more clear that Steve does not approve – evidenced by his excusing himself whenever I'm present. I couldn't care less. Now, he's just focusing on being Jezebel's trainer, which is exactly how it should be.

While the entourage secures a seating area out on the balcony, I head straight to the bar to buy a round. It will give me a chance to sneak in a few drinks before I get there. My game plan is to get too drunk so that I am incapable of having sex, even though I don't think I've ever been incapable before. But Jezebel doesn't know that. I order a few shots of tequila for myself along with drinks for everyone else.

Just as I'm about to down the second shot, Steve sidles up at the bar next to me. Cringe. He watches me as I throw down the second shot of tequila. I wonder what he wants. Surely not to buy a round of drinks – he's a tight-ass, after all. Probably just wants to make sure I'm getting him one. But the real reason is much worse; he wants to give me a pep-talk, something I'd prefer to avoid like the plague.

"Look dude, I can tell by now that you're not going anywhere," he says staring straight ahead into rows of liquor bottles lined up behind the bar. "I realise that I have to accept that. I only want what's best for Jezebel."

I nod slowly, pretending to listen but really figuring out an exit strategy.

He continues, "What Jezebel needs right now is focus. Intense, laser-like, tunnel vision – fucking focus, man."

I slide the full tray of drinks onto my arm, ready to carry them away. But Steve turns to me, and looks me directly in the eye as if to stop me. "Just don't go breaking that focus, okay."

"Of course not. I want what's best for her too. Now, if you don't mind..."

He faces his whole body towards me now, up in my face. "Whatever you do to her, I do to you."

What the hell does *that* mean? I think as I simply nod and move away. Fucking weirdo.

On the way back to our area, there are four guys in their twenties who look like they're all bulked up on steroids, blocking the entrance to the balcony area. One of them sees me holding a full tray of drinks but makes no effort to move aside. "Excuse me," I say as I try to edge my way through, but the same guy intentionally bumps into me, spilling a few of the drinks.

"Jesus, really?"

This prompts Roid Guy to square up. "Watch where you're going, bro."

His other mates, who all look similar – over-muscled, way too tight shirts, and so much hair product that it shines like grease – laugh and egg the ringleader along. I know these types. They are younger, immature and look for trouble. Most likely suffering from roid rage and an inability to attract women. They speak like they're on coke – most probably are. Roid rage and coke are an unfortunate combo. They usually pick the same targets – men who have a gorgeous girlfriend hanging off their arm, which they don't. I noticed them ogling Jezebel on the way in, and then scowl once they realised she was with me. Now they want to assert their dominance, which only happens when they have safety in numbers. Get one of these douche-bags on their own, and they'd cower like the pumped-up pussies they are.

"Spilt some of your lady's drink. What's a hot bitch like her doing with a loser like you?"

"I'm the loser? Okay, I'm fine with that. But don't disrespect my girl."

"Whatcha gonna do about it, huh?"

Roid Boy's getting up close now, his pecs twitching, his mates laughing in the background. Christ, first Steve and now this doofus. What have I done to deserve this? I could feel my anger rise to a simmer, but I maintain my calm. I wasn't going to start a fight, not tonight. Jezebel was having a good time, and the last thing I wanted was to ruin it.

"Oh, I don't know," I retort, giving the man a sardonic smile. "I thought maybe you could use a drink. It might help cool down those overheated muscles of yours."

His friends roar with laughter. The guy's face reddened, but he maintained his smug grin, refusing to back down. He raised a clenched fist, and before I could dodge it, a punch landed squarely on my cheek, knocking me back. My tray of drinks went flying. My vision blurred momentarily, the taste of copper filling my mouth.

People backed away, making room for the impending brawl. A few even began cheering.

As I regained my balance, wiping a trickle of blood from my mouth, Jezebel appeared next to me, her face a mask of concern and anger.

"He's not worth it, Archie," she hisses, her eyes flashing with fury.

"Maybe not," I grumble. "But he needs to be taught a lesson."

"Ah, your bitch missus come to your rescue, eh?" Roid Boy says while fist-bumping a few of his mates. "What you doing with this loser, baby?"

"You picked the wrong boyfriend to mess with tonight," Jezebel tells him.

Feeling emasculated, I get up to let fly at this dickhead, but before I can make a move, Jezebel steps forward, her body poised like a panther ready to strike. The guys in front of us look taken aback. She was a woman, yes, but she was also a trained MMA fighter.

"What's this?" the ringleader sneered. "Your lady really is stepping in to save your ass?"

Jezebel's eyes narrowed, a cold smile on her lips. "Not saving. She's just fighting her own battles." With that, she lunged. A swift punch to his gut, a roundhouse kick to the side of his head. He didn't have time to react before he was on the ground, groaning in pain. His friends, still processing what had happened, barely had time to react when Jezebel turned on them. One tried to grab her from behind, but a swift elbow to his gut and a back kick sent him sprawling. Another one, clearly the bravest among them, advanced, fists raised. But Jezebel was quicker, her fists a blur as she danced around him, landing punches and kicks with precision until he too, like his friends, was lying on the ground, gasping for breath. The fourth and final douche-bag came at her with a bottle which she expertly kicked out of his hand, stunning him with a short right jab to the nose, breaking it instantly. She followed this up with three ferocious knees to his balls. His eyes rolled back in his head before slumping to the ground, curled up in the foetal position.

The Roid Ringleader was on his feet again, holding a glass and seemingly ready to attack my girl, but Jezebel kicked that out of his hands also while effortlessly following up with a brutal uppercut punch that catches Roid Boy square on the jaw, breaking it instantly and sending a few teeth flying from his mouth. He lays motionless, out cold.

The entire bar was silent as Jezebel dusted herself off. Every eye in the room is on her. A club full of Sydney's elite youth, staring at this woman who is more glamorous than any of them, who just beat the living shit out of four big guys. Even the bouncers are gobsmacked, unsure what to do.

Jezebel walks back to me, a satisfied smirk on her face. "We should probably leave," she said, grabbing my hand and leading me towards the exit, the crowd parting for us as we leave, still staring in awe at this goddess.

And that's when I knew. No matter where we went, what we did – Jezebel was more than capable of taking care of herself. And although I still felt extremely emasculated, I loved her even more for it.

As we step into Jezebel's apartment, she wastes no time. With a sense of urgency, she pushes me against the wall, the door clicking shut beside us. I can't help but surrender to the electrifying energy between us. Buttons fly as she rips open my bone-white Ralph Lauren dress shirt, sending them scattering across the floor. Honestly, I couldn't care less.

"That was so hot how you stood up to those guys after they insulted me," she whispers in my ear before gently biting my ear lobe, flicking her tongue under my ear.

"It was so hot watching you beat the crap outta those dickheads," I reply.

Although I did find it hot, I am increasingly losing touch with my role in the relationship. Wanting to hold out on sex and having Jezebel literally protect me from getting bashed tonight has me confused about my role as a man.

"You know I was just about to step in and sort them out myself, right?"

Jezebel responds by kissing me on the mouth with such passion I feel a surge of energy flow to my loins. So much for getting too drunk for sex. Things escalate quickly, the intensity building as we move toward her bedroom. My shirt and jacket join the casualties along the way, but any words I might have tried to say are silenced by another fervent kiss from Jezebel.

In her bedroom, I attempt to exercise some restraint, trying to avoid heading directly to the bed. But Jezebel is having none of it, pulling me close and effectively toppling us onto the mattress. Her tight long-sleeve top becomes a casualty as well, discarded in her wake. Her gaze lingers on my chest, appreciating my tanned, toned physique.

"You're so beautiful," she murmurs, and even though I try to slow the pace, it's clear she's set on igniting the flames. Before I can fully process the situation, Jezebel is undoing my fly and yanking my pants down with a determination that's almost overwhelming.

"Whoa!" I can't help but exclaim as I suddenly feel incredibly exposed. There's nothing but my red undies between me and Jezebel, and her eyes are fixed on the unmistakable bulge beneath. A pang of unease washes over me, quickly turning into a sharp sensation of discomfort as Jezebel grabs my cock. I feel an instant stab of pain and instinct takes over. I sit up in one swift motion, a startled shout escaping my lips. In my haste, I manage to simultaneously propel Jezebel off me. She tumbles backward, landing awkwardly on the edge of the mattress before bouncing and ending up on her arse on the floor. Her shocked expression is priceless, and there's a moment of silence as we both process what just happened.

"What the fuck?"

"I am so sorry," I rush to say as I scramble to help her up from the floor.

With a fluid move, she rolls back onto her shoulders and springs back up to her feet in a single motion, like a textbook Jackie Chan move. Her words drip with playful challenge. "So, you wanna play rough, huh?"

Staring at her, my eyes widen in both surprise and slight panic. My head shakes involuntarily, "No, that's a definite no—"

But before I can even finish my sentence, Jezebel seizes me and flips me over her shoulder with impressive ease, depositing me onto the bed. I lay there momentarily stunned, my gaze now upside-down, looking up at her.

Trying to regain my composure, I begin to sit up. "Can we just—"

"Shut up," Jezebel cuts me off again, her quick movements reminiscent of a Brazilian jiu-jitsu technique as she half somersaults, half cartwheels onto me, pinning me down on the bed, my arms trapped beneath her knees.

"Jezebel, please!" I plead, a mixture of anxiety and discomfort creeping into my voice.

Her gaze sharpens, and she doesn't let up on her hold. "You like that move, don't you?"

"Not really—"

A tug at my arm forces me into a less-than-comfortable position.

"What was that?"

"Argh! I mean, yes! Great move. Excellent move." More of my masculinity is squeezed out with the pain. I alternate between groans and laughter at the situation.

Mocking my vulnerability, she continues, "You think this is funny, huh? What are you gonna do now? You're totally helpless."

Struggling against her hold, my voice tinged with desperation, I reply, "You know, this technically constitutes assault."

A wicked grin crosses her face, "Really? I call it self-defence. You threw me off the bed, you naughty, naughty boy."

"It was an accident! Your mattress is like a trampoline!"

Rolling her eyes, she counters, "I'm the bad one, huh. Perhaps I need to be punished then?"

Taken aback by her playful twist, I stammer, "Umm..."

Leaning closer, her gaze intense, she teasingly inquires, "What kind of weapon you got to punish me? What are you packing down here?" Her hand ventures where it shouldn't, touching me through my undies which, despite all the pain and discomfort, still resemble a tent.

As she grips me, I grimace from the pain, fighting to hold back tears in between bouts of laughter. Jezebel is smiling too, enjoying herself. Arousing herself. But my laughter turns to crying without me even trying. And then, she notices.

"Are you… crying!?' She releases me suddenly, sitting up. Any last morsel of masculinity drains out of me with my tears. Stunned and embarrassed, I sit up, wiping my eyes. "What is wrong with you?" she asks incredulously as she stands up. "Seriously, we've been dating for over a month now. What is it, you don't find me attractive?"

The fun and games are over. Swallowing hard, I reply, "Of course I find you attractive," my voice revealing my internal struggle.

"So, what is it, are you gay?"

"I'm definitely *not* gay."

"Training for the priesthood? I don't get it."

That last comment makes something click in my mind. Is this a way out? A way to protect myself from the truth I can't reveal? A light bulb moment. "Not quite, but…" I manage to say, hesitating before letting the words tumble out, "I am a born-again Christian."

She looks at me, puzzled. "Excuse me?"

"Born-again Christian," I repeat, my voice surprisingly steady. "After the wedding incident, I did some soul-searching which… led me back to the church."

Her eyes narrow, suspicion evident. "Which church?"

"The church, you know… The church of Jesus Christ."

"Don't bullshit me, Archie!"

"I'm not, I swear!"

"What church? There are many forms of Christianity."

Unsure where this newfound confession might lead, I offer, "I like to mix it up, you know."

Jezebel's eyes narrow further, her tone sceptical. "No, I don't. Most people generally stick to one."

"I'm not most people. It's all the same to me. God, Jesus, praying to a higher power."

Her expression remains dubious. "You better not be lying to me."

"I'm not, swear to God," I offer weakly, wondering if "swearing to God" is considered blasphemy. "I just want to be a better man for you."

For a moment, she softens, her tone gentle as she tries to understand. "Have you been to St. Pat's?"

"St. Pat's?"

"St. Patrick's, down the road. Father Bob."

"Oh yeah, Father Bob. Church on the corner, right?"

In an unexpected turn, her eyes light up, and I can't help but feel a glimmer of hope. "That's my church!"

"Huh?"

Pulling out a necklace from under her top, she reveals a cross pendant. My gaze fixes on it, a mixture of emotions swirling within me. "You don't have to abstain from sex before marriage in Catholicism," she explains, "but we can discuss that later. And I fully respect your choice not to do it just yet, okay?"

My heart pounds in my chest as I realise she's offering me a way to navigate this dilemma. I feel a mix of relief and guilt, knowing that I'm deceiving her but also sparing myself from revealing my mortifying truth.

"Thank you," I manage.

Chapter 14

Stage 3: Bargaining

"There has to be something you can do, doc..." I plead as I sit in Dr. Singh's practice.

Since my last date with Jezebel, I've been in mental turmoil. What have I just gotten myself into? I don't have a religious bone in my body, I keep thinking. Mostly, I have that dreaded feeling that somehow this STD is going to be the end of me. And now, Dr. Singh is seemingly elated, which only worsens my mood.

"Congratulations, Archie. You may have claimed the name of a newly discovered sexually transmitted... Archie Flynn Disease."

"I'm sorry, what?" I snap, disbelief colouring my tone.

"Very exciting news. We're still awaiting some data to come in from around the world, but so far, everything is pointing to a first-of-its-kind STD."

"What was that part about Archie Flynn Disease?"

"As a new strain of STD, you get the honour of having it named after you. Congratulations!"

"No. Fucking. Way. No way. No disease, sexual or otherwise, is getting named after me."

"Oh, I'm afraid it's not up to you, Archie. It's simply protocol."

"I don't give a shit. It's my STD, I own it. My copyright. Trademarked. Therefore, you legally have no permission to name it after me. I get to name it. There is absolutely no way my name is going up there with the likes of gonorrhoea, herpes and crabs. Do we understand each other, doc? Only *I* get to name this disease. And you know what I'm gonna name it? Bane Disease. Because this thing is the bane of my fucking existence. My mental health is suffering. And naming the disease after me certainly is not going to help that. Do you really want me back on the meds?"

"I understand this is upsetting for you."

"Upsetting? I am on the verge of necking myself, doc!"

"Okay, forget the name for now. We need to take a sample."

I pause, dread filling me. Just when I thought this day couldn't get any rosier. "A sample? What exactly does that entail?"

"There's a needle," Singh says casually, producing a scalpel, "followed by a small incision."

"No fucking way!"

"The needle is for a local anaesthetic."

"A needle into my penis!? No, you're gonna have to put me under, knock me out for this one."

"Oh, I'm afraid you're not going under for this, Archie."

"Come on, doc, please. I'm begging you."

"This is a medical centre, not a hospital. We don't put patients under here."

"There's no way I'm letting you near my junk with a needle and scalpel while fully conscious. I'm sorry, but it's not gonna happen!"

"Listen, Archie, I can tell you are on edge. I can see you have already progressed to the bargaining stage of your grief. This is a positive. But if you want this thing to go away, we need to find out as much as possible about it. And the best way to do that is to send a sample off for testing."

I feel close to tears again. "Why is this happening to me, Dr. Singh?"

"Don't play the victim now, Archie," Singh says with a paternal tone. "There are plenty of patients much worse off than you, trust me."

The doctor's words resonate. At least I still have my penis. Some people have lost much more. I nod, my voice trembling. "Okay, just get it over with."

"Now, I won't lie, it will still be somewhat painful, but this will help alleviate most of the pain. Is there anything I can do before we get started?"

"Get us a bottle of vodka?"

I enter my father's hospital room, walking funny like I've shat myself. Dad is watching TV from his hospital bed, but he notices my strange gait.

"What's wrong with you? Why are you walking like you crapped your pants?"

"Nothing, I'm fine!" I say as I carefully settle into the chair next to his bed. He observes me closely.

"My ass, you're fine," he retorts, turning down the TV volume. "It's that thing on your dick, isn't it?"

"Dad, please, I'm not in the mood."

"Better not have been messing around," Robert says, staring at me with a sideways glance. "You've been messing around, haven't you?"

"No, Dad! Actually, quite the opposite. I think I've met someone."

"What? What do you mean? If you've met someone, that means you've been messing around!"

"No, that's the thing. We've been on plenty of dates and we're taking things slow."

"That's great, I'm proud of you Archie!" He beams with pride. "For a while there, I was afraid you were gonna end up alone like me."

"You're not gonna end up alone, Dad. You have me," I say, giving his knee an affectionate slap-grab. "You know what I mean?"

Suddenly, I feel sorry for my old man. Why couldn't he move on from Mum and find love again? Or had he given up on love altogether? And why can't I properly connect with a woman? I've never had my heart broken, after all. What excuse do I have for being so inept at love and intimacy? And am I falling for Jezebel? How am I supposed to know what love is? All I know is that she does something to me. Something inside that I can't explain. Is *that* what love is?

"How did you know when you were in love with Mum?"

"Whoa, the big L word, look out!" Dad chuckles.

"I'm not saying..."

"It's okay, I'm just teasing," Robert says, his expression changing as he considers the question. "You just know, that's all I can say," he finally answers as he changes the TV channel. "No more wandering eyes. You have eyes for her only. What's her name and when do I get to meet her?" he asks, snapping me out of my trance.

"Jezebel."

"Jezebel? That's a beautiful name."

"Yeah, I like it too."

"Bring her by, I'd like to meet her. I'll tell you if it's love."

I contemplate it. Do I want Jezebel to see my dad in the hospital? Yes, she'd probably find it sweet. She has empathy, and I like that about her. "Sure, Dad. That's a good idea. Oh, and if she brings it up, I'm a Christian. I go to church and stuff."

This prompts the old man to burst out laughing. "You? Go to church? Jesus H. Christ, what have you gotten yourself into?"

"Oh, and don't mention, um…" I gesture toward my crotch, "my affliction."

"Don't mess this up, son."

"Speaking of which, do you have a bible I can borrow?"

"Actually…" Dad opens a drawer next to his bed, "they keep one here for us, to prepare for the inevitable." He hands the bible to me.

"Oh, you probably need it more, so…" I hand it back.

"What are you saying – I'm gonna kick the bucket soon!?"

"No, Dad. You're the only one who thinks you're going to die." I stare at the bible. "But, you know, you're in here, sick, and I'm not, so…" I hand it back.

Robert brushes off my refusal. "Ah, I won't read it anyway. It's like Shakespeare, doesn't make any sense to me. Plus, it sounds like you have some homework to do, so take it. Take it!

I accept the bible. "Okay, okay, I'll take it, Dad." I feel the weight of the book. "Jeez, it's pretty thick, huh? I wonder if there's a summed-up version."

Chapter 15

The Confession

As I stroll towards St. Patrick's Church, the oldest surviving Catholic church in Sydney, its presence commands attention on the Eastern side of the overpass. With origins dating back to 1844, the majestic sandstone structure stands proudly amidst the surrounding modern skyscrapers. This cathedral serves as a bridge between the old and the new – a symbol of the early colonial town of The Rocks blending harmoniously with the bustling contemporary metropolis and financial hub.

Nestled at the junction of two bustling inner-city roads, the church features two imposing spires flanking the entrance. The front façade showcases three intricately carved statues, with the central figure unmistakably depicting Jesus Christ himself. I observe the iconic image – the man, the legend – or perhaps just an ordinary individual with exceptional kindness who claimed the ability to heal through the potent influence of the placebo effect. Regardless, guilt creeps over me merely gazing at the edifice, let alone contemplating stepping inside.

My previous experiences within church walls have been confined to weddings, funerals and my scripture class days at Sydney High School. The idea of what to wear for this occasion confounds me, leading me to acquire a "church outfit." My ensemble consists of corduroy slacks, a polo shirt, and a "church" sweater adorned with a knitted magnolia pattern on the front.

Stepping through the arched front door, I'm consumed by an inexplicable sense of unease. Despite the church's warm and inclusive ambience, I battle a nagging feeling of being an imposter. Who am I trying to fool? In my heart, I know the truth – I'm the one perpetrating a charade. The church is near-capacity, the congregation harmonising in song. My gaze shifts towards the back pew, an appealing haven where I could blend in as an anonymous observer. However, almost as if she senses my hesitance, Jezebel Ekas turns from the front row, smiling radiantly, and motions me to join her. How can I resist that inviting smile? I force a smile in return, reluctantly walking down the aisle, whispering under my breath, "Goddamn it."

I settle beside Jezebel in the pew, her Sunday best attire radiating her pride in having her "man" by her side. Meanwhile, I'm lost in contemplation of how I wound up in this predicament. "What an imposter," I berate myself, my choice of a sweater over a polo shirt emphasising my lack of belonging.

The priest begins a sermon on the complexities of love's bonds. Amidst the sacred surroundings, my mind fixates on the irony of using the word "bondage" within these hallowed walls. The priest shifts into a prayer, Jezebel bows her head, and I instinctively follow suit. Yet, rather than being immersed in the prayer, my thoughts drift to basements and images of bondage. I even visualise myself struck by lightning the instant I leave this sanctified place. A feeling of being watched overcomes me. I open my eyes mid-prayer and turn my head, meeting the gaze of an attractive young woman – far younger than myself, barely out of high school. She smiles and winks at me. The encounter is surreal, and I'm momentarily taken aback. The old me probably would've winked back and asked her if she would like to take part in bible studies after church. But the Archie 2.0 version just concluded, "That was bizarre," before quickly redirecting my attention forward, unsure of how to react.

I bow my head in prayer once more, only this time I actually pray. I don't really know how to pray, and I haven't done so since I was a kid in trouble and out of desperation. I ask God almighty to cure me of this affliction. I make a promise to change my philandering ways and commit to this incredible woman next to me forever. No more wandering eyes. *If you would just do this one thing for me, I promise to be a better man.* I finish praying and open my eyes to find Jezebel looking at, or reading, me again. She smiles. I smile back.

As the priest concludes the prayer, the congregation celebrates through a hymn. Everyone rises, joining in the musical chorus. Struggling to keep up with the song's lyrics, I feign familiarity and sing along with a bit too much enthusiasm. Jezebel, amused, hands me a hymn book and points out the lines. I accept the book and belt out the words. Glances from fellow attendees, including the cute young woman, confirm their curiosity. I make a conscious effort to avoid eye contact with her.

The priest wraps up the hymn, addressing the gathering. "Is anyone among us grappling with inner conflicts today?" No one steps forward. "Don't worry, it's normal to experience turmoil from time to time. We all sin. Well, except for JC, of course."

"Jesus Christ," I mutter, unable to contain my thoughts within the sacred setting.

The priest looks directly at me, as if to say, "Feeling conflicted, my son?" There is a long silence which becomes uncomfortable as he stares straight through me. My God, I think. He knows I am a fraud and is going to expose me. I shift nervously in my seat. Then the strangest thing happens – as if through mental telepathy, I hear the priest say, "Why don't you come to confession, son?"

I turn to Jezebel to see if she heard it to but she just continues to stare straight ahead.

I take it as a sign and at this point I am desperate to try anything to get rid of this thing. I tell Jezebel that I will be confessing my sins after the sermon. She gives me an encouraging rub on the back. And so, extremely reluctantly, I approach the front of the church towards the confession booth.

I sweat as I wait inside. Father Bob enters and sits down in the adjoining booth. I peer through the screen mesh dividing them.

"I can see you are conflicted, my son of Christ," the priest states.

How does he know that? "Ah, yes, sir. I am."

"Your conscious is not clear, is it?"

I shake my head in shame, sweat running down his forehead. It's so hot in here. "No, Father... It's not."

"That's okay, my son." The priest then speaks louder, "For God loves all his children, no matter how guilty the conscious is. So, spill."

"It's some pretty personal stuff, just to warn you."

"I understand, my boy."

"This is all strictly confidential, right? What happens in confession stays in confession, yeah?"

"Of course."

"Like, legally? You know, like a therapist, you legally can't tell anybody what I'm about to tell you, right?"

"Yes, son. But you must understand, I am not a therapist. I am a man of God. But you have my word, boy. What happens in confession, stays in confession."

"Okay. Good." I'm not sure where to start. Can I trust this stranger? "Umm… I know that you know."

"Know what, my son?"

"That I'm not, you know, a church guy."

"That's okay. Jesus loves all of God's creation. Church person, or not."

"No, you don't understand. I am *supposed* to be a church guy."

"I'm not sure I *do* understand."

"My girlfriend brought me here today."

"Jezebel is your girlfriend?"

"You know her?"

"Of course. She is one of our most devout members."

"Great. Well, she thinks I'm a born-again Christian."

"You mean, you lied?"

"Yes."

"Oh boy, that is a dreadful sin."

"I know, but it's not my fault. I've got this… issue, you see." The urgency to confide in this unfamiliar priest swells within me. The dividing screen shields his expression, sparing me some embarrassment. "I've got a sexually transmitted infection. If Jezebel finds out, I'm afraid I'll lose her."

"Trust and honesty are vital in a relationship, my son."

"I get that, but you don't understand, Father. I mean, take a look at this thing!" I rise, loosening my belt.

Father Bob protests, "Oh, no, please don't."

But it's too late. My pants are down, and I press myself against the divider. Father Bob averts his gaze, then does a double-take. "Oh, dear!"

"Father, see this? Do you see what I'm grappling with here?" My voice trembles with emotion.

"Okay, okay, just put it away and lower your voice."

"Please, Father, can you help me? I'm desperate." Tears threaten to escape again. I haven't cried in three years and I'm going for three times in one week. "Just pray it away or something. Bless it, whatever you have to do. I'll come every Sunday for the rest of my life if you can just make it disappear. Please, Father."

"I'll assist you. Now, sit back down. Please, remember this is a place of worship!" Father Bob's urgent whisper conveys his seriousness. I return to my seat, my distress palpable.

"I'm sorry, Father. But I've never felt like this about a woman before... I can't bear to lose her." I wipe a tear away.

"I'm not sure what advice I can offer you, my boy."

"I don't need advice. I just need you to heal this. Heal me. Or else, I'm afraid it's going to be the end of me."

"Heal you?"

"Yes. I see it as God's way of punishing me for my selfish and reckless life."

"Reckless? To what extent... how reckless?"

"Um, what do you want, Father? An estimate? I don't know, I lost count a while back. But if I were to guess, it's probably in the thousands."

"What are you seeking through so many relations? That's what you need to ask yourself. You won't find God through meaningless sex."

"I don't know... physical connection. Companionship. Power. Validation. It's not like I dislike women. I love them. I just seem to love too many of them."

"You need to search within."

"Search within? I'm not sure I understand."

"God is within. You seek God in others, in women. Try seeking fulfillment from within. 'I' is an inside job, my son."

"I will search within, but I still need your prayers, blessings, Hail Marys, whatever you got. In return, I promise to leave my reckless ways behind. If I can just catch this break, I'll devote my life to Jezebel alone, for good." My sincerity is profound. "Please, Father, I'm begging you. Please. I'll change. I've learned my lesson. I know God wants me to be better, and so do I. I want to be a better man. I've realised I've hurt many women. Not physically; I've never harmed a woman that way. But emotionally. I suppose you could call me a heartbreaker. Connecting with women on an emotional level has always been challenging for me."

"I'm afraid I can't relate."

"Of course, you're celibate, right? How is that? The doctor says my sex life is over as I know it. But that's what motivates me each morning. I'm lost without it."

"Perhaps it could be beneficial."

"It's been nearly two months since I last had sex. I can't even relieve myself because of the pain. Can you imagine that, Father?"

"Yes, no, I mean... we're getting off track!"

"Right. Where was I?"

"Saying you'll change."

"I promise, Father. Just help me get rid of this, and I swear I'll change my ways. I swear on my faith. I might even propose to Jezebel, despite not believing in marriage."

By now, Father Bob appears ready to conclude our conversation. "Say ten Hail Marys. I'll pray for you."

"Thank you, God; thank you, Father."

Chapter 16
Make-or-Break

Jezebel and I are strolling along the harbour foreshore from West Rocks to the area beneath the bridge. Even without the sun's warmth, the harbour's natural beauty remains a constant wonder. The Opera House forms a stunning backdrop, making our joined hands a picture-postcard image of romance.

Glancing down at my hand intertwined with Jezebel's, I realise this is new territory for me. Holding hands isn't something I'm accustomed to, or perhaps I've never let relationships progress this far. Yet, here I am, hand in hand with a woman I haven't even slept with. How times have changed.

"Did you mean what you said at the wedding about not wanting kids?"

Jezebel's question pulls me from my thoughts. "Oh, you remembered that?"

"Your speech? Are you kidding? It was the highlight of the entire event."

"I would've thought the *Dirty Dancing* move stole the show."

Jezebel laughs, her joy contagious. "You're right, that was a highlight… but seriously, Archie, did you mean it?"

Rain starts to fall, prompting us to seek refuge beneath the bridge. Leaning against the wrought iron railing, we take shelter. As the bridge looms above, I watch the Watsons Bay Ferry set out from Circular Quay on its route to the harbourside suburb. Jezebel's question deserves careful consideration.

"I'm not entirely sure. Children, well…"

"Do you really see them from a return-on-investment point of view?" Jezebel asks, her incredulity barely hidden.

"They're certainly costly!"

"Archie. They're human beings. You were once a kid too."

"And what do they give you in return, really? Except for sleepless nights, tantrums, snotty noses and stinky diapers."

"Um – maybe unconditional love, for starters."

"For you, maybe. A father is only loved for as long as he provides."

"What made you so cynical?"

"I'm not cynical. Think about it. I'd get love maybe for the first thirteen years." This makes Jezebel chuckle. "But then they become a source of grief for the next eight years. I might get the love back after that, once they've passed adolescence, but it all depends on how much money you're willing to give them."

"Oh my God, you're incorrigible!"

"But I'm right, aren't I?"

"No. But yes, you'll have all those tantrums and diapers, but you'll also have the good stuff."

"Like what?"

"The beautiful memories. The first word. The first steps. Hearing 'I love you, Daddy' for the first time."

"Hmm... not sure the pros outweigh the cons. And it's not like you can just send them back, you know. Kids are forever. There's no return policy. They're just always... there. I won't lie – that idea terrifies me. I like my life the way it is. My freedom is valuable. Call me selfish. But I'd rather be selfish, free and happy, than trapped in a deal I can't back out of."

Jezebel nods, her gaze dropping. I can see her disappointment, feel it in the air. I gaze out at the harbour, realising I've never truly pictured myself as a father. The thought sure is frightening, mainly because it would mean sacrificing my sleep, something I value highly. Do I have what it takes to prioritise someone else's needs over mine, I wonder.

"Saying that..." How do I put this delicately? "With the right woman, if she truly wants a family, I'd be open to it."

Jezebel looks at me, trying to read my sincerity. "You're just saying what you think I want to hear."

"Nope, I'm being genuine. It's time I took myself out of the equation for a change." I see her demeanour lighten. "But don't expect me to handle diaper duties."

Jezebel playfully slaps my arm. I wrap my arm around her shoulders, drawing her closer. As she leans in, we share a kiss, accompanied by the sound of the ferry's blaring horn across the harbour and the raindrops pattering beyond the bridge.

Every day, I carve out a specific period that I dub "me time." This personal respite usually falls between one and three p.m. and spans at least an hour. When "me time" arrives, I create a sanctuary by closing and locking my office door, flick my phone onto do-not-disturb mode, recline on my sofa, and delve into a business or self-improvement book before surrendering to a half-hour nap.

This time serves a dual purpose. First, it's a momentary escape from the cacophony of the working day, offering much-needed tranquillity. Second, this interval rejuvenates me for the rest of the afternoon. I've discovered that I'm considerably more productive after lunch if I manage to slip in a quick nap. At times, I wonder if I should've been born Spanish, where the post-lunch siesta is a more accepted practice.

Recently, I've swapped out reading for streaming guided meditations through my AirPods. On this particular occasion, I lay on my sofa, wearing an eye mask, headphones securely in place, as a gentle, soothing voice directs my breathing. Just as I teeter on the verge of drifting into slumber, my office door slams open. Shit, must have forgotten to lock it.

Enter Bryce, clutching his worry beads. "Hey matey, what's going on?"

My deep meditation/nap comes to an abrupt halt. I tear off my eye mask. "What the hell?"

"Oh, sorry, forgot about your 'me time'," Bryce says. "Your door was ajar."

He closes the door behind him and comfortably sinks into my office chair. "So, I went and got the snip."

"What?"

"A vasectomy."

"You got your tubes tied?"

"It's pretty wild, man. It's like I'm firing blanks now." Bryce juts his pelvis forward. "Boom, nada."

Still reclined, I gaze at the ceiling. The tranquillity of "me time" has been well and truly shattered. A profound sorrow suddenly washes over me, rendering Bryce's chatter about shooting blanks inconsequential.

"Archie? Archie, come back down to Earth."

"Hmm?"

"What's eating at you? Something on your mind?"

"Tomorrow, I'm introducing Jezebel to my dad."

"Whoa, whoa – slow down, man, that's a big step."

"You're telling me. Can't remember the last time I brought a woman home to meet Pops."

"And now's the time because...?"

I think of the L-word, but halt myself before saying it aloud. "Because I really care about her."

"You barely know her! You've been seeing each other for, what, a month?"

"Almost three months."

"Three months? Wow, that flew by."

"You're telling me."

"You might want to reconsider. This is a significant step. Introducing someone to Robert Flynn is no small matter, especially given his condition. It'll be a lot for her to handle."

I shoot Bryce a pointed look.

"Sorry," he says. "I just think you should take your time. Presenting her to your dad is a massive deal, what with his health and fragile state. No need to rush it."

I give Bryce a brief glance.

"Just sleep on it, alright?"

"That was exactly my plan. Right now."

"How many bosses would let you nap on the job, huh?"

"I know, I'm pretty fortunate."

"Am I not the coolest boss, or what?"

Bryce shuts the door on the way out. Outside my office I hear him shout, "Selby! How many coffees is that today? Slow down on the caffeine, mate. Look at you, you're shaking. Relax, Selby!"

Chapter 17

Milestones

J ezebel and I stroll down the corridor of ward eight, heading towards Dad's room. Her attire leans towards the conservative today, a floral dress gracefully falling around her calves. On the other hand, I've gone for a more relaxed approach, clad in blue jeans, a black t-shirt, and sneakers.

This is a significant moment for me. I struggle to remember the last time I introduced a woman to my old man. Jess from high school, maybe? Then there was Annabel from England, who joined us during our summer escapade to Byron Bay for my twenty-first birthday. Dad got along well with her, and they had some engaging banter. I remember the three of us sharing laughs on the deck, gazing out at the azure waves cascading onto Wategos Beach. Dad would often ask me why I let her slip away after three months. I try to remember the reasons for our break-up – did she want me to relocate to London with her? I offered the excuse of not being able to cope without sunlight and sandy shores. But deep down, I know that's not why I ended things with Annabel. It was just my way of calling it quits around the crucial three-month mark, that juncture where reality normally sets in for me.

As for Jezebel, she told me she hasn't faced a partner's family since her toxic past relationship. She recalls her ex's rudeness towards her mother quite vividly. That should've been a glaring warning sign, she realises now. He never displayed any interest in her family, not to mention her close friends. Paying a visit to her parents felt like an insurmountable chore for him, while hanging out with her friends was a rarity, thanks to a well-prepared array of excuses.

And when he started to steer her away from her friends, that's when her nightmare truly began. The control he attempted to exert over her life was outrageous, going so far as to decree she couldn't spend time with her friends, was the catalyst for his first violent episode. She was determined not to be controlled. But when she resisted, he resorted to physical violence. He would apologise afterwards, swearing it wouldn't happen again. But it did. Repeatedly. Apology after apology, pledge after broken pledge. Jezebel regrets the length of time she spent in that toxic relationship, fully aware deep down that things wouldn't change.

Yet, the fear of leaving kept her trapped. She eventually enlisted her close friend Clara's support the day she walked away. The controlled anger he displayed in front of Clara served as a chilling reminder that if she didn't escape, her life could be at risk.

I haven't discussed my past relationship struggles with Jezebel yet. Should I? Is it necessary to reveal those intimate details, or is it wiser to just let them remain in the past? Perhaps it's best to wait.

We finally arrive at Robert Flynn's room. I guide Jezebel forward, saying, "After you." However, she stops abruptly in her tracks.

"No, you first."

I offer her a smile and step into the room.

Pops sits up in his bed, engrossed in a rugby league match blaring from the television. He's clearly infuriated by a referee's decision, exclaiming, "Come on, what was that? It was nothing! You can't tackle anyone anymore!?"

As I enter the room, he notices me and addresses the game's apparent downfall. "Archie, this game has gone to shit – they're sending people off for leading with the shoulder now!"

"Dad, there's someone I'd like you to meet." Jezebel promptly enters the room. He reacts instantly, hitting the off button on the television and hastily straightening up in his bed while smoothing his hair.

"Jeez, Archie, a little warning would have been nice."

I chuckle. "This is Jezebel. Jezebel, meet Robert Flynn, my dad."

"Hello, Mr. Flynn."

"Please, call me Robert, or Rob," he offers, his gaze intently fixed on Jezebel while smiling proudly at my choice of partner. Jezebel blushes a bit and hands him the flowers.

"For you?"

"Really? I just adore flowers!" Dad lies rather convincingly.

"No, you don't," I chime in.

"Shut up, Archie!" Robert retorts playfully, accepting them gratefully. "What do you know? Just because you never bring me any."

"That's a lie," I shoot back. "I do," I tell Jezebel, "and you hate them," I say to Dad.

"Are these native Australian?" Robert inquires, peering at the bouquet. "I can spot native Australian flowers when I see them. That right there is a Waratah," he states, sniffing the bouquet.

"Waratahs have no scent," I correct him.

"Whatever, Archie," Dad says with a shrug.

"And that's not a Waratah, it's called a Protea, from South Africa."

"What are you, a florist?" he asks, genuinely impressed by my knowledge. Jezebel finds our playful banter amusing. Dad carries on, "You know, the only thing more beautiful inside this room than these proteas? You, my dear."

Jezebel blushes again and lets out a soft laugh. "Oh, thank you, Robert. I see where Archie gets his charm from."

"Definitely not from his mother!"

Jezebel seems uncertain how to respond to this, and offers a nervous smile.

"Seriously, son. You're punching way above your weight here."

"You know, I knew you would say that," I interject. "And you're kinda right, because Jezebel's a fighter."

"A fighter?"

"I'm a martial artist."

"A martial artist? Wow, I've never met a professional martial artist before. American?"

Jezebel nods. I catch on that Robert is about to become intrigued, so I guide Jezebel to the chair beside his bed.

"Californian?"

"Wow. I'm impressed."

"I have a knack for picking accents. It's my useless superpower."

"I can see that. Have you ever heard of mixed martial arts? Or MMA?" she asks.

"Is that where you fight in a cage to the death?"

Jezebel chuckles. "Ha, not exactly. It's an octagon. We fight until one of us either taps out or is knocked out."

"Wow. But you're far too pretty to get your face all beaten up."

"Tell me about it," I add from my spot by the window.

"But you're gonna retire early, aren't you, babe?" Jezebel replies with a smile and a flash of her irresistible eyes.

"Well, that's why my face is still intact, and my record unbeaten. My defence is rock-solid."

"Ha!" Dad's face lights up. "I like her already, Archie! She's gonna keep you in line."

"I knew you would, Dad."

"Are your fights on TV?"

"Pay-per-view," Jezebel answers, glancing at the TV above Robert's bed. "Can you get that in here?"

"No," I reply on his behalf, "but I'll see if I can arrange it. She's got a big bout coming up on Sunday. I should warn you, though, it can get quite intense."

"Yeah, I'm not sure I can watch two women beat the living daylights out of each other," Pops confesses.

"But you're okay watching a bunch of men go at it?" Jezebel inquires, glancing up at the TV.

"I don't mind rugby, you know. It's very strategic, tactical," Robert opines, pondering his next statement. "But I've got to be honest with you. This new stuff, it feels a bit barbaric. Just pummelling each other into submission. No rules."

"Careful, Dad."

"It's fine," Jezebel reassures me. "MMA involves a lot of strategy too."

"Really? Educate me."

"Well, one of the most utilised martial arts in MMA is Brazilian jiu-jitsu. It was actually designed so that the smaller person could defeat a much larger opponent," Jezebel explains.

"Really? How does that work?"

"You close the distance so they can't strike you. You grapple with them, aiming to take them down to the ground. Then you employ carefully crafted moves using your hands, arms and legs to wrestle them into submission."

"Huh," Robert responds, mouth slightly agape, gazing at Jezebel. "Is that so?" She nods affirmatively.

"I could've used Brazilian jiu-jitsu back when I was growing up in the hood."

"Seems like you're passionate about sports."

"It's all I've got," Robert answers. "Well, sports, a couple of cute nurses... and Archie, of course," he adds, his enthusiasm for me somewhat less evident.

"Thanks, Dad."

"Just don't mess this up, son."

"Good grief." I hang my head, playfully exasperated.

"Because she will kick your ass."

Jezebel laughs.

"She's a keeper, I can tell," Dad adds.

"Okay, I understand, Pops. Thanks."

Jezebel can't help but laugh, which only fuels Robert further. "But if you do screw it up..." he says, diverting his attention to Jezebel, "just know that I'm available." He delivers this with a cheeky wink.

"Alright, visit's over," I declare, joining in the laughter that Jezebel and Dad share.

"Ooh, looks like you've got some competition here, Arch," Jezebel teases, a smile playing on her lips.

"What? I won't be around much longer," Robert adds. "I deserve a bit of affection before I check out, right?"

"You're incorrigible, Pops."

Robert grins widely, nodding at Jezebel. "What a character I am, huh?"

Chapter 18

Stage 4: Depression

I was in the midst of a video conference call when my office was invaded by two uniformed police officers. One was a burly male with the arrogant air of an ex-private school rugby captain, and the other was his female partner, a young blonde woman with a stern demeanour. I couldn't help but think about the cliché of young, blonde female cops in Australia.

"Are you Archie Flynn?" asks the rugby cop.

I glanced at my name tag on the door they had just walked through. "What are you, a detective?"

A subtle exchange of glances between the officers ensued, their expressions unimpressed. The blonde cop decided to speak next, her voice serious. "You're under arrest, Archie Flynn, for indecent exposure."

"What?" I tried to protest, but before I could react, the rugby captain had spun me around and was in the process of cuffing me. "Do you know Father Bob?" I blurted out, realising this was about what happened during confession. Damn it, I hadn't anticipated that he would report our confidential conversation.

"What kind of sicko exposes himself to a priest?" the rugby cop observed.

"Think about what you just said," I mutter, knowing I was probably digging myself into a deeper hole. "In fact, do you mind if she handcuffs me instead? I'm kind of into the whole BDSM thing."

The rugby cop's response was a shove against the wall. "Asshole," he sneered.

"That statement will be used against you," the blonde cop chimed in, scribbling notes in her small notebook. My patience for people with a tiny amount of authority was wearing thin.

"I thought what happens in confession stays in confession," I protested.

Just then, Bryce's face appeared around the door, and he mouthed, "What the fuck!?" before shifting his attention to the policemen. "Um, I have a mandatory mask policy for visitors to my office," he cheekily remarked. "If you don't mind covering up, I'd hate for there to be a COVID outbreak in the firm."

I couldn't help but suppress a smile.

"Never mind, we're leaving," the blonde cop said as they led me through the open-plan office. The entire staff of Bryce & Co. watched from their cubicles as I was escorted away, my head hung in shame.

And this was only the beginning.

"I don't see much social distancing happening there either," Bryce called out as we approached the exit. "At least a one-point-five metre distance is required, if I recall correctly."

The rugby cop turned his head and shot Bryce a glare that could have melted steel.

Later, alone in a jail cell, I stared at the floor with a sense of despair settling over me. Rock bottom had never felt so real. "How did I end up here?" I wondered aloud; a question I would ask myself over and over in the coming months. My mind was mired in depression. "All because of a fucking STD."

My phone had been confiscated, and the feeling of nakedness without it was unsettling. My phone had become an extension of myself, and now I was left with nothing to occupy my time except my thoughts. Was I being punished for past sins? The thought flickered through my mind, but I quickly shook it off. I'm an atheist; I don't believe in that sort of thing. Plus, I'm not that bad, am I? I've always been upfront about my promiscuity. When my girlfriends asked, I told them the truth – and if they couldn't handle it, they left. I might break hearts, but I'm not a womaniser.

I am not a womaniser.

My train of thought was interrupted by the cell door creaking open. A short, stout male guard with a moustache walked in. "You've got a visitor," he said as he unlocked the cell door. I was led out to the visitors' room, my mind a swirl of questions and uncertainties.

I was fully expecting Bryce when I walked into the visitors' room, so when I saw Jezebel on the other side of the glass partition, it threw me for a loop. How did she even find out

I had been arrested?

As she approached the glass, something about her eyes gave it away. Hurt. Pain. Betrayal. Shame and embarrassment coursed through me as I took a seat across from her.

"Father Bob spilled the beans to you too, huh? What happened to 'confession is confidential'?" I said, trying to break the tension.

"No. I couldn't reach you, so I went to your office."

"Bryce?"

"Archie, what happened at church?"

Ah shit. Perhaps Father Bob didn't spill the beans after all, but clearly she had heard something through the grapevine. "I, ah, asked Father Bob to heal an, ah, affliction…"

"Umm… what exactly?"

Oh boy, this was excruciating. But there was no out this time. No more lies, no more delaying or deceiving. I had to come clean. This was it. Sitting inside the visitors' room of Surry Hills Police HQ with a glass petition separating us, I was about to bare it all to the first woman I ever truly loved. And I hadn't even told her that I loved her yet.

"I have an STD."

A prolonged silence. A silence so deafening I'm pretty sure I heard one of the police officers in the next room fart, and as much as I wanted to laugh, now really wasn't the time.

"An STD?"

I nod my head.

Jezebel's mind kicks into overdrive. "What kind?"

Here we go, cards laid out on the table. "They don't know yet… it's a new kind."

Jezebel's expression says it all, a mixture of confusion and disgust. "Okay, that's weird."

"You're telling me."

"And you told Father Bob this?"

"Yeah… and I may have shown him."

Jezebel's eyes nearly pop out of her head. "You showed him your…?"

I nod. Jezebel hands her head, rubs her brow. Another prolonged silence. Eventually, she speaks. "So, *that's* the reason you haven't slept with me – because you've got some nasty STD on your dick."

"Yeah."

"You're not really a born-again Christian."

"No. I'm not. I'm sorry."

"The one thing I asked of you, Archie, was not to lie to me."

"I was trying to protect you. And I didn't wanna lose you."

"So you are just a regular fuck-boy, huh?"

"Fuck-boy? Is that like an American term for womaniser? No, I love women. And I have made love to many women. Yes, it's true. But it's you I love."

The words slipped out. Did I really just say that? I had never told a partner I loved them and meant it, until now. Jezebel had stirred something in me, something I couldn't quite grasp. It was love. Had I just confessed my feelings in the most unromantic setting ever? Nicely done, Arch. Real smooth. I dared to look up at Jezebel, hoping to decipher her reaction. A heavy silence settled between us. Jezebel allowed the words to hang for a moment before tucking them away, perhaps for later discussion, or maybe for private contemplation. And then dropped the bombshell question.

"What's your number?"

"My number?" I repeat, my mind racing to keep up.

"How many women have you slept with?"

The question felt like a noose tightening. "Umm... ah..."

"Over fifty?" I wanted to flee, to escape. Far away. "More than a hundred?" The truth was, I had lost count about five years back. But I knew it was well over a hundred. "Over *two* hundred?" Curiosity was now getting the better of Jezebel; I remained mute. "Over five hundred!?" Her disbelief was palpable. I maintained my poker face, refusing to reveal anything. "Can it really be over a thousand!?" The shock in her voice was unmistakable.

"To be honest, I'm not entirely sure. I stopped counting..."

"*Lost* count, you mean."

"It's just a number, Jezebel. It doesn't define me. What does matter is that you're not just another number."

"Not yet."

"No, not ever." I leaned in closer to the glass. "I don't want anyone else, just you. That's the truth."

Jezebel stares at me, tears pooling in her eyes. The silence stretched on, an endless void. Then finally, her voice emerged. "You've got some serious, deep-seated issues. I don't have time for nonsense relationships. At some point I'll have to return to the States, so I just don't have time for this. I've been through enough shit. I want the real deal."

"Yes, and so do I. And I will get better. I'm going to attend Sex Addicts Anonymous. Please, please give me a chance to prove to you that I can do better."

"I need some time…" Her sentence trailed off as a tear rolled down her cheek. She got up to leave.

"Wait, Jezebel."

And with that, I watched her exit the visitors' room, my eyes welling up also.

Then Bryce suddenly appeared and took her place, his familiar grin showing through the glass.

"Keep your chin up," he said. "I'm here to bail you out, bud!"

Chapter 19

Progress, Not Perfection

I find myself in Dr. Singh's practice, seated on the treatment bed, while he shuffles through a thick stack of papers. I gaze at the floor, my expression devoid of emotion.

"Alright. Do you want the good news or the bad news first?" Dr. Singh inquires.

"Christ," I respond, my voice heavy with uncertainty, "I don't know... I guess the good news."

"The good news is we've identified a match for your STD."

"The bad?"

"In Guinea."

"You mean Papua New Guinea?"

"No. Just Guinea. It's a country in Africa."

"Africa? How is that even possible!?"

"Doesn't matter. The point is, it's not a new strain. So, we haven't stumbled upon a new disease," Dr. Singh says, his tone tinged with a touch of disappointment. "Hence, we can't christen it Archie Flynn Disease. That's the bad news."

"We can't? Oh, what a bummer. I was really hoping to proudly display the certificate on my wall," I quip.

"It's labelled Costras Disease."

"Costras?"

"It's Spanish for 'scabs'. A doctor from Spain claimed the naming rights before we had a chance."

"So, how did they manage to treat these scabs?"

"They didn't. The infection spread and posed a threat to vital organs, so... unfortunately, surgical intervention was necessary."

"I beg your pardon?" I can't believe what I'm hearing.

"That's actually the bad news."

I can only stare at Dr. Singh, my eyes wide with disbelief. "Listen very carefully, Doc. Nobody – and I mean nobody – is amputating my... well, you know. Are we clear?"

"We might not..."

"NO!" I interject sharply. "Absolutely not. No one, nothing, ever. Do you understand me?"

Dr. Singh is taken aback by the ferocity of my tone. He retreats, putting some distance between us, and nods.

"I understand completely, Archie. I assure you, no one is going to subject your... um, that part of your anatomy to any sort of amputation."

Chapter 20

Lockdown!

I'm slouched in the lounge, draped in a tracksuit, as winter rain pelts down outside. My laptop rests open before me, and a near-empty bottle of red wine sits by my side. My attention toggles between the television and my work, not really focusing on either. My appearance reflects the internal struggle I'm facing – I even stopped shaving, which says a lot for a guy who takes his personal grooming to Tom Cruise-like levels.

The laptop's monitor abruptly springs to life, revealing Bryce's bright and cheerful visage on the screen. His exuberance contradicts my own downcast demeanour.

"Hey, buddy-boo, how about this, huh? Back on Zoom again, eh," Bryce says with a bit too much enthusiasm. "But don't get any ideas, you're returning to the office as soon as this outbreak is over."

"I hope this lockdown sticks around then. I get to avoid mingling with people, because let's face it – people suck. There's no more FOMO because nothing's happening anyway. And I can drink while I work," I state with a touch of pride, lifting the wine bottle to my lips and taking a direct swig. "Cheers." My slightly slurred words suggest a more-than-slightly tipsy state.

"Geez Louise, this is where the boss-friend line blurs. I'm not sure how I feel about you drinking on the job. Is everything okay, mate?"

"Sure. Everything's just peachy in the world right now, isn't it? We've got pandemics, conspiracies, division. And to top it off, I've contracted an incredibly rare, sub-Saharan sex disease on my appendage, and there's not a damn thing I can do about it. Yeah, everything's just swell, Bryce."

"Relax. Vaccines are on the way. We'll be back to our normal lives soon. Plus, we've had it easy compared to previous generations, right? Think about our grandfathers, shipped off to the other side of the world at nineteen years old to fight in a war that had nothing to do with them."

I'm not receiving the sympathy I need right now. Bryce continues to elaborate.

"What's become of you? Why aren't you drinking from a wine glass?"

"Less clean-up," I retort before indulging in another swig from the bottle. Wine trickles from my mouth, running down my chin. Bryce gazes at me through the laptop screen, a mix of concern and disgust evident on his face. "And how about you, boss? Everything going well?"

Bryce glances at his remote workspace, his tone thoughtful. "This whole work-from-home arrangement is taking its toll on our marriage. We're spending too much time together, you know? We're actually getting to know each other. Like, *really* know each other. It's strange – I think we're actually better off *not* knowing each other."

"Well, at least you have someone. The first woman I've ever genuinely connected with, I screwed it up."

"Oh boy, she seems to have had quite an impact on you."

"She definitely did. But you'll be pleased to know, I think it's over."

"Pleased? Why would I be pleased? If she makes you happy, you can't just let her slip away."

I remain silent. Bryce's reaction surprises me. I expected him to be ecstatic about the return of the eternal bachelor Archie, the source of his amusement and most outrageous fantasies. Over all our years of working together, Bryce always seemed happiest on Monday mornings, eager to hear of my weekend escapades. And escapades there were – and initially I enjoyed sharing them. I felt like I was helping Bryce, allowing him to live vicariously through me. But that enthusiasm waned, and before long I stopped caring.

I knew I needed to address my inability to form emotional connections with women, and I was finally ready to confront it – all because of Jezebel. But now she's gone.

Bryce continues, "Seriously, man. I've known you and your... ah, romantic escapades for a long time. And I've never seen you like this."

"Like what?"

"Truly in love."

"Ha."

"Look at you, all beat up. Depressed and shit. This isn't you. You're Archie Flynn, man.

You're the master, my hero. If she's the one who can finally tame the beast, you can't let her get away."

Bryce's emotions are genuinely stirring.

"She's not just another notch on your belt. You can't let her be the one that slipped through your fingers."

My gaze locks onto Bryce's face on the screen. I feel myself welling up slightly. "It's not that simple…" Can I reveal to my closest friend that my virility is under threat? "I can't be with anyone anymore."

"What… uh… are you crying?"

"No," I assert as I hastily wipe my eyes.

"I believe you are."

"I'm not crying!"

"Arch, this is new – you're so vulnerable and shit."

"Shut up."

"It's kind of beautiful."

"Shut up, Bryce!" In my frustration, I slam the laptop shut, tipping over the wine bottle in the process. "Goddamnit!" I curse as I pick up the fallen bottle. A few seconds later, my mobile phone starts ringing. I eye the screen – it's Bryce calling.

I walk into the basement of St. Patrick's Catholic Church, feeling like I'm walking into a circus. The sign above the door reads "Sex Addicts Anonymous", which my priest/therapist, Father Bob, thought would be a brilliant place for me to face my "appetite for carnal adventures".

Yeah, I confronted Father Bob about "what happens in confession, stays in confession", but he said he did it out of love and it was for my own good, and that it will set me on a path towards repentance and healing and all that crap. What was I supposed to say to that? Instead, I apologised for showing him my willy and agreed to come here knowing it would improve my chances in my upcoming court case. Plus, it was the only legal social gathering I could attend during lockdown, and I needed to get out of the house. Cabin fever is real. But, if I'm going to be really honest, the actual reason I'm here is for Jezebel.

If I can prove I am making an effort to address my issues and improve myself, maybe I still have a shot.

I find a seat and slump down, trying to look like I couldn't care less about being here. But the room is anything but indifferent. It's like a glitter bomb went off in here. Mostly LGBT folks, turning a support group into a flamboyant Pride parade. Not one chick in sight. Well, perhaps a few could pass for women – it's hard to tell these days.

The meeting starts, and Fabio, a walking embodiment of fabulousness, stands up and announces, "Hey there, I'm Fabio, but just call me Farbs. I'm addicted to my own charm, charisma and stunning jawline. Can't resist a good wink at myself in the mirror, know what I mean?"

The room burst out laughing, all except for the chairperson, who looks like one of those bears from the Blue Oyster Bar in the *Police Academy* movies. I almost chuckle myself, and then I realise I might just fit right in, in the most awkward way possible.

One by one, the group shared their stories. Graphic stories. About their sexual escapades. And I mean graphic – it's like X-rated story hour. These guys don't hold back.

Julian is up next, a diva extraordinaire. "*Hola, mi gente.* I'm Julian, and my vice? Well, it's not just tacos that I'm craving, if you catch my drift." More laughter from the room.

I'm beet-red as Julian dives into details that should never be shared in public. I consider making a run for it, but my curiosity and discomfort hold me captive. Julian tells the story of his rock-bottom, when he was on all sorts of party drugs which just made him horny, and he used to frequent a notorious gay beat in Elizabeth Bay down the back of Kings Cross, back when it was the city's seedy redlight district. Julian talks of the infamous wall, which had a glory hole. He used to back up his ass against the hole and let any stranger penetrate him. I start to feel a bit sick as he says this, while the rest of the room just nods in compassion and understanding. This is not the group for me.

I feel personally violated by the end of Julian's story. Then Reggie (short for Regina, apparently) takes the stage, a vivacious trans woman who radiates divine energy. "Hello, beautiful souls! Reggie here. I can't seem to resist the tall, dark, and emotionally unavailable types." Reggie looks me square in the eye as she says this. "You know, the ones who ghost you after leaving a trail of socks at your place? I guess I'm addicted to my own heartbreak."

I can't help but chuckle. Reggie's got a way of turning her pain into a vibrant spectacle. I applaud her, especially since Julian's was a tough act to follow.

But as the parade of stories continues, I'm squirming in my seat, feeling like I've stumbled into a secret sexual underworld. These people are way more open than I ever thought possible, taking the concept of oversharing to a whole new level – and not one that I am prepared to enter. I pray that I am not called up by the Blue Oyster chairperson.

I must have unintentionally manifested what I did not want because, just like that, the chair-person locks eyes with me. I look away but it's too late. He asks if I want to share. My pulse picks up and beads of alcohol-induced sweat form as I head up to the front through the rainbow crowd. As I face the room, I notice Reggie give me a slow wink while lasciviously chewing her gum.

"Uh, hey. I'm Archie, and I'm a sex addict. I guess my thing is the usual stuff... you know, bedroom acrobatics, maybe a game of blindfolded, naked Twister."

"Ooh, that sounds like fun," says some flaming flamingo.

My voice is barely above a whisper compared to the fireworks that preceded me. The room ripples with understanding chuckles, and I feel like that guy at a stand-up comedy show whose punchline landed with a thud. I talk of my past obsession and compulsion for sex, the need for validation, and low self-esteem but massive ego – all that jazz. Finally, I tell them about how my philandering has caught up with me in the form of an STD. I talk of the unfortunate timing of it coming along just when I met the most amazing woman of my life, and I'm now at risk of losing her forever. I tell them how I lied to her in order to hide it, but now I've come clean I don't know what's gonna happen. Strangely, it feels good to get it all off my chest to a room full of complete strangers.

As the meeting wraps up, a whirlwind of colour and charisma approaches me.

"Hey there, newbie. You're fresh, huh? Don't sweat the graphic stories. We're here to hold each other up," says Reggie.

I manage a half-smile. "Yeah, it's been an... experience."

"Don't worry, hon. You'll get used to it," Reggie explains. "This is where unicorns and rainbows gather to share, even the messy parts. Remember, we're all on different paths, but we're all aiming for growth – catch my drift?"

Walking out of the meeting, I'm still feeling a bit overwhelmed and slightly disturbed by the whole process, but something's shifted. Maybe this vibrant and diverse crew aren't exactly my people, but they've given me a glimpse into lives even more colourful than my own. And who knows, maybe embracing their unlikely support is exactly what I need to untangle the chaos in my own love life.

I've got Jezebel's VIP pass tucked away as I sneak into the Sydney Entertainment Centre. I feel like I've earned the right to semi-stalk after making an effort to improve myself through Sex Addicts Anonymous. The place is half-empty thanks to the super-flu, not the best scenario for staying incognito since I wasn't exactly invited to this fight. But on the other hand, it means masks are mandatory so I can stealth my way in wearing a hoodie, mask and sunnies, even though I look suss as fuck. But at least no one will recognise me. Better yet, no one will question me. I'm just another one of those ultra-cautious super-flu public participants. I could be immunocompromised, after all.

Hipster Athlete Steve is ringside, so I decide to slip in behind him out of sight. I know that C-U-Next-Tuesday would rat me out. I settle about ten rows back, still getting a good view of the action. Just in time, the two fighters step into the octagon, the ref in between them. A gasp escapes me as I catch sight of Jezebel's opponent.

She's like a female Ivan Drago from *Rocky IV*. Blonde and huge. Pure-bred Aryan. Her name's Yulia Kalichikov, and she towers over Jezebel. The ref separates them before the third round starts. As they circle, fists up, something feels off about Jezebel. Maybe it's her posture or the way she's moving – there's a lack of her usual confidence, and it's unsettling.

Jezebel's not herself. And I know what the problem is – she can't visualise her usual strategy of picturing her ex as her opponent. That's what's fuelled her unbeaten streak. But now, she can't shake thoughts of me. At least that's what's going through my slightly drunk noggin. The Russian giant across from her transforms into me, no matter how hard she tries to shake it. She sees me, Archie. I can even see her blink hard as if to erase the image, but it's too late. Kalichikov lands a straight jab right on Jezebel's nose.

Jezebel feels the sting and I know her nose is broken.

"Fuck."

I see her mouth, and hear her voice inside my head. Her eyes well up instantly. This is not a good start. Her broken nose joins the list of visible injuries: a black eye, a cut above her eye, and a lip that's swollen and split. She doesn't have time to dwell, though. Kalichikov starts with a barrage of body shots, and Jezebel drops her elbows to protect her ribs. She's taking a pounding, yet in the midst of it, she manages a swift uppercut which catches the Russian giant flush on her jaw, much like the one she dealt to that coked-up douche-bag from the bar. Only this one doesn't break her jaw. She does stumble backwards, but manages to stay on her feet.

Jezebel moves in, but slower than usual. She lets loose a barrage of punches at Kalichikov's head, but the Russian has her forearms up blocking the blows. I can see what's coming. Jezebel's gonna wear herself out. She uselessly punches in frustration, letting her emotions get the better of her.

I stand up and say, "Slow down Jez!"

My voice is easily audible, given how empty the stadium is. I see Steve look up from the corner, his eyes squinting to identify the voice behind the mask.

Then it happens. Jezebel tires, her guard drops slightly, and Kalichikov delivers a punch like a Russian freight train. Jezebel goes down, hitting the mat with a thud. Kalichikov pounces, straddling Jezebel and raining punches down on her. Blood splatters the canvas, and I can't help but wince, feeling every blow as if it were on me.

I can't bear to watch any longer. Without thinking, my body propels me out of my seat, bounding down the rows ahead. I hurdle over Hipster Athlete Steve and scale the octagon barrier. Steve's eyes widen in shock as he witnesses the masked figure entering the ring, leaping onto the back of the towering Russian.

"Get off her!"

My scream rings out, echoing in the arena. Jezebel's faint voice barely reaches my ears as I cling to Kalichikov's back. She moves, crashing us into the barricade. Pain jolts through me as I let out a pained grunt.

My actions push Steve into a rage. He's not going to be outdone, so he climbs into the ring too. Kalichikov expertly flips me over her back, sending me somersaulting through the air until I crash onto the canvas below.

Steve rushes to Jezebel, concern evident in his voice. "Are you okay?"

"I'm fine," Jezebel replies, her gaze shifting toward me. Kalichikov prepares for a body slam, and I'm immobilised, helpless. To make things worse, Kalichikov's bulldog-like trainer climbs into the octagon.

"Stay down," Steve warns Jezebel, but it's too late. Kalichikov slams her weight down onto me. The referee attempts to intervene, struggling to separate her from me. Then the Russian bulldog's trainer jumps in, raining blows down on me. Out of nowhere, Jezebel swoops in, yanking the bulldog off me. But Kalichikov swiftly tackles Jezebel, catching her off guard. Exhausted, Jezebel can't retaliate, and Kalichikov locks her into an arm bar on the floor.

Steve rushes in, trying to break Kalichikov's grip on Jezebel. The bulldog charges at Steve, knocking him aside. Amidst the chaos, the referee also joins the fray, trying to separate the five of us. Somehow, I manage to get to my feet, though the world blurs before me. There's the taste of blood in my mouth.

"Jezebel," I mutter, charging forward, unintentionally crashing into the ref, Jezebel, Kalichikov and Steve in a chaotic pile-on.

Steve wrestles me into a headlock, while Jezebel struggles with him, and Kalichikov continues grappling with her. The bulldog confronts the referee, and more people from both sides rush into the octagon. The situation spirals out of control. Security and police swarm in, attempting to defuse the chaos but only making it worse. The octagon is now a sea of bodies, a full-blown brawl caught on camera. Every person not inside the ring films the whole shit-show on their phone.

Chapter 21

Aftermath

I'm stuck in the police station, my eyes glued to the television screen broadcasting the horrifying fight replay. It's on every major news channel, having gone viral worldwide. Jezebel and, unfortunately, Kalichikov have become overnight sensations. I can't help but feel a hint of pride in that – maybe it'll raise Jezebel's public profile.

But what I'm not proud of are the black eye and the aching shoulder, a constant reminder of Steve (moron) twisting my arm behind my back. He was supposed to be on my goddamn side! Qudos Bank Arena has slapped me with a lifetime ban, and now I'm waiting to see what the justice department dishes out.

The same young blonde police officer who nabbed me earlier is typing away at a computer across from me, filling out some report. "Second offence," she remarks in a tone that gets on my nerves. It's like she's savouring the tiny bit of authority she holds over me, talking down as if I'm some trouble-making school kid. I can't be bothered with her antics, so I give a half-hearted nod. "Might as well consolidate them into one court order. If you don't shape up, you're asking for it," she continues, waiting for me to reply. But I'm not giving her the satisfaction, just returning her stare. And yep, she blinks first, shifting her gaze to the TV. "What were you thinking?" she asks.

I remain tight-lipped. I'm over it. Plus, I know I'm not legally obliged to give her an answer.

"Planning on giving me the silent treatment, huh?" she quips. I nod a slow affirmation. She shakes her head, engrossed in her paperwork. "Real mature..."

A surge of violent frustration washes over me, an urge to flick her on the ear or something. But I quickly rein it in. I've never hit a woman, not even flicked an ear, and I sure as hell don't want to start now. Thankfully, my anger gets interrupted by a familiar voice from behind.

"Going for a hattrick, are you mate!?" Bryce's voice rings out as he walks in, a wide grin splitting his face. "You're setting new records." A moment of silence hangs in the air as Blondie shoots Bryce an exasperated look.

"Do not encourage him," she says to Bryce.

"Lighten up, constable. Just having a laugh," Bryce replies. "I'm here to bail him out... again."

I swivel in my chair to face Bryce. His presence immediately lifts my mood. He's holding out some worry beads. "Thought you could use these, mate," he says.

I stand outside Jezebel's apartment door, the worry beads clutched in my hand. As the door opens, there's no surprise in seeing who's on the other side – Hipster Athlete Steve.

It seems suspicion works both ways, as evinced by Steve's quick response. "She doesn't want to see you," he states, barely letting the door open fully.

"What brings you here?" I ask.

"What brings *me* here?" Steve retorts incredulously. "What brings you here, more like it. Shouldn't you be home, isolating? News flash: lockdown is in effect."

"Well, shouldn't you be at home too, then?"

"Actually, no. I'm Jezebel's chosen bubble-buddy."

"Excuse me?"

"Seriously, catch up. Single folks can isolate with a chosen person, a bubble-buddy."

"Well, news flash: there's a new bubble-buddy in town."

Steve smirks, obviously enjoying my shock at his victory in the bubble-buddy race.

"Considering I'm her boyfriend..."

"*Were* her boyfriend. Breaking news: it's over."

"Sounds like fake news to me."

Steve's demeanour changes, and he steps out into the hallway and closes the door behind him. He squares off with me, getting serious. "I know about your reputation, man."

"My reputation? What, you been digging around to find any dirt you could use to drive a wedge between us? Did you hire a private eye or something?"

"Didn't need one. Your rep's already out there, spreading like a virus."

"Reminds me of you, because I'd like to avoid you like the plague."

"I'm serious. Bad reputations spread like wildfire, kind of like you around women's beds... if you catch my drift."

"Look, I get that you're infatuated with Jezebel, and that's your deal, not mine, but—"

"Whoa, hold on a second there, buddy," Steve interrupts, holding up a finger. "Just back up."

"We're not buddies, and never will be. Maybe you'll be her bridesmaid at our wedding someday, but we still won't be buddies."

"Your wedding!? You've got quite the sense of humour, huh?" he taunts, then asks about my eye. "Is that eyeshadow? Oh, right, no. That's a black eye. And your arm's looking a little twisted there, who did that to you..."

I can't stand how Steve thinks he's a comedic genius. That urge for violence wells up again, and I'm not a violent man. "Yeah, speaking of that, why did you attack me out there? I was trying to protect Jezebel."

Steve laughs at my words. "Oh, come on," he says, projecting loud enough for Jezebel to hear inside, "you couldn't protect a fly in a slaughterhouse."

"That's not a saying," I reply, which gets him riled up.

"You want to be clever? Want another round?"

"You want to fight again with your big mouth?" I say, mimicking his stance. "You want to tango with the devil?"

He starts shuffling, doing the Ali shuffle, and shadow-boxing, his punches stopping just short of my face. But I don't flinch. I'm beyond caring. I've got nothing to lose, and only Jezebel to gain. I can't help but stare at this guy's antics, until I finally blurt out, "Were you dropped on your head as a baby or something?"

Steve comes close, his face inches from mine. "Don't mess with me. I could take you down anytime."

"Yeesh, you could take me down with your breath. Could you step back? I might puke."

Steve's face flushes red with anger. "My breath doesn't smell."

"Of course you can't smell your own breath, but to me it smells like a steak and blue cheese milkshake or something."

He clenches his fist again, knuckles white. He's gearing up for another strike, but I sense he might not hold back this time. Fine by me. If I can get this guy taken away into custody, maybe I'll have a shot at talking some sense into Jezebel. But that plan's dashed as Jezebel's door swings open.

Even with her battered appearance, she looks divine. "I want both of you to leave, please."

"Jezzie?" Steve protests.

"No, Steve. I need some alone time right now. Please go." Jezebel glances at me, a hint of regret in her eyes. "Both of you."

"Together? That doesn't sound like a great idea," I suggest.

"You're right," Steve agrees. "You should go first."

"I'm in no hurry," I reply. "Be my guest."

"Neither am I," Steve counters.

"Did you really pick this douche-bag as your new bubble-buddy?" I ask Jezebel.

Steve takes a step towards her. "Yeah, I'm her bubble-buddy, and I'm going back in—"

His words are cut off by Jezebel. "Would you both stop it? You're acting like a couple of children," she says before slamming the door shut, leaving us both stranded outside, staring at the closed door, dumbfounded.

"You know what," I say as I step away from Steve, "if you're not gonna brush your teeth or chew some gum, I think I will leave first, for my own safety."

"Fine. So long, dickwad."

"You really should see a dentist. Could be halitosis," I say, walking down the hall.

Steve watches me leave and bangs on Jezebel's door. "Jezzie, open up, it's Steve." But the door stays shut. I turn and watch him hold his hand in front of his mouth, breathing onto it, trying to catch a whiff of his own breath. Confusion is written all over his face. "Jezzie, please. I don't have halitosis... whatever that is."

On the other side of the door, I can hear tears in Jezebel's voice. "Please, Steve, just go away!"

Chapter 22

Robert James Flynn 1946 – 2022

I slump in front of the television, nursing a drink, and watch the Wallabies beat the Springboks in rugby union, a rare feat these days. Normally, a Wallabies victory would light up my mood, but not today. My face remains a blank canvas.

In simple terms, I look like garbage. It's not that I'm willingly trapped indoors. Typically, I'd be out, self-medicating with booze, sometimes drugs, and always a revolving door of women. But now, I'm just letting myself go. My usually sharp grooming has given way to a week's worth of beard growth, and my hair stands in wild disarray. There's even a hint of a beer gut forming.

Still, it isn't completely my fault. Greater Sydney is under lockdown, Melbourne as well, even Canberra, the nation's capital. I hate it. The double-whammy of heartbreak and being unable to escape through meaningless encounters with strangers is slowly eating at me. All I have left for now is alcohol. I can't even distract myself with porn and self-indulgence. The throbbing ache in my groin is a constant reminder. I shove a handful of butternut popcorn into my mouth, crumbs spilling in every direction, as my thoughts wander to the possibility that my STD might just be my undoing.

Just when I'm lost in my spiralling thoughts, my phone's shrill ring pierces the air. I glare at it, popcorn tumbling from my mouth, before begrudgingly answering.

"Talk."

"Archie, it's me," says Dr. Singh. I glance at my watch. Why would the doc be calling me at 10:38 on a Friday night? A shiver runs down my spine, a sinking feeling settling in.

"Yes?"

"It's about your father…"

My heart skips a beat.

Nestled within Sydney's upscale Eastern Suburbs, a little way down the coast from the famed Bondi Beach, Waverly Cemetery commands its spot atop sandstone cliffs, gazing out over the expanse of the Pacific Ocean. Gravestones occupy much of the view, varying in shape and size – some are monumentally massive, resembling tombs that would probably outvalue most people's homes. I consider myself fortunate to have secured a plot here, although it came at a price. While I'm not a believer in burials, viewing gravestones as a needless expense, I recognise how much my old man adored the ocean. I wanted to grant him the finest posthumous view that money could buy.

Gazing out at the endless blue ocean, the rhythmic symphony of waves crashing against the cliffs infiltrates my thoughts and distracts me from the burial service. I'm not truly present. And I still appear to be a dishevelled mess, having skipped the shave, even for my father's farewell. At least I managed to tidy up my hair, and I've donned my best black Hugo Boss suit. About thirty attendees have gathered, mostly acquaintances of Robert's who outlasted him and likely wonder who'll be the next to bite the dust.

I didn't even get to bid my father goodbye, and yet I feel utterly flat. Perhaps I'm in a state of denial. What were Dr. Singh's words? The five stages of grief. On a brighter note, I sense I've reached the fifth stage concerning my unfortunate "never having sex again" predicament. I've accepted it. In fact, I'm feeling better for it. Who needs sex anyway? For procreation? What's the point of bringing a child into this world if their end is inevitable? Life is a gift, yet it comes with a grim caveat: death. What kind of twisted cosmic joke is that, God?

Engulfed in these existential musings, I fail to register Father Bob calling me. "Archie… Archie?" his voice eventually breaks through. I snap out of my reverie, nod, and ascend to the front. I haven't prepared a speech, though I don't need to. I've decided to speak from the heart.

"Well, Dad was, ah, my pops, my father… obviously," I begin, stating the glaringly obvious and earning a nod of agreement from a sunglasses-wearing stranger on the front row – a small source of amusement and support for me. "He was more than that, though.

He was a mate. As many of you know, Pops raised me mostly on his own after my lovely mother took off when I was eight."

A few gasps ripple through the crowd, particularly from some of the elderly ladies. The stranger nods once more, a silent gesture of solidarity. I nod back in appreciation.

"As most of you are aware, I'm an only child, so it was just Pops and me. Can't have been easy, especially during my teenage years – I was such a little shit."

A chuckle ripples through the crowd, triggered by the individual up front. For the first time, I become aware of the faces before me, scanning each one. Just as I'm about to continue, someone catches my eye. A woman wearing a broad-brimmed black hat and dark shades – it is unmistakably Jezebel, standing at the back, trying her best to blend in. Feeling my gaze, she tilts her head down slightly.

"Ah, well... I didn't get to say goodbye to Pops. But I know he wouldn't want us to mourn today. He'd want us to celebrate his life. And the fact that we managed to secure the last plot in arguably the most exquisite resting place in Sydney, which wasn't cheap mind you, well... he deserved it. Because he wasn't just my dad... he was my mate." It was at this point that I expected the tears to come. But they didn't. I just felt so numb.

"I remember after Mum left. I asked Dad if she was ever coming back. He said he didn't know. I then asked if she left because of me. He said, 'No Arch, nothing to do with you.' He then told me that even though she's not here, that I'll be in her thoughts every day for the rest of her life. And that one day, she'd regret leaving, and will come back for you. But in the meantime, we got each other. And that's something to be grateful for... Well, Mum never came back. But one thing's for sure, Pops and I had each other's back ever since."

I see others tearing up in the crowd. Pretty sure I see Jezebel wipe her eyes. But still nothing comes. "So, please, join me in The Rocks for a few drinks, in honour of the irreverent old soul."

I linger around the graveyard, acknowledging the condolences from each individual as they make their way out. The mysterious stranger wearing the hideous sunglasses comes forward, shuffling with a walking stick.

"I always thought Rupert had balls of steel," he offers.

"It's Robert, actually. But thank you," I correct him.

"No, Rupert!" he retorts forcefully.

"Alright, Rupert it is. And you are...?"

"I'm Jimmy the sweeper," he says matter-of-factly.

"Thanks, Jimmy the sweeper. See you at the wake."

He nods and shuffles off. Next in line is Jezebel. We stand there in silence, both seemingly waiting for the other to start. Eventually, it's Jezebel who breaks the quiet.

"I just wanted to... uh..."

"Thank you, Jezebel." I take in her appearance. She looks stunning, even in all black. Although I can't determine whether the hat and glasses are hiding bruises from her brutal bout with the Russian psycho, or if they're part of her mourning attire.

"I'm so sorry about your father."

"He liked you... perhaps a little too much."

Jezebel smiles slightly, and looks away shyly.

"I'd like to see your eyes."

Jezebel removes her sunglasses, revealing a black eye, along with some minor cuts and bruising around her head and neck. It stings to see her like this.

"Ouch... that crazy Russian bitch."

She smiles. "It's just a sport, Archie. You don't look so hot either. A shave would've been a good idea."

I rub my beard, unsure of how to respond. Jezebel takes the lead.

"You shouldn't have climbed into the octagon. You could've got seriously hurt."

"Yeah, I'm sorry about that. I was drunk."

"I know... but it's nice to know you care. And I'm sorry for hitting you, that wasn't cool."

"It's okay."

"No, it's not, Archie." Another pause. "Coming from an abusive relationship, domestic violence... it's not okay."

"Oh yeah, that prick."

"He used to lie. A lot. Cheat. And lie. Every time I confronted him about it, things turned violent. That's why I despise lying so much."

"Thank you for opening up. I understand your perspective now."

"Again, I'm sorry about your father. I was looking forward to getting to know him. He seemed like a real character."

"He was. Thanks. I'm glad you got to meet him before he, you know…"

Another extended silence ensues, during which neither of us is quite sure where to direct our gazes. The pressure to break the silence falls on me.

"Listen, um, sometimes, in order to love someone, you have to keep them at arm's length."

"Excuse me? Did you pick that up from a movie or something?" She's giving me that look, a hint of a smile in her eyes. I was attempting to be profound, and she's having none of it. Why does this woman manage to both rile me up and charm me so effectively? I part my lips, but no words emerge.

"Like, what does that even mean?" Jezebel asks, a genuine air of curiosity about her.

"Uh, well… see…"

"What movie did you get that from? I know I've heard it before, it's on the tip of my tongue."

"How about we just erase that scene?"

"For your father's sake, probably best. He's probably rolling in his grave right now. Oh my God, I'm sorry, I shouldn't joke about that."

"Talk about too soon."

"I'm so sorry."

"It's fine. Actually, he's probably laughing in there right now," I say looking down at Robert's coffin in the open grave. "Are you coming to the wake?"

"Is that an invitation?"

"You don't need an invitation. People just show up."

"Then I suppose I might just show up at the wake." With that, she pivots on her heels and strides away. I can't help but notice how enticing her figure looks in that tight black skirt, which is neither too long nor too short. An instant surge of arousal catches me off guard, and suddenly, I'm grappling with guilt for entertaining such carnal thoughts amidst my father's passing. It's been a while, and I am terribly, frustratingly horny.

The wake unfolds at The Waterloo, Robert Flynn's cherished pub in The Rocks. An establishment steeped in history, it's one of Australia's oldest pubs, dating back to 1843 – an antiquity by Australian standards.

Dad always had a thing for its history. Fashioned from Sydney's ancient sandstone, it stands nestled on a tight corner, on a street with a slight leftward slope. Overflowing with character, its interior oozes history and echoes with countless tales. I recall Dad coming home, a tad tipsy, recounting stories after being given tours by Ivan, the publican. Dad would tell me about the cellars and a hidden tunnel, back when I'd pretend to listen. Oddly enough, I find myself genuinely intrigued now that he's gone. The pub's cellar boasted a clandestine passageway to the harbour, once employed for rum smuggling and forcibly recruiting inebriated sailors. Should a patron collapse inside the pub, they might find themselves tumbling through a trapdoor, traversing underground passages, and awakening aboard a ship out at sea. Consigned to strenuous toil on the deck, they were known as the Shanghaied Sailors. "That would be one hell of a hangover," I muse, sipping rum as I scan the attendees gathered to commemorate Dad.

But Jezebel's nowhere to be seen. In response, I'm drawn towards the bar, discreetly avoiding eye contact with the other guests. "Being the son of the deceased man has its perks," I think to myself. "No one likes fumbling through awkward conversations with the grieving." There's not much anyone can say except apologise or offer condolences, but that's typically the limit. I can simply nod my head politely and move on with a, "Thank you, but I'd prefer some solitude right now." And they seem to understand. With a smirk, I sidle up to the bar.

That's my plan – solitude in the cellar of an ancient pub. But first, a necessary stock-up. Ivan, leaning against the bar, pours beer with a quizzical eyebrow arched at me. He's like a relic from old Sydney Town with his wispy moustache curling up at the ends and his lengthy grey sideburns. There aren't many like Ivan left.

"Hey Ivan, mind if I check out the cellar?" I inquire.

"Not at all, old boy, not at all," Ivan responds, momentarily pausing his beer pour to retrieve the key. Ivan's referred to me as "old boy" since I was a kid, a peculiar moniker I still find amusing given that he's more than twice my age.

"Might grab a bottle of that rum Dad used to rave about but couldn't afford. The... ah..."

"Mount Gay, 1703."

"Really? Sure it's Mount Gay?"

"Absolutely. As Jamaican as they come. Got an issue with 'gay'?"

"How much?"

"For you, today, on the house."

"Come on Ivan, that's like a two-hundred-dollar bottle."

"Two-fifty... Archie, take it." Ivan fixes me with an unwavering gaze, a few seconds of dramatic silence that almost borders on unsettling. To be honest, it's the kind of look that could make a guy feel like a trapdoor and a secret tunnel to the sea might be in his future.

"You're not planning on Shanghai-ing me, are you, Ivan?"

Ivan erupts in hearty laughter, the sound resonating throughout the pub.

"Good to see you've inherited the old fella's sense of humour," he remarks, placing a whiskey glass next to the exquisite blue and gold Mount Gay bottle. "You know, your old man was the funniest guy that ever came in here. He always made my job more enjoyable when he walked through the door."

"This could double as an urn," I quip, admiring the impressive bottle of Mount Gay.

"Well, it was his favourite," Ivan remarks, guiding me towards the trapdoor, unlocking and raising it. It reminds me of that scene from *Fight Club*, where the bartender reveals the secret trapdoor to the underground basement.

"Light switch is on the left at the bottom of the ladder," Ivan instructs. I take the plunge into the darkness below, feeling like a total badass.

I descend the steep staircase into the basement, immediately hit by the musty, stagnant aroma resulting from a lack of proper ventilation. The room spans about four by five metres, its walls fashioned from raw sandstone. A window, firmly shut with wooden panels, stands before me. Presumably, this is the entry point to the tunnel that leads down to the harbour. Taking in the space, I gently place the rum bottle atop an ancient wooden wine barrel. I unseal the bottle, yank out the cork, and inhale the fragrance of the top-shelf liquor. My face contorts as I pour nearly half a glass.

"Time to suppress those feelings, Dad. I've barely navigated the five stages of Dick Grief. Your turn will come later. But this one's for you." I hoist my glass to an imaginary presence across from me, downing the rum in a single, swift motion. A gasp, followed by shudders and a cough, escapes me. "Holy shit," I exclaim, slamming the glass onto the barrel top before doubling over, still coughing. "Never quite grasped what you saw in this stuff, Pops. Now, what was your fascination with this basement all about?"

After regaining my composure, I pour another equally substantial glass. This time, however, I opt for a small sip before shifting my focus to the framed, aged newspaper articles adorning the wall. My gaze locks onto the date: September 3rd, 1808.

"Crikey," I mutter to myself. "Didn't realise newspapers existed back then."

My eyes remain on the text, absorbing the article's discourse on rum's role as currency in Sydney's early settlement days. It features an image of the original Sydney Hospital, detailing how its construction was funded with rum.

"You've got to be kidding me," I mumble to myself, growing comfortable with soliloquies. "Rum as currency... intriguing."

Being a financial adviser, I hold a modicum of knowledge about Australia's initial struggles in establishing a reliable currency. But the notion that rum was genuinely used as a substantial means of exchange hadn't quite registered. I delve into the rest of the article, reading each word with rapt attention, more as a distraction from my current reality. I'm not ready to deal with Dad yet. Where was I – ah, the concept of what humans invest value in has always intrigued me – from the Dutch Tulip Mania of the seventeenth century to the current Bitcoin phenomenon, a topic I'm still forming an opinion on. However, that didn't hinder me from purchasing some during the pandemic, watching it steadily ascend to new all-time highs (followed by crashing lows). Capital in its myriad forms captivates me, especially when it takes the form of rum. Only Australians could make rum their national currency, I muse to myself.

My thoughts swirl in a concoction of introspection and the rum's gentle influence, and I barely register the sound of footsteps descending into the cellar.

"Archie?" a voice, somewhat familiar, breaks my reverie.

Continuing to scrutinise the newspaper article, I respond without looking up, "I'd rather be alone right now, if you don't mind."

"Having family around at times like this can be important," the voice replies, coaxing an ember of irritation within me. My gaze shifts to a woman, appearing to be around fifty-five, blonde, tanned, with a complexion that might be cosmetically enhanced. She's wearing an elegantly tailored suit with subtle deep purple pinstripes, exuding an air of affluence. There's no mistaking it – she's Pamela Flynn.

"Pamela…?" A whirlwind of emotions engulfs me, making me stumble over my words. "What are you doing here?"

"Came to pay my respects, of course. Bob was my husband. The father of my child," she responds matter-of-factly, brushing aside the unspoken query that tugs at me.

Holding back an onslaught of emotions, I simply say, "We haven't seen or heard from you in twenty fucking years."

"Archie, I can explain…"

"How about an apology?"

My mind races; this is such a load of nonsense. But I allow her to speak, eager to hear her reasoning. How dare she waltz back into my life now, only when Dad's gone? I can almost envision him up there, spewing curses and fury.

"I'm sorry. I'm truly, truly sorry. Your father was right, it had nothing to do with you."

"You were at the funeral?"

She nods.

"Boy, was he an amazing lover," Pamela comments, a cheeky glint in her eye. "Your father really knew a woman's body."

"Alright, can we just fast forward to why you abandoned us without a trace?"

"Your father couldn't offer me the lifestyle I aspired to, Archie. That's the stark truth."

"Are you telling me it was all about money?"

Pamela nods, a touch of sympathy in her eyes.

"What are you, a gold digger? He worked hard, provided for us, put food on the table. Wasn't that enough?"

"No… It wasn't. Not for me."

"For years, I thought you'd run off with some other man. Frankly, I'd have preferred it if you were sleeping with some other jerk."

"I never cheated on your father."

"What about me, huh? Clearly, you didn't give a damn about me."

"That's not true. You were everything to me. But I couldn't take you away from your father. I was already plagued by guilt from leaving him."

"Where did you go? You never called, never wrote."

"I travelled, darling. I needed to get away, and I did write. You didn't receive my letters?"

"What letters?"

"I sent letters, postcards..."

"Postcards from where?"

"Oh boy, let me think," she says as she leans up against a barrel and stares at the ceiling as if accessing her memory bank. "First, Europe. I spent two years in London. Then, South America..."

"You left us to gallivant around the world," I mutter sarcastically as I refill my glass and down half of its contents.

"Archie, I was just twenty-one when I married your father."

"Not my fault; I wasn't even born yet."

"But you were conceived. I had you seven months later."

"Is that why Dad married you?"

"Absolutely. His parents, your grandparents, were devout Catholics. You know that, right?"

My thoughts drift to the church, to Father Bob, and then to Jezebel.

"So, it's like that. You abandoned us for a globetrotting adventure. Mother of the century."

Pamela takes the initiative to pour herself a glass of rum, and downs it in a confident gulp. "This isn't easy for me either, you know."

"What do you want?" I ask, a twinge of sincerity in my voice.

"What do I want?" she says, staring upwards again. "I want us to be friends again," she replies between sips of rum.

"Go to hell, Pamela."

"Archie, please..."

She steps forward to embrace me, but I shove her away.

"To hell with you."

"Please, don't..."

"Get the fuck out of here!"

"I'm sorry!" Pamela blurts out, tears streaming down her face. She moves to embrace me again, and this time I don't resist – instead breaking into tears as well.

"Fuck you," I repeat amidst my tears as we cling to each other, weeping together. Unbeknownst to us, we're lost in the moment, oblivious to the footsteps descending the stairs, and Jezebel's voice calling my name. But as soon as she sees us locked in an embrace, her face falls. She quietly retreats.

We eventually break apart, wiping away our tears. "It's too late," I murmur. Pamela tilts her head, seemingly not understanding. "I want you to leave. And I never want to see you again."

"Darling, please."

"Don't darling me! Get the fuck out!" I shout, emotions running at an all-time high.

Pamela ascends the stairs in tears.

Emerging from the cellar, my mind is a fog of thoughts and emotions. I glance around the room, hoping to spot Jezebel, but she's nowhere in sight. Returning to the bar, I notice Father Bob, sitting alone with a glass of whiskey. He looks up at me, takes me in. "You look like you've just seen a ghost."

"Yeah," is all I can say, staring ahead across the bar, taking in all the attendees. "In a way, I did. Have you seen Jezebel?"

He answers bluntly, "She just left. She walked out of the basement and headed straight for the door."

"From the basement?" I frown, my mind racing. Pulling out a stool, I settle beside Father Bob. "Give me what he's having," I tell Ivan, who returns a half-wink, half-nod as he makes the drink. Father Bob raises his gaze to meet mine as I lean against the bar. "I need to apologise again for exposing myself to you, Father Bob."

Just as the words escape my lips, an older lady, prim and prudish, appears, her voice faltering as she speaks. "Oh... Archie, I wanted to express my condolences, but I hope I'm not intruding."

I assure her, "No, not at all."

"Well..." she hesitates, and an uncomfortable silence stretches. I raise an eyebrow, prompting her to continue. Father Bob covers his face with his hands, and Ivan pours a whiskey, shooting a quizzical look at Father Bob. "My condolences," she finally manages, and I offer her a small, sympathetic nod, seemingly to myself.

"Thank you. I appreciate it," I respond, and as she shuffles away, I return my focus to Father Bob. "Do you think she heard me?"

"Of course she heard you."

"Oh, whoops. Sorry about that. Now, where were we?" I ask just as Ivan sets my whiskey on the bar.

"I believe you were apologising for showing Father Bob your dick," Ivan reminds me. Father Bob cringes, hanging his head and massaging his brow.

"It's not what you think, Ivan," I explain.

"I'm sure there's a perfectly good explanation," he replies.

Father Bob's tone is weary as he replies, "It's alright. Let's move past it, Archie."

Another silence descends, and I contemplate my next step. Suddenly, a spark of clarity cuts through the haze in my mind. "What's it like being a priest?" I ask Father Bob, who exchanges a glance with Ivan before responding.

"Honestly… It's an enlightening experience," he says, taking a sip of whiskey.

Perching on a stool next to him, I continue, "And what about the whole celibacy thing? You must have to… you know, relieve yourself, I assume. But does it ever lead to…"

Father Bob fixes me with a deadpan look. "Lead to what?"

Persisting, I lean in and whisper, "You know… questionable situations?"

Father Bob's reaction is swift. "I don't know exactly what you're getting at, but I'm pretty certain the answer is no."

"I'm only asking because I'm now off-limits with sex. This could be forever. So, priesthood seems like the only option I got."

"You cannot be serious."

"What if I am? Could you teach me the ways of the church?"

"Choosing priesthood for the wrong reasons won't work, Archie. You must have the right intentions."

"I do," I assert defensively. "And how much does it pay? I've heard Catholicism can be quite profitable."

Father Bob seems to be at his wits' end with my questions. "Archie, I'm genuinely sorry about Robert. But right now, you need to give me space, while you need to take time to grieve."

"Okay, Father. Thank you," is all I manage to reply before Bryce appears behind me, catching me off guard.

"Hey there, how are you holding up?" Bryce asks, pulling up a stool. Father Bob takes his cue and makes a quiet exit.

"Hey Bryce, appreciate you being here," I reply.

"It's expected. You're my best employee," Bryce says, downbeat.

"Yeah, about that…" I pause as Bryce sips his seltzer and casts a sideways glance at me.

I'm about to tell him that I am going to hand in my resignation. The idea had been brewing beneath the surface for some time, but after Dad's death and the ghost of mothers past turning up, the idea of quitting my job and pissing off somewhere – maybe California with Jezebel, if she'll have me – had all of a sudden come front of mind. But this was not the right time and place to be having this discussion. Despite being more than a little tipsy and eager to quit right then and there, I reel myself in.

"It's alright," I continue, putting my arm around Bryce's shoulder.

"He was such a great guy," Bryce says, tearing up. He had met Dad on a number of occasions, and they'd always had a laugh, enjoyed a beer together. His death seems to have affected him more than I expected.

Karen comes over to join us. She pats her husband on the back, her embarrassment evident. Bryce is too overcome with emotion to respond, so I step in. "He had a special connection with my dad."

"I know, he's been a mess. My condolences, Archie," Karen says, genuinely surprised. I nod, and she offers comforting words while rubbing Bryce's back. He takes off his glasses, nods in gratitude, and wipes his tears away.

"I'm so sorry for your loss," Karen expresses.

"Thanks, Karen."

"Oh, and I've changed my name," she continues.

"Excuse me?" I'm puzzled.

"She switched her name due to the whole 'entitled Karen' thing," Bryce interjects, recovering from his emotional moment.

"Really?" I ask.

"Yep. I noticed I was starting to get discriminated against. As if being a Hitler wasn't bad enough. So, I legally changed it."

"To what?" I ask.

"Becky."

"*Becky*?" I'm taken aback.

"Yes, Becky. What's wrong with that?" she challenges.

I shake my head, biting my tongue and holding back my thoughts. But Bryce speaks up, voicing what's on my mind. He's good like that.

"Sounds like Karen's sister, right?" Bryce's remark earns laughter from me and a playful hit from Karen/Becky.

"Honey, I thought you're supposed to defend me," she playfully scolds him.

"Ow!" Bryce rubs his shoulder. "Don't blame me!"

"Half your fault. Shouldn't have married a Hitler! Maybe I'll divorce you and ditch the name. How about that?" she threatens.

"Wow, that's harsh, baby."

Sensing the need to lighten the mood, I chime in, "I can understand your frustration, Karen."

"Becky," she corrects.

"Sorry, Becky. But if you're looking to vent about the situation, perhaps the manager over there..." I begin, but Karen cuts me off.

"Seriously, screw you both!" Karen's exclamation garners laughter from Bryce and me, but it also draws attention from the elderly guests nearby.

"Seems like we're causing a scene. I'll leave you two galahs to it. Bryce, no overindulgence tonight if you want any... um..." Karen says, departing.

"No worries, Karen – I mean, Becky," Bryce says, to which Karen responds by flipping the bird as she struts away. I finish my drink, signal to Ivan for another, then turn my attention back to Bryce. "Are you alright?"

"I am now; I've accepted that Robert's gone."

"How did you even..." I trail off in astonishment.

I noticed when Bryce called when he first heard the news of Dad's death, that he was in denial, asking if the doctors had double-checked for vital signs of life. Classic denial. Next, I saw him over a video call and he was seriously pissed off that the doctors couldn't save Dad, or at least prolong his life. Anger. Then, he paid me a visit at home and we had a deep conversation about Pops. He kept saying that he wished he could go back in time and tell Robert to get his prostate checked earlier. And that he would now be getting his own prostate checked. Bargaining. And now, here he was more upset than I am (sadness), before telling me he's accepted Dad's death. All inside a few days. Why can't I grieve like that?

"What?" he asks.

"You just went through the whole grieving process in two days."

Bryce looks confused. "What are you talking about?"

"Forget it," I dismiss as Ivan serves me another drink.

"What were you and the priest talking about?"

"Oh, just discussing my potentially entering the priesthood..."

Bryce splutters and nearly spills his seltzer on the bar counter.

"I've done a lot of introspection..." I can now hear myself slurring my words. "I've been trapped in the rat race, chasing status, burning the candle at both ends. I've missed out on appreciating life's simpler pleasures. Everything happens for a reason, Bryce. I believe my affliction is a calling – a life of celibacy."

Bryce studies me for a moment, then nods slowly. "I get it."

"You do?"

"Yeah, I understand that you've had enough booze," Bryce says, sliding the bottle of Mount Gay towards him and studying the label. "Nice looking bottle."

Chapter 23

Stage 5: Acceptance

I fix my gaze on the towering statue of Jesus Christ that commands attention at the rear of St. Patrick's Church. A frown forms on my face as I attempt to persuade Father Bob of my earnest desire to become ordained. Naturally, Father Bob remains sceptical, questioning both my motivations and my capacity for patience.

"The seminarian stage requires four years of theological study," he explains.

I cut in, determined to make my point. "Can we expedite the process somehow?"

Father Bob looks taken aback. "What do you mean?"

"I'm not interested in becoming a priest four years from now," I assert. "I want it to happen *now*."

"You lack patience, which suggests you are not cut out for this," Father Bob retorts. "Even after completing seminary, you must serve as a transitional deacon for at least a year, possibly taking up to five years before ordination."

"Well, you know what they say – 'Grant me patience, Lord, but hurry'," I quip, smiling at my own joke. Father Bob doesn't smile; he just gives me that same deadpan look he always does. I take out my phone. "There must be a quicker route."

Father Bob regards me with disbelief as I start typing away. After a few moments, I hand the phone over to him. He reads an article from the Vatican website about online ordination courses. "It seems I'm right," I remark, a hint of satisfaction in my voice.

"Why do you truly wish to become a priest?" Father Bob asks. "And please, don't use your... condition as a reason."

I lean against the pew, furrowing my brow. I glance back at the statue of Jesus for some inspiration, searching for it in that solemn gaze. Facing Father Bob again, I speak with conviction, "I want to be a better man." Father Bob remains quiet, observing my sincerity. I seem unyielding in my determination.

"You don't need to become a priest to be a better man. Would you consider yourself a spiritual individual, Mr. Flynn?" Father Bob probes.

"I think my experiences with my penis have brought me closer to God," I say, the realisation dawning on me as I speak.

"That's good then, but please do not mention those two words in the same sentence ever again," Father Bob winces. "God can have unusual ways of guiding his children. But still, there's no need to become a priest."

"Alright, I'll refrain. But can we have another therapy session?"

"It's not therapy. It's confession. And no, confession is Sunday only."

"Ah, yes, the Sunday service..."

The Sunday service that Jezebel just so happens to attend. It just clicked that this could be the perfect way to see her again. I had tried to call her the day after Dad's funeral but she didn't answer. I texted her and she replied that it was time for the both of us to move on. I asked why. She said she saw me with the blonde lady in the basement of the pub, and though I tried to explain to her that she was my long-lost mother, she didn't believe me. And why should she. She said the woman looked way too young to be my mum. I told her I would introduce her to Pamela to prove it. But she went quiet, which is good because I'm not too keen on contacting Pamela. Not yet, anyway.

But this way, I can see Jezebel without being too pushy. I'm just another regular church-goer. And if I see her in person, I know I can tell her all about my visit from Pamela.

"That's sorted then, see you on Sunday, Father!"

Father Bob regards me closely, his gaze meeting mine. He sighs, as if conceding to an inevitable conclusion.

"See you on Sunday," he says reluctantly.

I'm in Dr. Singh's office, absorbing the news just delivered – that the specimen taken from my privates wasn't a sexually transmitted disease but simply a run-of-the-mill wart. I find this hard to believe.

"You mean like a genital wart?" I question.

"No, just your garden-variety wart – just one that took a fancy to the end of your wicked willy," Dr. Singh retorts with a chuckle, clearly pleased with himself.

"Wait a minute. So, we've gone from potential castration to just having a run-of-the-mill wart?" I confirm incredulously.

"That's right. A rather sizable, ugly, yet, strangely regular wart," he explains.

"But warts don't hang around for that long."

"They can when there's an abundance of blood flow – like when you're sporting an erection, for example. I can only assume you get an abundance of them."

I roll my eyes. "Now, how do I kick this unwelcome hitchhiker to the curb?"

"Simple, dip your wicked willy in apple cider vinegar twice a day until it waves the white flag and disappears."

"Dip my dick in apple cider vinegar? You're pulling my leg."

"No jest, this is the remedy. You can look it up if you're sceptical."

I pause for a beat, my scrutiny fixed on Dr. Singh, searching for any indication that this is some elaborate prank. Surely not – doctors cannot joke around with their patients' diagnoses, right?

"Don't get too excited, Archie. You really should start practising safe sex."

The way Singh drops this line sets alarm bells ringing in my head. I rise from my seat, approach him, and lock eyes with the good doctor. "Did you engineer this?"

"Excuse me?" Singh replies with an air of studied neutrality that doesn't sit well with me.

"This entire situation. The diagnosis. You knew it was a wart all along, didn't you?"

"Don't be ridiculous. What would be my motive for doing such a thing?"

"Maybe, just maybe, you concocted a bizarre scheme to correct my reckless behaviour. A noble intention I'm sure, but—"

"Archie, as much as I wish I could influence you to change your wicked ways..." Singh interjects, his tone void of any deception, "that would breach doctor-patient trust, not to mention jeopardise my career."

His deadpan delivery still doesn't fully convince me. I narrow my eyes, sizing up the truth behind his words. He meets my gaze, seemingly engaged in a contest of wills, as if probing for an explanation within my own eyes.

"Are you absolutely sure about that?" I ask in a low murmur, my scepticism still lingering. "Because I'll know if you're lying." The doctor remains unflinching, maintaining his poker face. I lean back, still wary but willing to give it a rest for now. "I'm torn between wanting to punch or kiss you right now," I admit.

"Neither option is necessary, thank you."

"Apple cider vinegar, huh?" I clarify once more.

"Indeed, apple cider vinegar."

I make a hasty exit, but Dr. Singh has one last card to play. "Behave yourself now, Archie Flynn." His parting words stop me in my tracks just before leaving the room. "Wouldn't want you to catch a real genital wart." I lock eyes with him one final time, his expression remaining inscrutable. I nod, turn and leave.

I make a beeline for the closest supermarket. As I scour the Woolworths aisles, my eyes hunt for the elusive apple cider vinegar while, almost automatically, I dial Jezebel's number. She doesn't pick up. My excitement about my newfound wart-banishing remedy is contagious, and I want Jezebel to share in this bizarre victory. Maybe it could mend things between us – prove me capable of rekindling our relationship, even.

I opt for a WhatsApp message, hitting send with a flourish. My gaze then lands on the lower shelf right in front of me, and a grin tugs at my lips as I spot a bottle of organic apple cider vinegar. "You little beauty," I murmur to myself.

I typed another message for Jezebel:

Why are you not answering my calls? I have some exciting news!

No answer.

The moment I step back into my place, I carefully set a bowl down on my coffee table, right beside the apple cider vinegar. I've got a Penfolds 389 Cabernet Sauvignon Shiraz from the 2001 vintage, a McLaren Vale treasure I've been hoarding for the perfect occasion – perhaps even to share with Jezebel. But I've decided this peculiar moment is special enough. With determination, I uncork the bottle, pour myself a healthy measure of this top-shelf wine, and relish its sweet bouquet of dark cherry and subtle oaky tannins.

Wine in hand, I then grasp the bottle of organic apple cider vinegar and pour a generous portion into the bowl. Taking another sip of wine, I indulge in its flavour while my thoughts linger on the task ahead. I undo my belt and fly, shedding my jeans and red Ralph Lauren undies until they're bunched around my ankles. I position the bowl of vinegar on the corner of the coffee table, creating space to straddle around it, lowering myself into a crouch. My hand wraps around my member, and I give my arch-nemesis – the wart – a stern glare.

With that, I immerse the tip of my cock into the bowl, grimacing as it stings. "Oooh… shit," I mutter, Dr. Singh's warning echoing in my mind. That burning sensation signifies progress, but it's hard to focus on that when it feels like my manhood's ablaze. "Arghhh… ooooh, ahhhh… It burns!"

I think I hear a noise coming from my bedroom, but I'm too engrossed in my home remedy to acknowledge or care. I manage to gulp down some more wine, hoping to dull the pain. I need something stronger. Whiskey, or maybe even some of that rum, would do the trick.

"Arrhhhh, aaaawwww, oooooohhhhh, aaaahhhhh."

Just when I'm fully immersed in this dubious ritual, my heart freezes as a voice interrupts my suffering.

"Archie!?" I glance up to see Jezebel standing there, decked out in her activewear, handbag hanging off her shoulder, her face morphing through shock, disbelief and more than a hint of confusion. My own shock renders me paralysed as I take in her presence. Here I am, crouched like a madman, glass of red in one hand, the other holding my schlong, which is submerged in a bowl of apple cider vinegar. To add to my humiliation, my face is flushed and slicked with sweat.

"What on earth are you doing!?" Jezebel demands, her tone a blend of incredulity and exasperation.

My brain whirs into action, and I stand up, hurriedly arranging myself. "What are you doing here!?" I counter, caught between bewilderment and embarrassment. But my frantic question only adds to the bizarre scene before her. My attempt to conceal my "operation" with my hand falls short as Jezebel's eyes flicker towards the evidence. The expression that crosses her face leaves no room for doubt. I can almost hear her thoughts aloud. "What the hell are you doing!?" I roar, hoping that bluster will somehow shift the surreal situation.

"Your front door was wide open. I heard you shouting and I rushed in, and..." Her voice trails off as she takes in the sight before her. "What's happened to your... what in the world are you..." Her words falter. "I should just go," she decides, turning to leave me and my madness behind.

"No, wait, let me explain. It's just a wart!" I scramble towards her, desperation coating my words. "Please, stay. Have a drink. I've got a 2001 Penfolds 389 on the go."

"What's a 2001 Penfolds 389?"

"It's like a five-hundred-dollar wine. Seriously, it's next-level stuff."

"I could use a drink. Anything to erase the image I've just witnessed," she says while steadying herself on the kitchen bench. "I gave you the benefit of the doubt. Came to hear your side of the story about your mother, and I've walked into some kind of grotesque penis ritual. I mean, really. Why can't I just find a normal boyfriend?"

While she rants, and I don't blame her, I dash over to the coffee table, seizing the wine bottle and hurrying to the kitchen. I pour her a glass, offering it to her with a flourish. I think I hear another noise coming from upstairs, but my attention is fixed on Jezebel as she takes a substantial sip, clearly not registering the quality of the wine. I pour another glass for myself and take a sip as well, a shared moment of silent recovery after the chaos that just unfolded.

"Alright," Jezebel finally breaks the ice, her tone more collected now. "Are you going to tell me what on earth was happening here?"

"It's a home remedy – apple cider vinegar. I've got a... wart issue down there," I admit with an awkward cough, squirming at the topic.

"Are you absolutely sure that thing's just a wart?"

"Yes, quite sure. Just an especially stubborn one."

"Okay, if you say so."

"I know so! Dr. Singh confirmed it. And this vinegar trick is his recommended solution. He told me to, well, dip my... you know."

"Dip your... uh, yeah."

And then the unthinkable happens – footsteps descending the stairs. I register it. Jezebel registers it.

"Got company?" she asks.

"No," I say, suddenly alarmed that there is an intruder inside my home. "Who's there?"

Then – to my utter horror – Gemma appears in the corridor.

"It's me," she says.

My eyes bulge and my jaw drops as I struggle to comprehend her standing there, in one of her black latex dominatrix outfits, complete with dog collar and chains. She brandishes a whip with tassels attached to the end. I glance at Jezebel, whose expression registers shock like mine – only much, much worse.

"Gemma, what the fuck are you doing inside my home?"

"You didn't answer my calls or messages! So, I came to surprise you!"

"You cannot just break like this – I'm in a relationship now!" I say, motioning to Jezebel, who responds with a raise of her eyebrows.

"Uh, no. We are *not* in a relationship," she says as she gathers up her things.

How could this be happening to me!? Just as I finally start to see light at the end of the tunnel, I get hit with a double whammy. I grab Jezebel by the arm to stop her from leaving.

"Jezebel, please, let me explain."

Jezebel stares at my hand gripping her arm, then glances up at me. Her look is a warning, and I sense a kung-flu flip coming my way, so I let go. "It's not what you think. This woman's a client."

Jezebel takes in Gemma again who's casually leaning up against the staircase, swinging the tassels on her whip around in circles. I realise how ridiculous it sounds describing her as a business acquaintance, which is amplified when Gemma drops her next bombshell. "I've already got the coke all lined up already and good to go," she says glancing back upstairs to my bedroom. Fuck. I dare to glance at Jezebel, who only offers me a raise of the eyebrows that I read as, "Who *are* you?"

"She's from my old life, before I met you," I add before turning my attention to Gemma. "Gemma. Leave! NOW!"

Gemma shrugs. "Lemme grab my stuff," is all she says before ascending the stairs.

I cross over and shout up the stairs, "And I know you had a key cut. I'm changing the locks!"

Jezebel passes behind me, headed for the front door.

"Jezebel, wait..."

She turns back. "Archie. Do not contact me again. Ever," she says with conviction.

I don't argue. I let her go. I watch her go from the front door. She doesn't even look back. My lover. My best friend. My soulmate.

Gone.

Chapter 24

Father Bob

To say I was devastated over the loss of Jezebel is a colossal understatement. I'd blown it, and I knew it. There was no getting her back now. Not after her seeing me dip my willy in apple cider vinegar followed up by a slightly chubby dominatrix appearing ready to whip me into submission. There's no coming back from that.

Still, I refused to let myself sink back into depression. I needed to talk to someone, but who? Dad was no longer around. Bryce might listen but I know he'd be secretly stoked that he could live vicariously through my dating life once again. A part of me wanted to reach out to Pamela, but I couldn't bring myself to. Not after what she did – her pathetic, superficial and selfish reason for leaving.

The only person I could think of was Father Bob.

Inside the church, Father Bob was giving me a crash course in spirituality. The weather outside matched my mood. The rain tapped against the stained-glass windows, painting the holy images with streaks of water. Rainy days always had a way of making things a tad miserable.

Still, at least I was getting some guidance in the spiritual department. Father Bob was taking it upon himself to school me in the basics. "Have you ever turned to a higher power in prayer, Archie?" he asked.

Memories flitted back to my childhood, to those times when I was still a kid. The only instance that sprang to mind was after Pamela left – I prayed then, fervently, praying that my mum would return. It was a futile effort, though, one that eventually led me to lose faith – not just in my mum, but in God. He'd let me down, failed me. Or so I thought. Funny enough, I realised then that God had technically answered my prayers, just two decades later. Quite the delay. And the only other time I could recall praying was when this wart thing started plaguing me.

"In the last three months, I've started," I admitted at last, trying to be honest.

"Out of sheer desperation, I imagine? Due to this thing on your... well, you know?"

"Yes, Father. You could say it was out of sheer desperation."

"Remember, Archie, you can't just turn to God when you need something. That's not quite how the higher powers work," Father Bob explained, his expression serious. "In fact, prayers hold the most power when they're directed toward someone else, not just for your own desires."

"Got it, Father," I said, a thought forming in my mind. "So, if I ask others to pray for me, that's the way to go?" Another thought came rushing in, and I couldn't help myself. "And, uh, would you mind saying a prayer for me?"

Father Bob regarded me with a searching gaze. "When you pray, who do you think you're praying to?"

"God almighty, of course."

"How do you envision God?"

That question caught me off guard. In my mind's eye, I saw the stereotypical image of an old white man with flowing grey hair and a bushy set of eyebrows, perched at the pearly gates of heaven. But then, an absurd scenario played out – this elderly figure refused me entry, a divine rejection because of all my sins and the hearts I'd broken. Suddenly, God looked a lot like Santa Claus to me. It was strange; the resemblance was uncanny. Then the memory of my parents threatening me with no presents from Santa if I wasn't a good boy clicked into place. Then the realisation dawned – Christmas was about Jesus, and by extension, was God actually... Santa Claus?

"Excuse me?" Father Bob's voice was incredulous. "Did you say... Santa Claus? You think God is Santa Claus?"

I snapped out of my bizarre mental tangent. "What? No," I stammered, feeling a tad embarrassed. "Of course not."

"But you did say Santa Claus," Father Bob pressed, his curiosity piqued.

"I meant to say that one of my earliest memories involves Christmas. Back then, I believed Santa was the one behind it all, and he gave me a gift that changed everything." I managed to steer the conversation back on track, and it seemed to have Father Bob's attention. He raised an eyebrow, seemingly intrigued by what this "life-changing gift" could be.

"Have you seen *Star Wars*?"

Father Bob shook his head, no.

"You never watched *Star Wars*?" I stared at him, incredulous. "Now that's sacrilege – no pun intended."

Oddly enough, I managed to earn a small smile from him, the first time I'd seen him crack even a hint of one.

"You need to watch it, Father," I urged, standing up. "But stick to the original trilogy, forget about the rest. Anyway, the gift was a VHS of *Star Wars*, the original. That gift changed my life – not just by introducing me to the Star Wars universe, but also by teaching me about the concepts of good and evil. It's like the light side and the dark side. But more importantly, it shaped my view of God – being this all-surrounding force. Like an energy that can work with you or against you." I presented this as if it was the most logical thing in the world, that *Star Wars* could explain my understanding of God. Father Bob appeared a bit perplexed, which didn't surprise me, considering he admitted he'd never seen the film.

"Interesting. Very interesting. You know, it's not far off. You know who could harness this energy for good, better than anyone?"

"You?"

"No. Jesus Christ."

"Jesus Christ was a Jedi master."

"A what?"

"Never mind. Excuse me, I've gotta take a piss."

Father Bob cringed at my choice of words. "You can use the bathroom at the end of the hall, just past the confession box."

I entered the bathroom, a small urinal catching my eye. As I relieved myself, I couldn't help but glance downward. And then, there it was – the wart had all but vanished! I couldn't believe my eyes. All that remained was a bit of redness and peeling skin. I was like it had dissolved or just dropped off. A wave of emotion washed over me. I was ecstatic, overjoyed. It was like the heavens opened up.

"Unbelievable! It's gone. It's fucking gone! Father, it's gone!" I shouted, my elation spilling over.

Father Bob burst into the bathroom, seemingly alarmed. "What's wrong?" he started to ask, but his words died on his lips when he caught sight of me – pants down, beaming from ear to ear. "Oh, Lord, not again!" he exclaimed, covering his eyes as if to shield himself from the unexpected sight of my manhood once more.

"Father, it's a miracle! The wicked willy is history!" I gushed, quickly tucking myself back in. I dashed past a shell-shocked Father Bob, rushing out into the aisle of the church. I stood there, facing the grand monument of Jesus Christ.

"Thank you, JC! Thank you for this miracle. Bless you!" I even blew Christ a dramatic kiss before making a hasty exit, throwing in a triumphant "woo hoo!" as I jumped and clicked my heels together for good measure.

Chapter 25
Back in the Game

The first thing I wanted to do was call Jezebel to tell her the news. But her stark reminder to never contact her again dissuaded me. I have to respect her wish, no matter how painful that may be. Yet, the timing of it all... I came down with this hideous wart just as I met her. Then, just as I've finally gotten rid of it, she's gone.

So, I call Bryce. I tell him everything. What happened with Jezebel, the apple cider vinegar and Gemma. He finds it hilarious, of course. It takes him a while to control his laughter, but even then he laughs some more. And I cannot help but see the funny side. But that doesn't mean I am not shattered about losing her.

"I blew it. The one woman, Bryce. The one woman that I could see myself growing old with, and I royally fucked it up."

"I hear you, mate. But look on the bright side – you got a healthy cock again. Now, *that's* something to be grateful for." I know what's coming next. "You know what you need, man? You need a rebound."

"How did I know you were going to say that?"

"Because it's exactly what you need. How long's it been? Three months? You finally can rock out with your cock out again, plus you need to get over Jezebel. This is just what you need. Not to mention your blue balls. That's a serious health issue. You need to do this for your own well-being on a physical, psychological and emotional level."

I have to hand it to him. Bryce can be extremely persuasive when he wants to be – whether it be negotiating a deal at work or influencing me to get back out there so he can be entertained by my stories every Monday morning again.

It wasn't long before I had Bryce on loudspeaker while I stood in front of the mirror, a fresh look with slicked-back hair after a shower, and a towel snugly wrapped around my waist. If happiness had a physical form, it would be right here, written all over me. It's like my whole vibe has undertaken a complete turnaround. I tried my best not to think of Jezebel as I finally shaved my unkept beard away. I've got my bounce back, that glint of mischief back in my eye. Archie Flynn has returned, and he's damn ready to kick it into high gear and pop off a few caps.

But it's not just me riding this wave of elation. I can practically hear the grin in Bryce's voice through the phone.

"Mate, I gotta admit, you had me worried there," Bryce's voice dances out of my phone, resting on the bathroom vanity. "All that talk about quitting work and turning into a priest – man, I've been down in the dumps as hell. Karen/Becky's like, 'What's wrong with you, hun?' And I'm like, 'I think I lost Archie.'"

I chuckle, shaking my head, taking a swig from the beer bottle that's chilling next to me.

"Well, then she won't have a problem with you being my wingman, Bryce," I say as I deftly scrape away another patch of stubborn stubble.

"Consider it done, my man. I'm here for whatever you need to get the fuck back on the horse." Bryce's enthusiasm is infectious. "Remember that week I told you to take off for your old man? Well, scratch that – make it two weeks. Get back on the playing field, Archie. It's the best prescription. You need this, and I need this too. I won't lie, you've dropped the ball at work lately. And I'm sure that once you get your game back out there, you'll be kicking goals from left, right and centre once again, my boy."

"Okay, I hear you. First thing is I need to revamp my dating profile."

"Absolutely, dude. I've got some photography skills under my belt. Karen, I mean, Becky, is always making me snap her vacation pics and whatnot. Drives me crazy. But I'll be more than happy to snap some of you. Just tell me what you want, and I got all angles covered."

"Thanks, Bryce. I really appreciate it. Let's catch up at the Quay. We can get some shots with the harbour in the background, sound good?"

"Hell yeah, man. I'll bring my trusty DSLR!"

"You've got a DSLR? Perfect. How about half an hour?"

"I'm already stepping out the door."

"Oh, and Bryce, I'm taking you up on that two-week leave. Thanks."

I end the call, a smile stretching across my face. I finish up my shaving, a whistle escaping my lips. I rinse off the last remnants of shaving cream, dab some Davidoff Cool Water aftershave on my freshly shaven cheeks, and wink at my reflection. "Lookin' fine, sunshine," I murmur to myself, a sense of fulfillment coursing through me.

About an hour later, I'm posing for a photo as Bryce directs me with his Canon DSLR camera hanging around his neck. We're down by the harbour, right between the massive cruise ship dock at the International Passenger Terminal and Circular Quay where Sydney's ferries come and go. This place is buzzing with people, and I'm slowly losing my cool as Bryce tries to snap a decent shot with the Opera House as the backdrop. But it's a fantastic day, the sun playing on the waters of the harbour. Bryce, with his camera, hat and sunglasses, looks like he just jumped off the Carnival Cruise ship. And there's me, looking all groomed and dapper in my Versace blue-denim jeans, open-neck long-sleeve tee, and gold-rimmed Ray-Bans. We could almost pass for a gay couple on their honeymoon – the thought actually makes me chuckle.

"Alright, time for a natural shot," Bryce says. "Can you turn around and lean against the railing?" I follow his lead, doing exactly as he says, even though he's taking this way too seriously. "Perfect. Now, give that bum a little more oomph."

"What?" I protest.

"Your bum. Flaunt it. Chicks dig a good bum, and yours is pretty peachy."

I cringe as a few people nearby catch snippets of our conversation. "Please, don't refer to my butt as peachy," I demand, "ever again."

"Come on, mate, it's the truth. It's tight, and you gotta show off your assets. Now, turn around again."

"We're not shooting a music video, it's just a dating profile."

"I've come all this way."

"I'll turn around, but I'm not sticking my butt out."

"You want my help or not?"

With a heavy sigh, I reluctantly turn back, lean against the railing, and give my bum a little extra attention. "Like this?" I ask, slightly sticking my butt out.

"More. Like, really put it out there, man," Bryce says, focusing his camera. "Trust me, chicks dig this shit." I stick my butt out. "Yeah, that's the spirit," Bryce says as he snaps a few shots. "Alright, awesome. Now, keep your body as it is, but turn your head towards me."

I do as he says. "Like this? It doesn't feel very natural, honestly."

"Trust me, Archie. Now, hold your right hand up like a claw."

I do it, my face deadpan.

"Perfect," Bryce says, camera to his eye. "Now, we're gonna make a Boomerang. I need you to give me that move again, turning your head and putting your hand up like a claw while giving me a tiger growl."

"Fuck you," I say, dropping the pose and shaking my head in frustration. "I should've known this was a terrible idea."

"Chill, mate, just having some fun," Bryce says, a huge grin plastered on his face. "Chicks love a bit of humour." A couple of attractive women in tight-fitting activewear stroll past us. One of them, a blonde with a cap, sunglasses and a water bottle, notices us.

"Oh my God, you guys are adorable. Would you like me to take a photo of you both together?" she asks.

"Yes," Bryce says before I can even react.

"No!" I blurt out, leaving the woman somewhat taken aback. "No, thanks. We're good."

"Aw, come on, Arch, just one picture," Bryce pleads.

"No!" I assert firmly, "We're not... I'm not gay. I'm actually single."

The woman is speechless, hurrying off with her friend with her hand over her mouth.

"You need to work on your game, man," Bryce says, checking the photos on his camera screen.

"She's right. We look like we just stepped off the LGBT cruise. Let's get out of here, find somewhere less crowded," I suggest.

Bryce walks up beside me. "Whatever you say, partner," he says, attempting to hold my hand. I swat his hand away.

"What's wrong with you?" I ask, bewildered by Bryce. Sometimes I don't know if he's kidding or not. "Let's head under the bridge, fewer people."

"And better lighting. Good call. We also need a photo with a puppy."

"Why?"

"*Why*?" Bryce exclaims. "You serious right now? Because chicks are crazy for puppies, obviously."

"But I don't have a puppy."

"It doesn't have to be yours," Bryce says, spotting a middle-aged woman with her miniature schnauzer approaching. He walks over to her. "Oh my God, what a cute dog! Is that a schnauzer?"

The woman stops, caught off guard by Bryce's enthusiasm. "Yes, it is. You're familiar with the breed?" she replies.

"Bryce?" I interject, concerned.

"I had one when I was growing up. My first pet," Bryce says, crouching down to the dog, who seems to enjoy the attention. "May I?" he asks, and without waiting for an answer, he takes the dog from its owner and hands it to me. "Hold on for a second, please." The woman looks surprised, not quite sure how to react.

"Bryce!?" I protest again, but before I can return the dog, Bryce already has a picture of me clutching the startled-looking canine. My expression mirrors the dog's confusion.

"Got it," Bryce says, checking the photo. The woman snatches her dog from me, shooting Bryce a withering glare, and walks off with her schnauzer.

"Not the best shot, but it'll do," Bryce says, unfazed by the encounter. We continue walking along the harbour. "So, any news on the Jez-itsu front?"

"Her name is Jezebel."

"I know, but I mashed Jezebel with jiu-jitsu. Jez-itsu."

"I caught that. Quite clever, Bryce."

"Well, I don't think she was the right fit for you anyway, man."

"Yeah, I'm aware you prefer me flying solo."

"I think it'll be good for you. You've been through a lot. Stepping back into the dating scene could be just the ticket to reviving your mojo. I miss the old Archie, the authentic one."

Bryce spots another woman heading our way, this time a young mum pushing a stroller. "This is it, we need a baby shot," Bryce says, heading directly for the young mother.

"What?" I exclaim, tracking his focus. "Bryce, no!"

"We've got to show off your paternal side, trust me," Bryce insists, approaching the young mum. "Excuse me, could we borrow your baby for a quick photo?"

"Pardon me?" the woman says, clearly taken aback.

I step in promptly. "Sorry about my friend," I say, pulling Bryce away, "he's a few beers short a six-pack, if you know what I mean. Let's go, mate."

"What's the problem? It's a golden opportunity," Bryce protests.

"The photo shoot is over!" I conclude.

It doesn't take me long to line up a date at one of my favourite bars. Maybe Sammy is this stylish cocktail joint about three blocks away from my place, close to the CBD end of The Rocks. I'm at the bar, getting us two espresso martinis. One for me and another for my date, Melissa. She's twenty-four, a brunette with a slight resemblance to Kim Kardashian. Her short stature complements her choice of attire – a black leather skirt that's not too mini and a tight, low-cut white top that emphasises her generous cleavage. Her nearly black hair is pulled back into a tight ponytail. While she might wear a bit more makeup than I'd prefer, she does exude glamour.

I'm feeling good. I went for a solid jog around Barangaroo Point along the harbour foreshore, even throwing in some stair-runs to get those endorphins pumping and pheromones emitting. This is my first date since my personal issues got sorted, and I'm more than ready to dive back into the dating game. Melissa and I connected on Bumble earlier today, and after a few text exchanges, I lined up this date. With Jezebel still taking up real estate in my head, there's no better distraction than alcohol, a date and hopefully, the horizontal dance. I do miss Jezebel like crazy, but I'm respecting her request for no contact. If she wants to talk to me again, she will have to make the first move. The ball's in her court.

So, I'm moving forward. The sexual frustration in me is palpable, but I decide to hold off on any self-relief to conserve energy. Right now, I'm still fully loaded and feeling more energised than ever.

Melissa is a sports physician for the South Sydney Rabbitohs rugby league team. I'm a bit surprised she's not dating one of the players, considering how fit she is.

"It's unprofessional," she explains, taking a sip of her cocktail, "and most of them are just a bunch of jerks. I wouldn't touch them with a ten-foot pole, you know."

I like her attitude already. The date follows a fairly standard course. She asks about my job, and I try my best to explain it without coming across as a FinPrick, as I'm wont to do. Though I can tell she already thinks that I am one. She asks about where I live, and I mention that I own a house a few blocks away. In case you forgot – I don't own it, I rent, but she doesn't need to know that. Her eyes light up at that, which is pretty standard for dating in Sydney. I once had a first date where the first thing she asked was what kind of car I drive. I shit you not. So, I lied and told her what she wanted to hear – that I drove a BMW M3 but was looking to do my part for the planet and switch to electric, having just put down a deposit for a Tesla Model X which was shipping from California in a few weeks. She ate it up like a dog devouring a juicy steak, completely unaware that my eco-friendly car story was as fabricated as a unicorn's diet plan. Jeez, I can bullshit when I want to. But it worked a treat, and I took her home that night. Still, when daylight came and she saw no BMW in the drive, I had to come clean. She called me a lying asshole and stormed out. Sorted itself out, really. Sorry (not sorry), but that's what you get for being a gold digger. Show me a woman who doesn't see my worth in dollar value, such as Jezebel Ekas, and I'll treat her like a queen. Anyway, there I go off on a tangent again. Now, back to the present.

I make a mental note of Melissa's reaction when I tell her I own a house in West Rocks. The combination of caffeine and alcohol starts to kick in, and I'm full of energy, feeling my long-lost mojo returning. The conversation flows naturally, laughter is abundant and the chemistry is undeniable. However, I'm well aware that I shouldn't invite her over to my place just yet. So, I suggest another whiskey bar nearby, my hand casually resting on the inside of her forearm. Melissa reciprocates by briefly placing her hand on my knee.

We stroll a few blocks to a narrow cobblestoned laneway in The Rocks. Along the way, we pass a small park with a mural of old Sydney Town on a wall. We reach a staircase with a sign reading "The Doss House" hanging above. The staircase leads down to a basement whiskey bar with a charming beer garden surrounded by sandstone walls.

Inside, the ambience is moody, and it's so dark that I trip over a step leading up to the bar. Melissa finds it hilarious. I order whiskey, and she opts for a gin and tonic. We sit outside in the beer garden, and our conversation continues to flow effortlessly. Melissa starts playing with her hair, a clear sign of flirtation. Physical contact gradually escalates, and before long, we're both a little tipsy. I decide to lean in for a kiss, and she meets me halfway. Our kiss is fun and enjoyable, though nowhere near as intimate as the kisses I've shared with Jezebel. Yet, I use the view of the Harbour Bridge from my place as an excuse to invite her over. She agrees, saying she'd love to see it.

We walk up Argyle Street, passing through the tunnel to my place on the other side in West Rocks. I lead her inside, offer her a drink, and we barely finish one glass of wine before we're at it again – kissing passionately, our hands exploring each other's bodies. As we sit on the couch, I slide her underwear down from beneath her skirt. I kneel on the floor, pulling her closer, and I go down on her for a good five minutes. We switch positions, and she takes me into her mouth. I get hard, but strangely, not fully. It's odd for this to happen to me. Alcohol has never been an issue before. No matter how drunk I've been, I've always managed to perform. And besides, I'm not even drunk.

Melissa climbs on top of me, straddling me as she lowers herself down. I need to focus hard to prevent myself from losing my semi-erection. I grab her ample breasts, which have now popped out of her top. Skirt hiked up, top pulled down – we should be having a fantastic moment, but I feel myself going limp. Could it be the alcohol? It's not something I've encountered before. Despite my best efforts, it seems like I can't maintain an erection.

Eventually, Melissa senses something is off as I close my eyes, straining to keep things going. But it's no use. She stops abruptly.

"Oh my God," she exclaims, "that's a first."

"I'm so sorry, it's a first for me too," I admit, surrendering to the unfortunate situation.

"Well, that doesn't make me feel any better!"

"Oh no, it's not you. There's absolutely nothing wrong with you."

"What is it then – your dick's broken?"

"I think it's the Fosters flops. I'm too drunk."

"Whatever," she says cleaning herself up and gathering her bag to leave.

"Can I book you an Uber?"

There's silence except for the sound of her footsteps descending the stairs, the front door opening and subsequently slamming shut.

I stare down at my limp dick. "What's happened to you?"

Chapter 26

Revelations

I can't seem to catch a break. Finally, my dick looks normal again but appears broken. After the failed one-night stand with Melissa, I attempted to rub one out, yet couldn't bring myself to glory. Tried watching some of my favourite porn categories – nothing. So, I went further down the rabbit hole and viewed some real nasty shit which just seemed to turn me off even more.

So, I called Dr. Singh who, of course, suggested Viagra. I declined, citing my age as a reason to refuse having to rely on a drug to get an erection. The doc assured me that "this too shall pass" and, in time, I would get my libido back.

But I didn't have time. I was still holding onto a thin veil of hope that Jezebel would give me another chance. And if she did, I needed to be ready. I had to deliver. So, I did some digging online and found a local billionaire obsessed with living forever. Seems a lot of the world's elite are investing in the idea of longevity. One of the treatments this rich prick was receiving was "penis rejuvenation therapy" so I booked an appointment for an initial consultation and treatment.

The penis specialist told me that not only could he cure my erectile dysfunction, but make it harder and erect for much longer. I signed up right there. Not cheap, mind you. Two thousand bucks for the initial three-week sessions, the first of which involved shockwave therapy. So, that was kind of weird, my penis receiving a shockwave treatment. I was yet to notice any results, but trying to remain positive.

To take my mind off my broken willy, I decided to finally clean out Pops' place. I had been procrastinating over it and now the time had come.

At my father's apartment, surrounded by his belongings, attempting to clean out what's left is certainly a strange feeling. I'm still feeling like a hollowed-out tree, devoid of any deep emotion. Except for guilt, that little devil, because his passing hasn't really hit me yet. It doesn't help that I'm standing within the four walls of his dingy government housing unit, the very place I promised myself I'd help him escape from someday. I passed his neighbours in the corridor – a couple who look suss as fuck, in both a co-dependent and drug-dependent kind of way. I had offered Dad the chance to live with me in West Rocks, but he turned it down, knowing it would cramp my style. God bless him.

As I pack old books, clothes and random knick-knacks into cardboard boxes, Mavis, Robert's plump elderly carer who remind me of an old, female and ginger Ricky Gervais, waltzes in with a bunch of flatpack cardboard boxes.

"Will this be enough, Archie?" she huffs, her short, fiery-red curls bouncing with every step.

"Aw, you're a sweetheart, thanks Mavis."

"I'll just pop them down here, shall I?"

"Appreciate it, Mavis. I hope you have a lucky man in your life appreciating you."

"Oh, stop it you." Mavis blushes, leans the boxes against the wall, then pauses, as if she's wrestling with something. She hesitates, turns back towards me. "Archie, your father was a fine man," she mumbles, fidgeting with her hands. I stop what I'm doing, turning to fully face her.

"I know. But thank you."

"He treated me kindly, always. Never raised his voice, never a complaint, and most of all, never a sleaze-bucket," she says, her gaze focused on the floor. "I know how much he meant to you. You were good to him, visiting every week. You could see you were like a couple mates."

"We were. Best mates." I wait for more words to fill the air, for some sense of closure perhaps. But Mavis just nods gently, does a half-turn, and slips out the door.

Could Mavis read minds? Was she some sort of guilt-whisperer? I return my attention to the task at hand – sorting through my father's things – attempting to drown out the thoughts that threaten to swarm my mind. I pick up a small metal chest, about the size of a shoebox, complete with a vintage lock and key. Curiosity pushes me to unlock it, and as it creaks open, the first thing I see is an old photo album.

On the front, it reads, "The early years, Pamela and Archibald".

It's like finding a forgotten treasure chest, a portal to a time long before life took its twists and turns. My curiosity tugs at me, urging me to open this window into the past, to see a version of my father that I had never known, a time when my mother was still part of his world, and I was just a little bundle of innocence.

I gingerly open the album, its pages crackling as I turn them, suggesting it hadn't been looked at in years. It reveals images that seem to belong to a different lifetime. The photographs are aged and yellowed, capturing moments of a young couple deeply in love, their eyes reflecting the sort of passion I never saw in my father's eyes after my mother left. In one picture, they're lying on a picnic blanket, arms wrapped around each other, smiles as wide as the sky. My father's hair is a little wild, his face unburdened by the lines that would come later. Scruffy-handsome is a good way to describe him. Beside him, my mother looks carefree, laugh lines dancing at the edges of her lips. Her blonde hair is reminiscent of Madonna in the eighties, and she's wearing stone-washed denim jeans and jacket to match. She is a beautiful young woman.

Then, among the pages, I find myself. A tiny, fragile creature held in my father's arms, his beaming smile radiating joy and pride. His love for me is palpable even through the photograph, and I'm struck by the thought that this was a different man from the one I had come to know. My mother is beside him, her gaze fixed on me, her expression tender and full of warmth. In these moments, captured forever on paper, I glimpse the family I never really had.

As I trace my fingers over the photographs, a wave of emotion crashes over me. Tears unexpectedly gather at the corners of my eyes, a mixture of sadness and nostalgia. The ache of what could have been, the bittersweet reminder that once upon a time, we were a family – albeit briefly – hits me with an intensity I hadn't anticipated. These images show me a different chapter of my parents' lives, a chapter I had never been privy to, and the weight of all the unresolved questions and unspoken words between us settles heavily on my shoulders.

I lose myself in this time capsule, aching for the unity and love that existed before it all fell apart. The photos, with their sepia tones and faded edges, speak a language that transcends the years, reminding me that beneath the layers of pain and estrangement, there was a time when my parents were united in their journey, bound by a love that once burned brightly. I close the album with a sense of longing, my emotions a mix of sorrow and gratitude for these images that have allowed me a fleeting glimpse into a world that could have been.

But the album doesn't compare to what comes next. My eyes settle on a bundle of old letters bound with rubber bands tucked away in the dusty corner of the chest. I take them out, choose one, unfold it, and begin to read. The words are written in a flowing, cursive style.

I miss you more than words can say. I want you to know that I love you beyond measure, and none of this is your fault. I'm certain you're wondering why I left. There are things a seven-year-old shouldn't be burdened with, things that are beyond explanation. Your father and I faced challenges that a young heart like yours shouldn't comprehend. And having you at such a tender age made me realise that we get only one shot at life. Selfish as it may sound, I needed to chase the dreams that filled my mind. As I write this from Palermo, Italy, I can't help but imagine you here. It's a place you'd adore.

You're growing into a time where you can handle both yourself and your father. First order of business: teach him to use email, so I can finally retire these handwritten letters! You've always been your own person, Archie Robert Flynn, and I've no doubt you'll thrive. But that doesn't stop me from missing you every single day, fretting about your well-being. I hope one day you'll find it in your heart to forgive me, and maybe we'll cross paths once more. For now, your father needs you.

With unwavering love, Mum

The words strike me like a punch to the gut. There's a stack of these letters in the chest, each one an emotional landmine. A whirlwind of feelings and questions flood my head. Why did Dad keep these letters hidden from me? And still the reason Pamela left remains shrouded in mystery. I remember that I was a surprise, a curveball in her life's game plan. She hadn't envisioned a life dominated by motherhood. Once I was old enough to wrestle a jar of Vegemite open and make my own way to school, she jetted off to pursue the globe-trotting lifestyle she had always craved. A life that my dad couldn't provide.

I decide not to read any more letters for now. Best consumed in small portions. I gently return the letter to its rightful place, lock the chest and slide it aside, a solitary island among my father's possessions.

Chapter 27
The Big Resignation

I considered reaching out to Pam about the letters after reading every single one as soon I got home from cleaning out Dad's flat. But I didn't have it in me. Yeah, okay, she attempted to remain a part of my life. So what, she still abandoned me. But now I was holding resentment towards Pops also for having withheld the letters from me. I cannot comprehend why he would do such a thing except wanting me to turn against Pamela even more. But I can't be sure, and it's something I will never find a definitive answer to.

One action I did take after reading the letters and postcards, which were sent from exotic locations around the world such as Monte Carlo, Hong Kong and Rio de Janeiro to name a few, was to hand in my resignation to Bryce. I had spent my entire twenties taking myself and my career too seriously. Being mentored by Bryce, running the rat race, and keeping up with the Joneses had caused me to lose sight of the bigger picture. Working ten hours a day, five days a week, for a weekend where I would cut loose and indulge in mostly meaningless sex had become stale. That's not living. It was time for a shake-up. A change was in order. And Pam's letters were the final nudge I needed to flee the coop. I had enough money saved up to travel comfortably for at least a year not working, maybe more. With Dad gone and Jezebel no longer an option, there was nothing here for me. Yeah, there's Pam. But if that relationship were to rekindle, it would take time. It's my turn to abscond.

So, here I am inside Bryce's office and the space is filled with an air of tension as I prepare to deliver what might be the worst news of his life.

"I'm handing in my resignation," I say, trying to maintain a casual tone even though my heart is racing. "It's time for me to move on."

Bryce's face contorts with a mix of disbelief, shock and disgust. You'd think I'd just farted in his face. "What? You're fucking with me, right?"

I shake my head, my voice steady. "No, I'm not messing around."

He shoots back, "Bullshit, Archie!"

My attempt at casualness is clearly not working, and as I face Bryce's incredulity, I can't help but wonder if I'm doing the right thing. Yet, deep down, I know this decision has been brewing within me for quite some time. I've played out this conversation in my mind countless times, and though Bryce might think my father's recent passing is clouding my judgment, I'm resolute in my choice.

Bryce, sensing my determination, tries to reason with me, his voice laden with sympathy. "Come on, Arch, your father just died. You're not thinking straight. I told you to take two weeks paid leave."

It's a classic case of denial; the first stage of grief. And although I'm proud of myself for recognising it, I'm not clouded by it. This decision is a culmination of various factors, not just my father's passing.

Bryce's gaze sharpens as he awaits my response.

"I don't need time off, Bryce."

"Jesus, Archie. After all I have done for you!" He's angry now. We discuss the last decade or so of working together, and I thank him earnestly for all that he's done for me, including his mentoring.

This subdues him somewhat, until I say, "But it's time for my next chapter."

Now Bryce goes through the stages of bargaining and even offers me a generous sabbatical package, hoping to convince me to stay. But despite his best efforts, I know this is my path. As he brings up the possibility of head-hunters stealing me from under his wings, I assure him that's not the case. "I'll be going out on my own."

It's true. The pandemic has taught me, and a lot of people, that I can work remotely, even run my own venture from anywhere in the world. The realisation came to me when I met my mother, and the sudden reappearance of Jezebel has added fuel to the fire of change burning within me.

Bryce's attempts at bargaining and reasoning continue, but my resolve is firm. This isn't about Bryce or the firm; it's about what I need to do for myself. As the conversation progresses, Bryce's emotions intensify, and I see him cycling through the stages of grief in front of me. He's moved from denial to anger to bargaining, and now the sadness is kicking in, and I can't help but feel the weight of my decision. But I need to stand my ground.

When I see tears welling in Bryce's eyes, I know that my words are getting through to him. He's a mentor, a friend, and more than just a boss. We share a moment of understanding, and the tension starts to dissipate. As the conversation concludes, we're both on the same page, even if it's not easy for either of us.

"I don't like it... but I accept it."

I cannot believe it. While it took me over three months, Bryce went through all five stages of grieving in under ten minutes, beating his previous record of grieving my father in all but two days. The guy's a freak, but in the best possible way.

"Hey Arch, can I ask a favour?"

"Sure."

"One last story. I know you went on a date the other night. Tell me all about it, for old times' sake."

"There's really not much to tell. It played out great, I took her home, but I couldn't go through with it."

"What do you mean?"

"I wasn't into it. It was devoid of any meaning. I couldn't get it up."

"Huh," is all Bryce can manage. "Interesting." I turn to leave. "Archie?" I turn back, and Bryce says something that takes my breath away.

"Don't let Jezebel be the one that got away."

I consider his statement, nod and exit.

As I leave his office, I can't shake the mix of emotions that course through me. This is the end of an era, the start of a new chapter that holds uncertainty, excitement and the promise of personal growth. I'm not just leaving a job; I'm leaving behind a life that I've known for the better part of a decade. But in my heart, I know that it's time for a change; a chance to spread my wings and see where this new path takes me.

Chapter 28

J.C. and Me

Once again, I find myself in the presence of Father Bob, in the confines of his private back office after Sunday service. The room is cloaked in an air of sanctity, but also a hint of mustiness due to its lack of ventilation. My eyes scan the walls, half expecting to see signs of mould.

"You really need to let some fresh air in here, Father," I suggest, concerned about his well-being. "Mould's the last thing you need."

Father Bob responds, "And the priesthood is the last thing you need."

I grasp the doorknob and swing the door back and forth playfully, as if my futile attempt at creating airflow might solve the problem. But it's not really about the ventilation. I'm here for more soul-searching discussions with the priest, who's convinced I'm not destined for the spiritual life, something I'm well aware of.

"Oh, never mind about that, I'm past that now."

"Because you no longer have your... you know."

"Might have something to do with it."

I launch into a candid account of my recent experiences, including my mother's sudden reappearance in my life and the letters I discovered, which have sent me into a spiral of confusion. Father Bob's response is a mixture of spiritual insight and psychological advice, the kind that can only come from a man who has spent a lifetime in the cloth. He emphasises the importance of introspection and internal searching, asserting that true answers are not found in external stimuli. Which is another way of telling me to stop the meaningless sex. I tell him about my recent almost-one-night-stand and how it didn't do it for me anymore and he is thrilled to hear it, says he's proud of me. His words resonate with me, and I consider the meaning behind his wisdom.

But suddenly, the conversation shifts, and my heart skips a beat as Father Bob mentions

Jezebel. My question hangs in the air.

"I noticed she wasn't in church this morning... Have you heard from her?"

Then it comes – the revelation that she's heading back to the U.S. feeling like a jolt of electricity fizzing through me.

"For good?" I manage to ask, my voice shaky.

Father Bob confirms my fears, and the reality hits me harder than I expected. Jezebel, the one who's been on my mind more than anyone else, is leaving, perhaps forever. The thought pierces through me like a dagger, leaving a palpable ache.

Determined not to let her slip away without at least trying, I'm out of Father Bob's office in a flash. At record speed I'm outside her complex, dialing Jezebel's unit number, my finger trembling as I press the buttons again and again, urgency pushing me forward despite the mounting tension.

Reaching her voicemail, I switch to another strategy. I navigate through her long list of friends on Facebook, hoping to find a familiar face, a lifeline. And there she is, Larissa – the friend I met during that fateful night out with Jezebel. My fingers fly across the screen, composing a message, then pausing. No time for back-and-forth, I decide, and hit the call button.

Larissa's voice on the other end sounds surprised. "Archie?"

Relief floods over me as I realise she answered. There's no time for pleasantries. "Larissa, do you know where Jezebel is?" I say, cutting straight to the chase.

"She's on her way to the airport," Larissa replies, and I can almost feel the seconds ticking away.

"I missed her," I mutter, frustration bubbling up. But Larissa isn't done.

"She's got a flight to L.A. at eight-thirty. You might still catch her if you hurry."

My heart races as I check my watch, the numbers blinking back at me. Five-thirty. Time's on my side, at least for now. A surge of determination fills me, a resolve to not let her slip away without a fight. "Thanks, Larissa. I'm gonna try."

"Go get her, lover boy," she encourages, and her words fuel my resolve. "Oh, and I should warn you, she's with that douche-bag, Steve."

"Okay, thanks for the heads up, Larissa," I say before hanging up.

Fuck Steve, I'm going anyway. With renewed determination, I'm on the move. The prospect of catching up with Jezebel before she leaves is all I need to spur me into action. I don't care if she leaves, even if I just get to say goodbye. Time is fleeting, but hope still burns strong within me.

I summon an Uber to ensure I reach Sydney International Airport in record time. In just a matter of minutes, a sleek black Subaru WRX driven by Muhammed pulls up to the curb. The sight of the fast car is strangely fitting for my current predicament. I hop in and offer Muhammed a tempting challenge – a fifty-dollar tip if he can get me to the airport as swiftly as the law allows. Muhammed doesn't back down and accepts the challenge, accelerating with a determination that matches my urgency.

The ride feels like a whirlwind as Muhammed expertly navigates through traffic, his black Subaru weaving in and out of lanes like a shadow in pursuit of time itself. As we enter the Eastern Distributor tunnel, the speedometer hits eighty km/h due to the speed camera limit. Once we're past the cameras, Muhammed unleashes the full power of the car, pushing it to a hundred km/h. It's a thrilling ride, and for a moment, I'm swept up in the adrenaline-fueled excitement. Muhammed's driving skills earn him the title of the best Uber driver ever in my mind.

The radio plays "Goodbye Stranger" by Supertramp, a song that triggers a memory of a wild night involving a one-night stand and the unfortunate discovery of a wart on my nether regions. In this intense moment, the song feels like the soundtrack to my own romantic comedy.

Before I know it – barely giving me enough time to buy the cheapest plane ticket I could find on my phone to get me through security – we've broken land-speed records and arrived at the airport. Muhammed's skilful driving made the journey feel like a mere five minutes. True to my word, I hand over a fifty-dollar tip in cash, appreciating the adrenaline rush and the driver's willingness to help me seize the moment.

Inside the departure terminal, I follow the signs and the advice of airport personnel to reach Gate 28. But before I can proceed, I'm reminded of the mask requirement. A small hiccup, but a kind lady offers me one for free, saving me the trouble of buying one. Mask secured, I navigate through security, which isn't too busy, and then rush through the various airport sections, finally reaching the gate. My heart races as I scan the waiting area, but Jezebel is nowhere to be seen. My hopes deflate, and the realisation that I might have missed her sinks in like a heavy weight. The thought of her slipping away, perhaps forever, triggers a wave of melancholy.

I decide a drink is in order to soothe my emotions and find myself propped up at the airport bar. A straight whiskey arrives, and I down it in one go, the fiery liquid providing a temporary respite from the turmoil within. I order another and sip it slowly, staring out at the aircraft moving on the runway, a world of departures and arrivals that mirrors the chaos of my own feelings.

Then, a voice breaks through the din of the airport. A voice I'd recognise anywhere. "Archie?"

I turn to see her standing there, looking as stunning as ever. Jezebel. In tight blue jeans and a light grey sweater, she exudes a casual elegance that takes my breath away. She questions why I'm here, and for a moment, I'm too caught up in her presence to form a coherent response.

But reality creeps back in as I notice Steve trailing behind her, hand luggage in tow. As much as I want to relish this moment, the sight of him by her side sets off an alarm in my mind.

But I don't give a fuck, and manage to mumble, "I came to see you."

Jezebel's gaze shifts to Steve, and a conversation seems to occur between them without words. I can't ignore the unease that bubbles up inside me at that exchange. The only thing I can make out is Steve saying, "This fucker from down under?" Jezebel requests a moment with me, and Steve reluctantly obliges, retreating to a seat that offers a full view of us. I brace myself for this pivotal conversation.

As the words spill out, I lay bare my insecurities, my history of seeking validation through women, and my transformation since meeting her. It's an unfamiliar vulnerability for me, but it's a necessary admission. Her eyes, usually so enigmatic, study me intently, and I find it hard to hold her gaze.

Her response is unexpected, her appreciation for my honesty both humbling and surprising. For the first time, she's seen beneath my armour, and it feels liberating. Our connection is unique, I tell her, something worth holding onto. But reality isn't as romantic as the Hollywood movies. Steve remains in the picture, a reminder of the practicality and convenience that sometimes outweigh matters of the heart.

"I'm going to give things a shot with Steve," she says.

My heart sinks. It's a choice that makes sense, but logic doesn't quell the disappointment. A gap between us remains, a gap that might never be bridged. I lean in, trying to convey my feelings in that moment, a last-ditch effort to make her reconsider. Her response is to hold my gaze, and the intensity of that connection is almost overwhelming.

A tear forms in her eye, and I can see the internal struggle within her. But then she utters those two words that pierce my heart. "I'm sorry." The finality of her words hangs in the air, and I can only nod slowly, acknowledging the decision that's been made.

With the weight of our unfulfilled potential heavy on my shoulders, I bid her farewell. "Keep your fists up and knock 'em dead, okay." She smiles at this. I head for the escalator, the sound of Lionel Richie's "Stuck on You" playing from the airport bar, adding a surreal touch to the scene. Turning as I step onto the descending escalator, I look back at her, holding onto that moment as long as I can. Our eyes meet, and I tilt my head slightly, a hint of a wistful smile on my lips. The cliché romantic comedy vibe isn't lost on either of us, and her laughter rings out as I slowly disappear from her view.

In that moment, as heartbroken as I am, I realise there's still beauty in this goodbye. A connection that was powerful, a love that was genuine, even if it wasn't meant to be forever. The airport's bustling chaos melts away as I step onto the escalator, carrying the memory of her laughter and our shared moments. It's a final image that lingers, a bittersweet end to a chapter that was marked by vulnerability, growth and a love that defied expectations. And involved no sex whatsoever.

Once more, the rain graces the day as I find myself dropping into St. Patrick's Cathedral on my way home from the airport. The lingering urge to apologise to Father Bob beckons me. My last attempt at reconciliation ended with a swift departure, a rather comedic exit from the possibility of becoming a religious man, spurred by my penile recovery. Not that I was ever destined to be religious in the eyes of Father Bob, or me for that matter. Nevertheless, I intend to clarify my actions at that last meeting and perhaps underline my newfound commitment to change, catalysed by Jezebel, him, and the subtle nudges of the church. Will I embrace a newfound religiosity? Not a snowball's chance in hell.

Giant doors block my path upon arrival, but that's just an obstacle for mere mortals. With a hearty push, I cajole one of the mammoths into motion and step inside, letting the door thud shut behind me. The church looms empty and serene, candles flickering like stars in the cosmos, casting a warm glow amidst the pews.

"Father Bob?" I call out, but my words are met only by their own echoes, rebounding off the cavernous walls. I venture toward the back office, positioned to the right of the confession booth. A polite knock on the door, "Father, you around?" goes unanswered. Without hesitation, I decide to venture in.

Inside, the room is vacant, but my attention is captured by the top drawer. The bottle of whiskey is conspicuously absent, replaced by something more modern and extravagant – Grey Goose vodka. A chuckle escapes my lips as I seize the opportunity. A hearty swig follows, accompanied by a satisfying sigh. "Well played, Father," I quip before carefully returning the bottle to its clandestine abode.

Yet, another intriguing discovery beckons – a priest's cassock hangs upon a hanger, complete with the obligatory clerical collar. My innate curiosity gets the better of me, compelling me to try on the attire. Buttons align obediently, and the collar, once in place, is surprisingly confining. I take in my reflection in the mirror, and, to my amusement, I admit that the look is rather fetching.

I saunter back into the church, my footfall echoing with authority. I stand at the pulpit, gazing out at an invisible congregation. "Ladies and gentlemen," I address my imaginary crowd, "I present to you, Father Archie... has a ring to it." I pivot and address the statue of Christ at the back. "S'up, JC, how's the priest's get-up work for me? You know, you didn't answer all my prayer, but you answered enough, so... thank you," I say as I place my hands together in the prayer position in bow my head.

Rain streaks the stained-glass windows, casting a vibrant spectrum of colours over both the statue of Jesus and myself, a moment soon punctuated by a flash of lightning illuminating Christ and lighting up the church in electric blue flashes. A resounding clap of thunder follows, as if warning me not to play God.

Then, I feel a presence, sense someone watching me in this sacred space. Startled, I turn, bracing for a Father Bob encounter, but to my surprise, it's not him. But someone stands by the entrance, the open cathedral door illuminating them. It's a woman, her rain-drenched and dishevelled hair a chaotic masterpiece of nature's design. Water drips onto the tiled floor beneath her feet. Her luggage by her side, she takes a deep breath, her bewildered gaze locked onto me. And just like that, as my eyes adjust to the light surrounding her silhouette, confusion mirrors itself in our eyes.

"Jezebel," I utter, still adjusting to the unexpected sight. I turn back J.C. and mouth a silent, "thank you."

"Archie," she responds, her voice a mixture of incredulity and exhaustion, "why are you wearing that?"

I step down from my impromptu stage. Simultaneously, Jezebel strolls down the aisle, each step marking her approach.

"I was merely contemplating the colossal error I narrowly avoided by not becoming a priest," I confess, injecting a note of wryness.

She responds with a smirk. "Not to mention what a sinful waste that would've been."

Our embrace ignites, lips colliding in the fervent dance of a thousand remembered kisses. The meeting floods my eyes with tears, a rush of emotion I've confined for years now. Yet, the fervour of our reunion quickly fans other flames that had been repressed for over three long months. The torrent of arousal surges through me, and a forceful reminder of my masculinity demands attention as I become rock-hard instantly. She has that effect on me. Which is a relief after my previous intimate experience, as well as saving me thousands of dollars on penis rejuvenation shock-treatment therapy. Thank you, Jezebel, I think to myself.

Overcome by the intensity of it all, she also becomes aware that my body is responding in ways that only Jezebel has ever provoked. With a breathless longing, she presses herself against me, and in that electric moment, restraint feels as far away as our past separation.

"Did Father Bob grant you permission to wear this?" Jezebel playfully quips, momentarily breaking our passionate kiss.

"What do you think?" I manage to reply, a mere whisper, before our lips rekindle the fire. She feels my undeniable response, my hardness pressing against her. Her touch electrifies me.

Her eyes gaze over my priestly ensemble. "You've got no idea how strangely hot you look as a priest."

"Father Archie scrubs up nicely," I jest, and her touch urges us further. She smiles. The mischievous kind, her eyes communicating a naughty lightbulb moment. Suddenly, Jezebel steers me towards the confession booth, my confusion palpable.

"What's the game plan?" I inquire.

"Just follow my lead," she insists, grabbing my hand and whisking me behind the confessional curtain. The door shuts, and before I can protest, she pulls me onto the seat, straddling me with an undeniable urgency.

"Jezebel," I manage to interject, but she isn't interested in objections.

"Quiet," she demands, ripping the cassock's buttons open with a force that fuels our desires. Our lips lock once more, and I'm acutely aware of her wetness pressing against my now insistent-as-it's-ever-been erection. Though I sense the potential for chaos in this escapade, her allure proves overpowering.

I'm caught between logic and longing, and Jezebel is quick to exploit my weakness. She releases my imprisoned arousal and regards it with a fervour that quickens my pulse.

"Beautiful," she murmurs, her hand working a magic that leaves me almost breathless. She stands, her soaked skirt lifted, and I find myself in a daze as she guides me into her warm, waiting depths. It's the perfect fit, gripping me like a tailored glove, each contour and curve meshing flawlessly.

With Jezebel the chemistry surges like a symphony, and her decision to forsake her flight and Steve for this illicit reunion only fuels the inferno. My staying-power is put to the test as she sets a pace that's slow and deliberate, each movement deliberate and oh-so-tempting. I had yet to relieve myself since my cock had been cured. Strangely, there was just no more urge to, despite the serious case of blue balls – until now, of course.

Her breath dances upon my ear, its weight hanging heavy with desire. My hands find her, exploring the contours beneath her clothing. Her perfect breasts press against my chest, her nipples standing in anticipation. A playful nibble at my earlobe pushes me to the edge, and I'm struggling to hold on, even though it's been under a minute.

The dam cracks, then shatters. A tidal wave of pleasure cascades over me, drowning every logical thought. Like a long-dormant volcano erupting. A guttural moan escapes my lips, and I'm engulfed in ecstasy. My body trembles, a world of stars and blurred visions encompassing me as I experience the most incredible, extended orgasm.

Amid the euphoria, Jezebel's exclamation of "Oh my God!" pierces through the haze as she's filled to the brim. Her eyes, wide with astonishment, lock with mine before everything fades into oblivion.

Blackout.

Afterword

If you've got this far, I'd like to thank you from the bottom of my heart for reading and supporting my work. Highly Flawed Individual is my first novel, conceived during COVID while living on the beautiful Magnetic Island, Australia in 2020. Three years later, after spending many early mornings and late evenings, in between working a full-time remote job and travelling the world, consuming way too much coffee and at times questionable amounts of alcohol, I somehow managed to complete my story. If you found it entertaining I would really appreciate a review on Amazon. Reviews help independent authors like myself to continue sharing their stories.

On that note, you haven't seen the last of Archie Flynn; his global misadventures are only just beginning. While you wait for the next book in the series to launch, you can read an Archie Flynn prequel novella for absolutely FREE! You will also join my quarterly newsletter to stay in the loop about future book release dates, as well as discounts and promos.

Thanks again, and all the best,

T.C. Roberts

https://books.timroberts.au/prequel

Acknowledgements

A special thanks to my excellent editor, Dominic Wakeford, who not only helped improve the story structure and prose, but was instrumental in positioning the book in the market and guiding me with the self-publishing process overall.

Printed in Great Britain
by Amazon

50709838R00121